Always Here

Banks Brothers Series: Book Three

Rebecca Braden

Always Here
Banks Brothers Series, Book 3

CHAPTER 1
BAYLOR

Broken branches and crisp leaves crunch under our feet as we stomp through the woods with our gear, heading toward the small cave along the hiking trail. It's astonishing how many people read the big-ass "Do Not Enter" sign and ignore it anyway.

When we come to a stop, Henry points his flashlight inside, sighing and shaking his head.

"Banks and Harris, you're up," he says, tossing a hand out and gesturing toward the cave.

He always picks us because we're the slimmest of the guys here. Karson goes in first, then I follow.

The air inside the channel is thin and suffocating, making anyone feel claustrophobic. As we crawl on our elbows and stomachs through the cave, Karson and I make our way through the tight passage to the hiker. The man has gone down a narrow shaft and gotten himself stuck in a crawl space.

"Hey, I wanted to talk to you about something," Karson says.

"Okay, what is it?" I ask, taking a controlled breath.

“I ran into Megan at Hideaway a couple of weeks ago and wanted to know if you’d be cool with me asking her out.” He asks slowly, carefully controlling his breathing.

The question makes me want to laugh, but I’ll conserve my oxygen for now. Megan is a piece of work, but he can figure that out on his own. I’m not sure why he’s asking me this. I haven’t talked to Megan in almost a year.

“Go for it, dude,” I tell him, then keep crawling. Thankfully, I’m not as broad as my brothers, or I’d be just as stuck as the hiker. Then again, if I were their size, I wouldn’t have been selected for the retrieval.

When dirt and small rocks fall from above, we both tuck our chins. We wait a moment after it stops, then resume moving.

“How is she in bed? She’s not into any weird shit, right?”

“Depends on what you think is weird.”

“Ah, that is not reassuring at all. I’m not going to get a finger in the ass, am I? That’s all I need to know. I’m not into that,” he says warily.

Chuckling, I decide to mess with him by reaching out and running my hand up the back of his calf. “How do you know you're not into it?”

Karson squirms, sending more dirt around us. “Ahh, stop it, you fucking asshole,” he damn near screeches. He huffs out a breath and answers the question. “During a college hookup, the bitch took me by surprise and took my ass-ginity. That shit is not for me. I hated every second of it.”

I can’t control the burst of laughter that erupts from me. Karson is not impressed and grumbles.

“That’s hilarious. I was messing with you, man. I don’t know how she is in bed. We didn’t get that far, and even if I knew, I wouldn’t say. Just a heads-up, Megan is a vulture. She’ll chew up man.”

“Damn, I was worried you might say something like that,” he says. “What about the new girl, Winter?”

Jealousy sparks my rage. Winter is mine, even if she won’t admit it yet. This ass eater knows it, too. Without thinking, my fist flies out and connects with Karson’s ass cheek.

“Off-limits. Don’t even think about it.” I snarl, my voice low and threatening.

“Damn, okay. G.I. Joe.” He grumbles.

Winter and I have settled into an uncomfortable friend zone. It’s a slap in the face every time she says we're just friends. Secretly, I’m biding my time, waiting for the right moment to lay the charm on her.

Winnie is a vision from every dream I’ve ever had, resembling an angel sent from heaven with her white-blonde hair, smooth porcelain skin, and crystal-blue eyes. She has a perfect pear-shaped figure; I’ve always preferred ass over breasts, and Winnie has a hella ass. The cute softness on her stomach makes her even more desirable, and those thighs. Fuck, I love her thighs.

Damn, I need to stop thinking about her. I’m in the middle of a rescue, getting a damned stiffy.

When we stop, I wait for Karson to slide down the small shaft because he’s smaller than I am. I then toss him the harness once he’s at the bottom.

“Sir, I’m with Cedar Creek Fire. We’re going to get you out of there. Hang tight,” Karson tells the man.

I can barely hear the muffled, wheezing man say, “Ok.”

“He’s losing oxygen,” Karson says, moving quickly.

Karson wraps a strap around the guy's legs, tosses me the end, and we work together to hoist and maneuver the man out. When his head emerges, he greedily gulps air. Karson gives the guy a quick exam to see if he can make it out on his own. Thank fuck he can.

As we exit the cave, the guy's kids run up and hug him. Hopefully, he learned a lesson today.

"Thank you both," he tells us.

"No need to thank us. Maybe next time, pay attention to the sign," I say, pointing to the sign with big, bold letters… DO NOT ENTER!

"Noted. I won't make that mistake again."

I shake my head and walk over to the truck to remove the gear we needed. We load it into the fire engine and head back to the firehouse. Today is the fifth time we've had to remove someone from the situation. The park needs to come up with a way to close off the entrance. Obviously, just the sign isn't working.

My dream of becoming a firefighter has been with me since first grade, when our class visited the firehouse. I realized this was my calling. After graduating, I earned a degree in fire science and promptly joined the fire academy. I can't picture my life doing anything else.

Today marked the end of my three-day shift, and I'm ready for it. The past three days have been a chaos of nonstop calls, ranging from stove fires and car accidents to one group of kids jumping off a bridge into a river.

Once I've showered and changed, I grab my gym bag and head out of the building. Right as I walk out the door, Henry stops me.

"Banks, you haven't RSVP'd for the firefighters' ball. I need to know if you have a plus one so I can send this in. It's coming up," Henry shouts as he stalks up to me.

Shit, I forgot about that, but now I have the perfect reason to ask Winter out. “Oh, yeah, ah, put me down as having a plus one.”

A broad grin spreads across the man’s face as he stops beside me. Henry isn’t stupid. He knows I’ve been pining for Winter for months. I spent four days watching over her and the kids while Ny and Briggs were out of town last summer. That’s when I realized I was utterly captivated by the audacious woman.

“I already did. I just wanted to hear you say it,” Henry smirks.

Asshole

“Has anyone ever told you you’re kind of a dick?” I grumble.

“All the time, kid. I’m just trying to give you the push you need. It’s been almost ten months,” he says with an amused laugh.

“I’m taking my time. Winter needed a friend, and I didn’t want to push her,” I say, adjusting the bag on my shoulder.

Henry claps me on the back as we walk. “I get it. You’re being a good man, but a word of advice.”

“Ok.”

“You'd better hurry. Ny told me Winter signed up for the speed dating event with Tink,” he says, dropping his hand.

There’s that jealous fucking rage again. Speed dating? Really? She'd rather speed date than entertain the idea of going out with me? That has to be a fucking joke. Does she not realize that the chances of her or the boys getting hurt by someone else are higher? I would never hurt them. The boys are my life.

“When? Tink is with Jamie,” I ask incredulously. I’m struggling to believe she’s actually doing it.

"No one tells Tink what to do. She's forcing Winter to go. Saturday night." He says, rolling his lips, trying not to laugh. He knows I'm seething right now.

"Guess I'm crashing a speed-dating event then," I grumble, then start stomping off.

"Good luck," Henry shouts with a chuckle.

This has to be a joke. It's Wednesday morning, and Friday night, Winter has girls' night at Birdie's. The kids and I will be at Briggs for poker night. I'm already planning how to cockblock the hell out of her. I just need Ny to make my plan work and keep Briggs from killing me for suggesting it.

Now in the car, I start the ignition and head to the school to pick up the kids. It's my routine when I'm off shift. Today we're going to get pizza and go to the arcade.

It helps that we're neighbors. I pick them up, and they hang out as long as they want because they only have to walk 30 feet back home. It was pure luck that the house next to mine went up for sale just as Winter was about to give up. I was ecstatic when I found out, and so were the kids. They come over every time they see me at home.

Sometimes I wonder if Winter picked the room directly across from mine on purpose. I can see her shadow in the window at night, and I know she can see mine. I felt like a creep the first time I noticed, but now I've accepted my creepiness and always search for her shadow before bed. I've also caught the angel looking into mine a few times.

There's a level of comfort in living next door to them because I'm close if they ever need me. The only time I struggle is when I'm on duty for three days straight. Now I'm not so sure. If Winnie meets someone, I'll be forced to see her with him. I'll know when he comes and goes, and when he doesn't leave.

A gag runs up my throat at the thought. I'm definitely going to try to stop that.

I park at the school, get out, and wait for Dylan and Daniel to come outside. When I see Ny walking up to me, carrying a sleeping Tulip, I can't help but smile. She and Briggs took to parenthood so easily.

"Bayrrito, I didn't know you were picking them up today," she says in her raspy voice.

I chuckle at our ongoing nicknames for each other. Journey has become my best friend.

"Nychos, good to see you. They wanted to hang out. I'm treating them to an afternoon of fun," I tell her proudly.

"That's how it works. They want to give you the world, but you have to pay for it."

A deep, hearty chuckle slips from my throat, and I nod. "Noted, and I don't mind. I enjoy spending time with them."

Journey shifts Tulip and kisses her head. "I know you do. They love living beside you. Dylan told me they come and go whenever they want."

Satisfaction fills me knowing they talk about me to my family. "They do. Although the first few times they did it, they scared the shit out of Winter, and she yelled at me for being too neighborly."

"That sounds like her."

"Hey, I need your help on Saturday. Briggs might kill us, but you'd be doing me a solid."

Ny gives me a sly sideways grin, as if she already knows what I'm thinking.

"Let me handle Briggs. Does this have to do with a specific event happening?"

"Yup."

"Yes, I can't see what the plan is, and it's about time."

Before I can ask her anything else, we hear the bell ring, meaning Dyl and Dan will fly out that door with Ox, Lux, and Harley any minute.

As if on cue, the little group rushes out together. Dyl and Dan's faces light up when they see me.

"Baylor," they say in unison. They damn near tackle me to the ground when they hug me, making me laugh and steady myself.

"We made these for you in class."

I watch as they both pull out cards they drew for me, with cute pictures and "Best friends" written on them.

"These are awesome. Thank you both. I have a big day planned for us."

"Yes, I love hanging out with you," Dyl says.

"Me too. I enjoy hanging out with Mom, too, but we get to do more manly things with you," Dan says seriously.

My gaze meets Ny's, and we both hold in our laughter at his brief comment.

"I'm glad you enjoy it. Say bye to Aunt Ny, and we'll go."

Both kids run over and hug her, while the other three hug me. They each walk beside me back to my car.

With them buckled in, I start the ignition and drive to the Fun Barn for pizza, arcade games, and a movie, if Winter says it's okay.

"Bay, can we stay overnight with you and play video games?" Dan asks.

When I look in the rearview mirror, I see him watching me with enormous eyes.

"Our dad never played games with us. He stole them," Daniel says. It tugs at my heartstrings to hear that.

The mere mention of the man always starts a raging fire inside. Their father is no man. He chose a harsh life over his family. Winter tried to get him help, but he never stuck with it. Instead, he took off six years ago, leaving them and only reappearing on rare occasions to ask Winter for money.

Then last year, he resurfaced and stole everything she'd worked for. To make it worse, he got her fired from her job. She had virtually nothing left. Had it not been for her friendship with Ny, she would have faced homelessness. What kind of man could allow that to happen to his kids?

The tension in my hand from gripping the steering wheel pulls me from my thoughts. I need to stop thinking about it. I take a calming breath and loosen my grip on the wheel.

"We'll ask your mom, but tomorrow you have school, so no staying up until midnight," I tell them.

That answer satisfies them. I'm pretty sure they would move in with me if they could. I get it. They crave a father figure. Winter is fantastic, but sometimes you need your father. I remember times growing up when I needed my dad. Mom would try, but it wasn't the same. Not everyone is as fortunate as my brothers and I were to have both our parents.

I shouldn't say this, but I'm glad their father will be in prison for at least ten years. That means he can't hurt them anymore while they are still young and impressionable.

I swear, sometimes it feels like I share parenting with Winter.

After parking outside, the kids and I got out and walked into the place. I prefer to come just after school lets out, so there are fewer people and shorter lines for the games.

We ordered our pizza and sat at the table. "How's school going?" I ask.

"Good. I want to play soccer next year," Daniel says, sipping his drink.

"I don't know if I want to fight with Uncle Sul more or play football next year. Uncle Sul said I should try football, then pick the one I like best," Dylan says.

"I don't enjoy fighting, but I like soccer, and my gym teacher says I'm good at it."

"I played soccer in school. I could help Daniel and Baxter play football. If you want help, Dylan," I tell them both.

"That would be awesome," Dyl answers, then leans back when the pizza comes out.

The conversation halts while we eat and play games. The boys don't want to watch a movie because they want to play video games at home, and who am I to argue with 11-year-olds?

CHAPTER 2
WINTER

“Hey, Winnie,” the whisky voice says before me.

I’ve been staring at this computer for hours, searching a catalog for authors to feature in the store’s new Indie Author section.

Slowly lifting my gaze, I see the broad-shouldered firefighter looking down at me through thick lashes that would make any woman jealous. A cheeky grin is firmly planted on his gorgeous face. My heart thrums to life at the sight of him.

“Not my name,” I respond curtly, refusing to show how that smile affects me.

Baylor Banks is a total babe and entirely out of my league, but he keeps showing up, spending time with the boys and me. I'm usually the no-nonsense type, and he’s the outgoing, gorgeous type. I’ve been trying to convince myself he’s completely off-limits, but damn, we have chemistry that even I can’t ignore sometimes.

I can't help but stare at Bay. His firefighter shirt strains across his rippled stomach, and his brawny arms are taut beneath the sleeves. He flexes his biceps, knowing I'm watching, making the large vein along his arm bulge. Heat rises in me the longer I stare.

When his lake-green eyes meet mine, I could drown in his gaze. I swear, Bryce and Ivey created gods, not men. A glint of amusement appears in Baylor's eyes as his charismatic grin widens.

"You made it just in time. I was about to close," I say, closing the catalog and locking my computer screen.

When he flashes his pearly white smile at me, my cheeks heat and burn. I'm sure they're flaming red right now. I bring my hand up to cool my cheeks.

Shake it off, Winter. Play it cool.

"What books do you plan to buy but never read?" I ask, propping my elbow on the counter and resting my chin in my hand.

Bay gives me a mock-shocked look before digging out a list. I know he doesn't read these books. I should read one and ask him questions to bust his ass.

"I'm offended that you think I don't read," he teases, narrowing his eyes playfully as he hands me the paper.

"I know you," I say, glancing at the list. I snort and giggle, then cover my mouth. "I didn't peg you as a romance guy. You usually bring me murder mysteries or sci-fi."

I sway my hips as I walk from behind the counter and through the aisles of books. Bay watches my every move every time we do this. I like giving him a show. The art of seduction isn't something I'm familiar with… but that doesn't stop me from trying.

For the past couple of months, Bay has come in weekly and given me a list. Then he follows me around while I pick the books out for him. He might be my best customer.

"Figured I'd try something new. Have you read any of those?" he asks, leaning into me to look at the paper.

I know he's doing it to get a rise out of me; of course, it works, and I inhale his warm, comforting scent. It's like wrapping a warm blanket fresh from the dryer around you.

Bay places a hand on the small of my back, leans closer, and grabs two copies of the last book. I nibble my lip as I take the copies from his hand. His proximity has my body melting.

"I've read all of them except the last one, but I want to. You'll have to tell me if it's any good," I say, then step away quickly. Friends. We're only friends. It can't be more than that.

"Or you could read it with me and compare notes?" he says, keeping the distance I put between us. Bay is attentive to my body language.

I tilt my head and glance at him. He's clearly joking. There's no chance this guy is going to read a smut book and then discuss it.

I burst out laughing and look at him again. "Sure," I say, then start walking to the front of the store.

"Why do you doubt me?" he asks, a bewildered look on his face.

"I'm not. I'm giving you until your shift at the firehouse is over to read that. Then I'm quizzing you."

"That's not fair. You know some shifts are busy."

"Excuses, excuses, Hotshot."

Behind the counter, I start checking out the books. After Bay pays, he leans on the counter. Mischief flashes in his eyes before a wickedly handsome smirk spreads across his face.

"How about I just give you a kiss, and we call it even?"

"Go," I laugh, pointing at the door.

"Can't blame a guy for trying, sweet lips. Talk later."

"Yeah, huh,"

With a shake of my head, I grab my things and lock up after he leaves.

I crave the absolute peace and solitude of driving alone. It's a chance to decompress and a perfect opportunity to sing the infectious songs as loud as I want. The energy and vibe of 2000s pop music are nostalgic and comforting. Jamming out to the pulsing tunes sends me back to simpler times, windows down, volume up, my head bobbing. For the length of the drive, it's just me, a perfect beat, and an open road.

Out front, I park and smile at my home. The three-bedroom house isn't huge, but it's ours. We went from shitty apartments to a home. The first thing we did was paint every room. Let's say the place is colorful.

Inside, it's an open-concept layout. On one side, there are two bedrooms, a bathroom, a laundry room, and an open den. On the other side is the main suite with an en-suite bathroom. It's perfect for us. A soothing gray covers the living room walls. A white sofa, a pink rug, and white tables brighten the space. Floral curtains adorn the beautiful French doors leading to the outside deck.

They completely remodeled this space. I almost collapsed when I saw the six-burner gas stove at the showing. I love to cook, and this space is perfect for it. The kitchen cabinets are white, with butcher-block countertops and stainless-steel appliances. I've never lived anywhere this nice before, and I'm digging it.

The scent of apples greets me daily; it's warm and inviting. It gives the feel of fall year-round, bringing a smile to my face.

For the first time in my life, I'm doing what I've always wanted to do. You'd think that at twenty-seven, I would have been more accomplished by now. All I can say is that it was worth the struggles in the end. After years of barely making ends meet, I now own a bookstore and a home. We're not financially rich by any means, but we're comfortable.

The move to Cedar Creek was one of the best decisions I've ever made. The twins love being here, and they live right beside their favorite Banks brother. I almost killed the man the first time the boys disappeared to his house to play video games. I thought I had lost my kids. They're eleven now, but they're still my babies.

It's the life I always wanted for them. Simple and easy. Now I only have to work one job, and they can enjoy being kids. They have friends at school and a big-ass family that loves them.

My primary focus has always been raising my children. Long ago, I thought I loved Troy. We met when I was fourteen, and I thought we'd be together forever. After I got pregnant at 15, everything changed. Troy was no longer the sweet, caring boy I'd fallen for. Not long after I found out I was pregnant, I discovered Troy had been using drugs and getting himself into questionable situations. But I still thought I loved him.

Once the boys were born, things only got worse. Troy wanted nothing to do with them. He withdrew, leaving for days, sometimes weeks, at a time. When he was home, he either yelled about everything or avoided us altogether. Any connection Troy and I once had was completely severed.

Truthfully, I should have known better, but my young mind didn't understand his behavior or the mistreatment. Even as he was destroying me, I stuck by him until I couldn't anymore.

By the time I was twenty-one, Troy had mostly disappeared from our lives. He would show up at my job every few months, but he never made an effort to see the boys. They haven't seen him since they were five. I tried to get Troy help, but he didn't want it. Only money. That's all he ever wanted.

While stirring the sauce, I reflect on my family. My parents, Milly and Patrick, are spiritual fanatics, and we haven't had a relationship since I got pregnant. They weren't the world's worst parents, but they weren't the greatest either. They tried to shape my sister and me into a false image of ourselves. They wanted us to follow and conform to a fallacious religion. That only made my sister and me rebel more.

I haven't heard from my older sister since the day she turned eighteen, thirteen years ago. She left me a letter saying she loved me and that she was going to do something great and see the world while doing it. I've always been proud of her for getting away. I think about her from time to time and miss her greatly. I wish I knew how she was doing.

With a sigh, I let my thoughts fade and strain the noodles. Once dinner was ready, I settled onto the sofa to look through the book I had challenged Bay to read. The boys are staying with him tonight, so it's just me.

Instead of reading, I think about Baylor rather than the book. Bay is the sexiest man I have ever met, and in his uniform, oh my god. I want him to use his firehose to put out the fire inside me.

At 6'3", with a strong, athletic physique, he's the slimmest of his brothers, and it suits him perfectly. I'm eagerly anticipating summer again, specifically so I can stare at him as he swims, watching his wet, muscular body flex. Last year, the sight of him almost brought me to orgasm. His low-hanging trunks and V-line had me rubbing my thighs together most of the day.

Baylor is naturally handsome. Dark lashes and defined brows frame his lake-green eyes. He keeps his hair in a crew cut and his face shaved. A straight nose, subtle cheekbones, and a strong jawline add character to his features. I love the easy smile that gives him that undeniable charm. And damn, does he have charm.

Whoa, is it getting hot in here?

When the heat starts to pick up, I lift the collar of my shirt and fan myself. I remind myself every day that we're just friends. That's all I want right now. Even if Bay has been a constant since the day he met us, he doesn't let the kids down, is funny, and shows the same protectiveness I see in all the Banks men.

I refuse to get caught up in all his manly gorgeousness because it would break the boy's heart if it didn't work out. It's a sacrifice I've grown accustomed to. Troy is the only man I have ever been with. After the shit he put the kids and me through, dating was never a priority for me.

I don't know how long I was lost in my thoughts before my phone rang. Not paying attention to the caller, I swiped to answer it.

"Hello,"

"Winter?" The powerful female voice came through the other end of the line, sounding oddly familiar.

"Yes, who's this?"

"It's Summer."

I slumped onto the couch, a feeling of elation in my chest, as if she somehow knew I had been thinking of her. My hand dug into my hair as I swallowed back a sob. The sound of her voice deepened my yearning to have my sister back.

"Summer? Is it really you? Where have you been? Are you okay?" The questions flew out in rapid succession.

"I'm okay, but I've really missed you," she said, her sigh audible through the phone.

"I've missed you, too. Where are you?"

"I'm in Virginia right now."

"Are you safe? Do you need me to come get you?" I asked, hoping she would say yes. I wanted to see and hug her again.

"I'll come to you if it's okay. I know it's been a long time. I understand if you can't forgive me." Summer's voice came out steady and controlled.

The sob in my throat almost broke free, and my chest constricted as I fought to keep quiet. What had happened to her? Where had she been? The thought that I couldn't forgive her had clearly been on her mind.

"Summer, you have nothing to apologize for. You can stay with the boys and me. I'll convert the den into a space for you. When will you be here?"

"Within the next two weeks, roughly. I'm sorry to spring this on you. I thought calling would be better than just showing up."

"Oh, honey, don't be sorry. The twins will be so excited to meet you."

When she heard about the twins, she let out a soft giggle.

"How old are they?" she asked. When I hear someone whispering in the background, I wonder if she ever married or had her own children.

"They just turned eleven. I can't believe I'll have teenagers soon," I say with a sigh. Are parents ever prepared for their kids to grow up?

"Hopefully, they're nothing like us when we were teens. We were rebels without a care in the world," she chuckles.

"They're good kids, but I worry about that every day. They're at the stage where they only want to play video games. I have so many questions for you, but I'll wait to ask them. Will you be flying? I can pick you up."

"Driving."

"Okay, I'll text you my address and make sure we have everything ready. God, it's so good to hear your voice."

"You too. I have to step into a meeting, but I'll call soon. Thank you, Winter. I love you."

"I love you too."

Once we said our goodbyes, I finally let myself cry. I never held it against Summer for leaving. It was our parents' doing. Summer was a tough, resilient woman who wouldn't be controlled.

I've refused to think about how much I truly missed her over the years. I never knew where she went or how to find her. It feels as if the universe is bringing her back to me.

We were so close at one point in our lives. All we had was each other. Now, I'll get a chance to know her again. Something must have happened for her to want to come home. I hope she's okay and that no one hurt her while she's been gone.

Guilt slams into me the more I think about it, making me want to cry harder. What if someone hurt her, and I didn't care that she was gone at the beginning? After watching and listening to all these crime shows, I wonder whether she chose to leave.

As I sit here on the back deck, I take in the night sky. It's a beautiful spring night, and the rain has finally stopped. The loud, rhythmic song of the katydids fills the air. As I breathe in, I feel the gentle wind, the humidity, and the scent of the revitalized, nourished soil.

The sound of a creaking door draws my attention. When I look over, I see Bay step out of his back door, one hand in his hoodie pocket, and give me a questioning look. It's almost midnight, and I'm usually in bed by now, but talking to Summer has my mind racing.

"Hey," Bay says in his whisky voice as he walks across the lawn to sit with me.

"Hi, are the boys sleeping?"

"Yeah. You're up late. Is everything okay?" he asks as he sits next to me.

I hate how my body gravitates toward him whenever our thighs brush. The dirty bitch is always reaching for him. She hungers to be claimed by him.

With an exhale, I look up at the sparkling sky. It's beautiful here. Most nights, the sky is clear and glittering with stars. It's the most beautiful sight.

"It is. My sister called me today."

"Is that a good or bad thing?"

He is always tentative. I don't talk much about my family. What I dealt with growing up was nothing compared to what others have been through. All I had was my family's constant preaching and their calling my sister and me sinners. Our parents never physically harmed us.

Now that I'm older, I realize we lived in a cult village. Over the years, I recall the fenced community and armed guards. The 'church' where the leader preached, and the audience praised him instead of God.

Yup, a cult for sure.

"It's been thirteen years. I'm not sure what she's been up to, but she'll be coming to stay with us."

"What's her name?"

"Summer Anderson. Why?" When I look into his lake-green eyes, I realize why he's asking. "You're going to have Beau look her up," I say with an eye roll.

"Maybe. Maybe not."

"She was a wonderful sister, Bay. Our crazy parents were the toughest on her. They had her life mapped out. Marry the leader's son, have ten babies, and be a submissive wife. Summer was a tough bitch. She would not be submissive. Do you want their names, too?" I ask sarcastically. He'll never find information on them. They haven't been part of the general population for decades.

I watch his brows knit together tightly. "Leader? Like, as in a cult? And yeah, I want their names, too."

"Yup. That's why I don't talk about it. Milly and Patrick Anderson."

Bay nods and looks up at the sky. The three names are permanently seared into his mind.

"Damn. What do you think your sister has been up to?"

"I don't know. The last thing Summer told me was that she was going to do amazing things. She was gone two days later."

"I hope she did."

"Me too. Do you think you can help me turn the den into a room for her?"

"You know I will. There isn't anything I wouldn't do for you," Bay says, looking up at the sky.

Damn it, I do know that. Scooting closer to him, we take in the darkness together.

CHAPTER 3
WINTER

When I talk to my customers, it fills me with such joy. I love all the book recommendations I get every day. Owning the Lore Labyrinth has been fantastic. I wake up excited to come to work.

Weekends for me are usually a long march through boredom. Not this weekend, though. Tomorrow night, I have ladies' night at Birdie's. Then, on Saturday, I have that stupid speed-dating event. I don't know why I let Tink talk me into going. I don't want to date a stranger.

I want to date Baylor.

With a shake of my head, I clear those thoughts and think about my sister coming to visit. Bay was not impressed that I agreed to let her stay with me, since I know nothing about her anymore, but it's my house, my decision. Summer would never hurt the boy or me. I know that in my heart.

His overbearing protectiveness is frustrating. Bay has been pushing the fence I put up a little more lately. I won't deny I want him, but I don't want to risk the relationship he's developed with the kids. No matter how badly I want to. What if he decides I'm not what he thought I would be and stops being a part of our lives altogether? It's not a risk I can take.

When I look out the front window of the store, I see the sun casting a long shadow. I glance at the clock and see I'm a little past closing time, then move through the store to close up just as a woman enters.

"Sorry, are you closing?" the woman asks with a hint of a Spanish accent.

"I was just about to, but I can wait," I say in a chipper voice.

"Thank you. I just got off work and rushed over."

"It's no trouble. Can I help you find anything?"

I watch the woman dig through her backpack, searching for something. She's pretty. Her black hair is in a tight bun, and she has green eyes. She's dressed in all black, wearing combat boots. She looks as if she just came from the set of an action film.

"I'm looking for these books. It's my sister's birthday."

When I take the list from her, a chill runs through me. The book list is grim. I've heard how gory and grotesque each one is. It's not my place to judge, but wowza. It's going to be a fearsome read. The books range from serial killers to haunted houses.

"I think I have most of them. I can order the others, but it usually takes a couple of weeks for them to arrive."

"No worries. I'll take what you have in stock," she says with a forced smile.

"Ok," I expected the woman to wait in the front for me, but she followed me instead.

"Have you worked here for long?" she asks.

"I bought the place a few months ago," I reply.

On my tiptoes, I pull the first book from the shelf and move down the aisle.

"Do you live in town?" she presses.

That's an odd question for a customer to ask.

I don't answer. She doesn't need to know.

"It looks like I don't have these two in stock," I say politely.

The woman nods and keeps following me.

"Do you have family around here?"

"I don't," I reply simply. I'm not telling this woman shit, and she's really starting to weird me out.

"You're not very talkative, are you?" She chuckles dryly.

"I don't answer personal questions from strangers. I like to keep things casual and book-related."

"Uh, huh, I get it. You can never be too careful."

She says she gets it, but she's utterly unapologetic. I want to ring her out and lock the doors. I've never felt so uneasy.

Neither of us speaks again as I complete her transaction. Once she's out the door, I quickly lock it and watch as she places her phone to her ear. At her car, she opens the door, tosses the books in without a care, gets in, and peels off.

That was the most off-putting experience I've ever had. I shake off the uneasy feeling and start closing up.

When the space is dark, I feel that tingly, terrifying sensation that makes the hair on the back of my neck stand up. You know the part of the movie where you scream at the blonde girl to run, but then she doesn't? Yup, that's me right now. My eyes scan the room, taking in the dark aisles where a killer could hide. The sensation no longer tingles. It's vibrating. Fear rears its ugly head and overpowers me.

Crap, I scared myself. I take a deep breath and hold it. I reach the last switch, ten feet from the back door, and then I do the logical adult thing. I flip off the switch, haul ass to the door, fling it open, and run out into the dim night.

When I slam into a body, I can't stop the scream that erupts from me before I hit the person in the face with my purse. My heart pounds so fast I'm pretty sure it's going to explode or stop beating. I'm not sure which yet.

"Hot dog, Winter," Gene groans, holding his nose.

"Oh my god, Gene," I shout, clutching my chest and doubling over as terror and relief fight inside me. I breathe in and out, trying to slow my racing heart. When I look up at him, he's holding his face in his hands, his eyes wide with shock. Gene is an older man who likes to dig through the dumpsters behind the buildings for what he calls 'treasures'.

"I'm sorry, young miss. I was heading to my usual hunting grounds. Are you okay?" he asks in a nasally voice, his thumb and forefinger clamping his nose. My eyes bulge when I see the red drops on his shirt.

Shit. I rummage in my purse, pull out some tissues, and help plug up the man's bleeding nose.

"I'm fine. I really should stop listening to podcasts. Like an idiot, I freaked myself out. Sorry, old timer. It was a reflex. Why don't you sit? I'll see if the cafe is still open and get some water," I say in a shaky voice. The adrenaline is still flowing through me.

Gene waves me off. "I got some in the truck. Don't you worry. Are you sure you just spooked yourself? Remember, I'm always back here from 7 pm to 10 pm on Mondays and Fridays. If you ever need me, just yell. I may be seventy, but I still have the hearing of a young buck and the fists of a champion."

Chuckling, I pat his shoulder. "I appreciate you, Gene. I promise my panic was self-induced. Thanks for looking out for me, though."

"That's what any decent person should do. I'll walk you to your car." He holds out his arm to me. I lift my lip, slip mine through his, and let him be my security guard.

At my car, I give him a gentle hug. "I'll see you on Monday. Sorry again about the nose."

"It's no bother. Have a good night, Ms. Winter."

In the driver's seat, I start the car and groan with embarrassment over what just happened. With the panic receding, I head home. Baylor picked the kids up from school like he usually does when he's not on shift. I know they'll ask to stay with him, but they need to come home tonight. If it were up to them, they'd live with him. I do not doubt that.

Exhaling with the relief of being safe at home, I park in the detached garage, get out, and head straight to my room.

The walls in this room are a soothing lavender, with white bedding and furniture. I wanted something calm and relaxed for this space. I open the dresser door and pick out leggings, scrunch socks, a tank top, and my only oversized hoodie. It used to be Troy's. I really should buy a new one and toss this fucking thing, or burn it. All it does is bring back bad memories.

I giggle when I open my phone and see a text from Baylor.

Hotshot:

We have dinner at my place.

Me:

But pizza rolls.

Hotshot:

Angel, DO NOT eat those. Come over.

My heart flutters every time he calls me Angel. I shouldn't like it, but I do.

In the bathroom, I take in the calm, serene feeling. I left it pristine white, giving it a spa feel when I entered. As I take my time, I turn on the water to heat while I strip down. Stepping into the shower, I relish the feel of hot water pelting me. Steam flows through the room like a cloud, and the aroma of my shampoo and body wash wafts to my senses, soothing me.

There is nothing better than a long, hot shower after a long day. Or the scare of your life. I am an idiot, I think, then chuckle out loud, reminiscing on my reaction tonight.

The shower's heat fades, prompting me to twist the handles and cut the water. I step out, towel off, and get dressed. Then I grab the gift I got for Bay. It's nothing special. I saw it in a gift shop while walking downtown and thought of him.

At his door, I knock and lose my breath when his sexy ass answers. He's in his tight jeans and a CCFD hoodie, sleeves pushed up. He has the fewest tattoos of the Banks men, with only one sleeve, but damn it, it's just enough to get me hot.

"Were they good for you today?" I squeak, I fucking squeaked like a schoolgirl.

When I brush past him, I can't resist absorbing his warmth and the comforting scent of sage and cinnamon. His smell is unique to him.

Inside his house, the design is the same as mine, but he has leather and wood furniture and natural-colored walls, making it look ultra manly, and every room smells like him.

"They're always good for me." I hear the door click and his jeans rustle as he shuffles behind me into the spacious kitchen. The scent of orange chicken and lo Mein noodles has my stomach growling.

When I go to make the kids a plate, Bay nudges me aside and makes us each a plate. I'm not sure what it is with these men. I have watched them all serve the woman and the kids before they get their own food.

"Boys, come get your plates." He calls out like it's the most natural thing in the world.

"Can we eat in the living room?" Dylan asks.

Before I can answer, Baylor does. "At the coffee table, and make sure you get napkins."

"Yes," they say in unison before scurrying off with their Chinese food.

Baylor sets my plate in front of me and then makes his. He finishes and takes a seat next to me. He forces me to face him by spinning my stool on its axis.

"You look like you had a bad day. Why?" Bay's jaw is lax, and his green irises bounce between mine, studying my every feature.

I'm stunned by his acknowledgment. I checked the mirror before I came over here, and even I couldn't tell.

"How could you possibly know that?" I ask, giving him a dumbfounded look.

"Because I pay attention, Winter. Your eyes get a dark tent underneath when you've had a long or stressful day," he says.

My heart dances, and the butterflies in my stomach flutter as he leans closer. He reaches out and gently uses his pointer finger to line each spot under my eyes. The rough pad is surprisingly tender.

"Tell me what happened, angel."

"A woman came in before I closed, and her entire vibe was off," I tell him, not bothering to hold back the shudder.

"How was her vibe off? Did she make you uncomfortable?"

He's always genuine about his concerns and questions. I like this side of him, but I also fear it. It makes me feel safe and cared for. I want that. Baylor makes me feel wanted, and it scares the shit out of me.

Without a word, Bay pulls his hoodie off. He reaches out, grabs the hem of my oversized hoodie, and starts lifting it. I swat his hands away, and he laughs, a warm, husky sound that makes my neck flush.

"What are you doing, you barbarian?"

"I know this isn't your hoodie, and I can guess who it belonged to. Talk," he commands, still lifting. "Arms up, Angel."

"Baylor, you can't just take my sweater off. I'm cold," I protest, fighting to pull the fabric back down. A playful glint dances in his eyes as he smiles at me.

"I'm aware. I have a replacement ready. Now, lift and talk, Winnie," he demands.

"That's not my name," I grumble, lifting my arms. "Yeah, she made me uncomfortable. Her book list was unsettling, and she looked like an assassin. Then she began to ask me personal questions."

"Do you have cameras at the store? What questions?" he says as the hoodie comes up over my head.

He doesn't even try to be discreet about how his eyes drink me in, as if I'm the only one who can quench his thirst. Baylor takes in every bump and curve of me. Biting his bottom lip, he balls up the old hoodie and tosses it into the garbage can, his eyes never leaving me.

My mouth opens and closes as my eyes bounce between him and the trash can. My gaze meets his, and I swear I can see a war raging in his bright irises. Once I recover from the moment's intensity, I start talking again.

"I have a couple of cameras," I think for a minute, sigh, and shake my head. "The section we were in is a blind spot, but the front camera probably caught her. She asked if I lived in town and had family around here."

Baylor holds out his hoodie so I can slip my arms into it. Wait, why am I letting this man dress me like a child? Oh, right, because it feels nice to be taken care of. That's why.

Once he has his sweatshirt over my head, he lets his fingers whisper over every inch of me he can reach. Goosebumps spread across my body from his touch. The shirt is still warm from his body. I want to bring it to my nose and inhale, but I won't… not yet, anyway.

"Can you send me the footage?" he asks, fluffing my hair and rubbing my neck with his tender palm.

Once he's satisfied and I'm comfortable again, he grabs his plate and starts eating. He's so damn cute and sweet. Why can't I get over my fear of being with him?

"Sure, but we can't do anything. All she did was creep me out. Are you worried?" I ask nervously, taking a bite of food.

"No, but at least I'll have a picture. If she comes back, call Beau or me," he insists.

"Again, there's nothing we can do about her asking questions. I didn't answer them. After she left, I freaked myself out," I say with a half-embarrassed chuckle because I am pathetic.

"How did you do that?" he asks, shoveling another bite into his mouth.

"I started imagining I was in a horror movie once all the lights were off. I ran through the store like a damned idiot. Then, as I flew out the back door, I collided with Gene and busted his face with my purse," I admit.

Baylor almost spits out his food when I tell him that part. It was not funny at the time. I was terrified and had beaten an older man.

"I'm sorry, but that's funny, Winnie. Is Gene okay?" He laughs hysterically.

"Yeah, but not his poor nose. He was a sport about it and made sure I was okay. He didn't even care that he was bleeding everywhere. I was so embarrassed."

"Don't be. That woman scared you. I have some news about your sister."

"I don't want to know," I say, stopping him before he says any more. "I want to hear about her life from her, Bay."

"And I need to make sure you and the kids are safe. You three are my responsibility."

"We're not your responsibility, hotshot. We're just friends. You don't have to take care of us." The words are a reminder for both of us.

Bay grunts and shuffles the remaining food on his plate. "You are and have been since the fourth of July. You'll see it one day. I want to do it, Winnie."

"You know the whole protective, possessive thing is hot sometimes, and other times it kind of pisses me off."

"So, what you're saying is you think I'm hot? I knew it," he snaps his fingers and gives me a heart-stopping, playful grin.

I can't help the stunned stare. Baylor is a beautiful, ridiculous man.

“Is that the only part you heard?” I ask with an arched brow.

Bay’s grin turns cocky as it widens. “It is. And you should know,” he leans closer, making my lungs still and my heart race. “The feeling is mutual.”

“You’re insufferable.”

“You like it. Eat,” he says, pointing to my plate.

God, it gets me hot when he’s demanding.

“I’m not sure I like you right now,” I tell him, then shove a big piece of chicken in my mouth, chew it, and show it to him.

Baylor bursts out laughing but doesn’t say anything else. Instead, he watches to make sure I eat. Jesus, he’s intense sometimes.

Once I’m mostly done eating, I slide his gift over to him. “Open it.”

I watch as he unwraps the small box and pulls out the St. Florian necklace. The pendant depicts St. Florian standing above a burning house, holding a bucket of water in his right hand. It means He is fire-resistant and features a firefighter's shield emblem on the back, depicting firefighter gear, a ladder, and a hose.

His face stays still as he removes the pendant and thumbs it. When he doesn’t say anything, nervousness coils in me. He hates it. Or did I cross a line? Hell, I don’t know.

“You don’t have to wear it. I saw it and thought of you,” I rush out, anxious that the gift might have been a bad idea.

“No. I want to. It’s the best gift I’ve gotten. Thank you, Angel.”

I watch his thick fingers struggle to unclasp it. With a giggle, I stand and step behind him.

“I’ll do it, princess,” I tease.

“Really? You’re such a charmer.”

Laughing harder now, I take the necklace, clasp it around his neck, and pat both his shoulders.

“Beautiful.”

“Pfft, I know.”

Sitting back down, we spend the next couple of hours talking before I head home with the boys. A sadness fills me as I enter my own home. A large part of me never wants to leave Bay, but I know it’s what I have to do.

CHAPTER 4
BAYLOR

After I dropped Winter off at Birdie's, I headed to Briggs. Outside his house, I saw my brother's cars in the driveway. Tonight is poker night, and the girls are all at Birdie's getting drunk. I have my two favorite sidekicks, Dylan and Daniel. When they ask to hang out, I always say yes. Besides, Winter could use a break.

Stepping out of the car, I grabbed my coffee. The boys leaped from the back seat, hurrying toward the entrance to escape the rain. It's a sprinkle, yet they act like they might melt if a drop touches them. It's late April, and spring is in full swing. Cool breezes and rain are common on most days.

Inside the house, Briggs steps into view. "About time, asshole."

"You said 7 pm, and it's," I check my watch and roll my eyes, "7:03 pm. Suck my dick, dude."

A baby's cry has my brows creasing.

"Blue sounds different." As soon as the words are out, Baxter steps out of the kitchen holding a newborn baby.

My eyes nearly jump out of my skull. “What the hell is that? Where did it come from?” I ask, quickening my pace to see the tiny human.

“I got this. You see, baby brother. When a man likes a woman,” Briggs teases.

“Shut up, smart ass. Whose kid is it?” I ask, looking down at the sleeping baby. I assume it’s a boy, given the blue blanket he’s swaddled in and the blue hat.

“This is my son, Everett Kingston Banks. Anna and I slept together the night before she lost her shit. She dropped him off at the garage three days ago. He’s two weeks old,” Baxter says tightly, but as soon as he looks at his boy, I watch the tension melt away.

Fuck, my heart hurts for my older brother. Not only did she break his heart, but she also left her child behind.

“Damn, Bax. I’m sorry, bro. That bitch just keeps swinging. Did you know she was pregnant? I know it’s a shit thing to ask, but are you sure he’s yours and not, you know?”

Bax grunts and shakes his head, then looks at the little boy in his arms with pure adoration. “Not a fucking clue. Anna had him tested against Gary. I was the next runner-up, and I gladly took the hit. Look at him? He’s perfect.”

Beau walks over and rubs the boy's head, then pats Baxter's back. “He is. Handing him over to you was the only decent thing Anna has done since that night. Don’t let her back in.”

Beau walks over, gets Blue from her playpen, and holds her. Suddenly, I realize that this is our life now. I mean, I don’t have kids, but I spend a decent amount of my time with the twins.

“She signed over all her rights. I told her that as soon as she walked out the door, she could never come back into our lives.”

I rub the back of my neck and keep staring at the baby. I can’t take my eyes off him. I’m guessing he has Baxter's blue eyes.

It's a shame that Anna went off the rails the way she did. She was a big part of our lives.

Sometimes I wonder if she was in love with Briggs, and if his marrying Journey fucked her up and sent her over the edge when she realized they'd never be together.

"I still can't believe how different she turned out. Her head is screwed. How the hell could she walk away? You're better off without her, Bax. You have us to help. That little boy is in the best hands." Briggs growls, shakes his head, and murmurs 'cunt' under his breath. He isn't wrong.

"I know. Anna married some rich schmuck. They moved to Paris, according to her socials," Baxter says, looking at me, silently asking if I want to hold Everett.

Of course, I want to hold him; he's my nephew.

I hook my arm, and Baxter gently places him in it. I forget how weightless babies are. He is cute. I take out my phone and snap a quick picture to show Winter. When I put it away, I move Everett's hat back and smile at the head of brown hair. I knew it.

"Has he been good? What did Mom and Dad say?"

"He's been great. Mom cried not only because she had a new grandbaby but also because Anna had broken her heart. Dad couldn't stop smiling and kept his opinions about Anna to himself." Bax answers and leans on the kitchen island, never taking his gaze off Everett.

Sitting at the table with my brothers, I hold Everett and think I'm not ready for little kids. I love the twins, but they're older and can wipe their own asses.

"He's cute, Bax. I thought you'd have ugly babies, but I stand corrected." I joke and smile at my big brother, making him chuckle.

"I was worried too, so you're off the hook for that comment." He laughs, actually laughs. The poor bastard has been miserable since that night; he has barely been around. This little boy helped bring our brother back to who he used to be.

"I always thought it was going to be Briggs to knock someone up and end up in this situation," Beau says, making everyone but Briggs laugh.

"Funny, dickface. I actually settled down before Journey."

"And yet you got drunk and married in Vegas," Beau fires back.

"What the hell is happening? We're over here talking like a bunch of chicks while the girls are at Beau's tossing back shots," I ask.

"We have all the kids, and the women deserve a break," Beau shrugs.

"Baylor," Dylan shouts as he walks into the room, the other boys following him.

I peel my eyes from the baby and meet Dyl's hazel eyes. "What's up?"

"Is balls a curse word?" he asks innocently, making all of us hold back our laughs.

"Because we have balls," Daniel says.

I have no idea how to answer the question, so I look to my brothers for the correct answer.

"Dad, is it a curse word? I told them it was," Ox asks Briggs. It takes Briggs a moment to compose himself before he speaks.

"I think we should see what your mom says about the curse word," Briggs says, looking back at all of us. "How old were we when we started saying balls without mom popping us in the mouth?"

"About their age. It's not a curse word, but maybe don't say it at school," Baxter answers, shaking the bottle he made.

"Whose baby is that?" Daniel asks, coming over to look. "It's so little," he says in awe.

"This is Everett. Baxter's son," I tell him.

"Did you have him?" Dylan scrunches his face and walks over to look. "I thought only girls could have babies because they have vaginas."

That statement breaks the composure of four grown-ass men. We all burst out laughing. I don't want to know how he knows that.

"Okay, enough talking about body parts. Don't say balls or that other word you said. Go play and do not curse," Briggs tells the boys. Ox innocently raises his hands and backs away. All four boys take off back upstairs, leaving us to our laughter.

Baxter walks over, taking Everett from my arms just as he starts to pout. He seems to know the child will wake. Bax takes his seat and feeds Everett, who goes whole hog on his meal. I always knew he'd be a good father. It's just a shame it happened this way.

When I flip my phone over, I see multiple missed calls from Winter. I'm not sure she'll answer, but I'll try calling her back.

Within two rings, she picks up.

"Is there a baby, Baylor? Or are the girls messing with me?" She asks.

I chuckle into the phone. "Yes, Baxter has a baby." I move the phone from my ear and send her the picture I took. "I just sent you a picture."

A moment passes before she squeals into the phone. "Oh my god, he's so precious. Does he have that new baby smell?"

My chest rumbles with laughter. "He's not a new car. You know that, right? We're friends, but I am not sniffing the baby, Winnie."

Winnie huffs into the phone. "I know that. Fine. Tell Baxter congrats. He is so adorable, and I get the first babysitting shift so that I can breathe in the new baby scent."

"That's weird, Winter."

"Don't you judge me. You sniffed your own foot the other night to make sure it didn't stink."

"They didn't stink, which means it was your feet I was smelling."

"It absolutely was not. We're not friends right now, stinky," she says incredulously and hangs up on me.

I put my phone away, chuckling to myself. "Winnie said, Congratulations," I tell Baxter.

"Winnie?" Briggs asks, sipping his beer.

"We're friends. She's made it clear that's all she wants right now."

"Uh-huh," Briggs says with a knowing look, but says nothing.

He knows I've wanted the short blonde beauty with crystal eyes since she showed up at the Fourth of July party, hungover from drinking with Ny the night before. When she finally came alive, I didn't miss her trying to hide her tiger stripes from having her twins. I wanted to lick and kiss each one.

"Are we going to play poker or keep talking like a bunch of gossip queens?" Beau asks, bouncing Blue on his knee.

"Yes, let's get the game going," I chime in, cutting off the conversation about Winter.

As I walk into Beau's, I hear the girls cackling about something. After we played poker at Briggs for a couple of hours, it's time to get the girls home safely. We all prefer that they do this here rather than at a bar.

Halfway to the kitchen, Winter jogs out, completely hammered. She stumbles and flings her arms around my neck, laughing.

Holding her back to keep her upright, chuckling. Winter looks up at me with one eye closed and swaying. She reaches up and places her hands on my chest to steady herself.

"Drink too much, Angel?" I smirk.

"No, Hotshot," she slurs. "We're playing truth or dare," she quips, as if I knew what kind of bad decisions they were making before I walked in.

Winnie stares and rubs my chest as if she's never felt one before. I knew she wanted me. That hungry look in her eyes gives it away.

"Wowza," she whispers, then keeps petting me.

Winter is a thing of beauty, even when she's drunk. Tonight her porcelain cheeks are rosy, and her mascara has smeared under her eyes. The high ponytail she had earlier is now on the side of her head. She is a gorgeous hot mess.

"Sounds fun. Are you and Ny ready to go?" I ask, trying to get her to focus so we can go.

Winter shakes her head vigorously. "I have to do my dare."

Before I can blink, she grabs my face, pulls me down to her level, crashes her closed lips to mine, and pulls back. Even though it was the briefest of seconds, I'm already addicted to her slick, warm lips.

Shit, I got a chubby.

Her mouth parts, and she looks at me like she's just seen a ghost before she shouts, "I did it," and takes off running back to the kitchen, laughing. I can't take my eyes off her white-blond hair flying behind her.

Beau walks over, laughing his ass off, and claps me on the shoulder.

"Bay," Journey sways on her feet in the kitchen doorway. "Did she use tongue?" she slurs, closing an eye as if that will steady her.

All I can do at this point is stare blankly. Was it a fuck with Baylor dare?

"That's a no." Ny turns and yells. "Lying bitch. Take a shot."

"Traitor," Winter shouts, loud enough for me to hear. My brain finally catches up, and I let out a nervous laugh. This is comical.

"What the hell is happening?" I ask Beau, who shakes his head.

"Hell, if I know. They act like a bunch of teenagers when they all drink together. Last time, they all got drunk and skinny-dipped at Ny's. Thankfully, by the time Briggs and I got there, they were dressed and admitted to it the next day."

"I'm glad I missed most of these gatherings."

Shaking my head, I follow Beau into the kitchen, where Birdie and Astor are dancing to 'Smack That" on the island.

"I see they're at it again," Noah says behind me.

Like a flip of a switch, Birdie and Astor stop dancing, hug each other, and start crying.

"Anna left her baby. How could she do that?" Birdie cries.

"Dear God," I mutter under my breath.

"Get used to it. It happens a lot," Noah whispers, walking over to retrieve his wife.

Anna shouldn't be considered part of this family, not even in memory. She isn't worth the tears shed over her.

“Screw her. Baxter is in good hands with Everett,” Winter says, then scrunches her face. Beau, Noah, and I laugh while she catches up to what she just said. “Wait. I said that wrong. What was I talking about?”

“Come on. I’m taking you and Ny home,” I tell her, rounding up the two women.

“Booo,” they all say together.

Drunk girls are exhausting. It’s been fifteen minutes, but it feels like sixty. I wait while the two girls say goodbye, then walk them to the car with Beau’s help to make sure neither falls.

“Thanks. Text Briggs and have him meet me out front,” I tell Beau when I see Ny in the back seat, her head back, eyes closed, and mouth open.

“Yup.” Beau laughs.

After I drop Ny off, I head home and carry a passed-out Winter into her house.

Settling her into her bed, I leave her some Tylenol, a sports drink, water, and a note thanking her for the kiss to fuck with her. It’s only fair.

CHAPTER 5
BAYLOR

I know I look insane walking up to Journey and Briggs' door, fully intent on cock-blocking Winnie, but the mere thought of her with anyone else is like a punch to the gut.

Tonight, I'm officially taking the gloves off and going all in to convince her it's a good idea for us to be together. She worries about the kids, but I'm not Troy. Maybe one day she'll realize that. Our father raised us to be good men to our women and children, not pieces of shit.

When I stop at the door, Briggs flings it open, looking like he might kill me.

"I should kick your ass, Baylor. I can't believe you got Journey to agree to this," Briggs grumbles, then growls when Journey comes out of the bedroom, dressed to impress.

"I believe I am capable of making my own decisions, Honey Bear," Journey purrs.

"See, it's fine. Ny is just signing headshots, and you'll be with her the entire time," I say, throwing a hand toward Ny.

"It's a speed-dating event, and she's your distraction. She's my wife," Briggs seethes. I get it. If I were in his shoes, I'd beat my own ass, too.

"Relax, baby. It's fine. I think it's cute he's going through all this trouble to cock-block Winter." Ny laughs and grabs her coat.

I give Briggs a duh look, but he glares daggers at me instead. Okay, so I crossed the line. I'll cross more when I get to the event. I had Winter's name replaced with Journey's this morning. She isn't participating in the dating. She'll sign photos rather than engage in conversation.

I know the woman who organized the event, and bribery goes a long way. I'll just need some of the guys from work to show up at her pet adoption event. Wait, that's the bartering system, not bribery, right?

"It'll go quickly, and I owe you babysitting hours."

"You owe me your left nut for this," Briggs says angrily.

"The right one is my favorite anyway. You can have the left. Wait, can I have kids with one nut? Potato chip, look it up and tell me, but be gentle with the news." I say dramatically, placing a hand on my chest while I wait.

Ny pulls out her phone and clicks. I knew there was a reason we became best friends.

"You're in luck, Tostitos. You can have kids with one nut."

Turning, I grin at Briggs, who has a permanent scowl on his face. "You can have the left one. Look, I know you're pissed. You got lucky. You found your person and accidentally married her. Some of us have to put in the work. Winnie isn't making this easy for me."

Briggs finally gives up on his anger when Journey pats his cheek with a smile. He would do anything to make sure she's happy. It's almost a guarantee she owns his left nut. Probably the right one, too.

"Fine, I give. Don't pull this shit again, though. I'll beat your ass next time," he tells me, then follows behind his wife, who is all too excited for tonight's shenanigans.

My life has felt monotonous and gray until now. The most eventful thing I had going for me was my job. I'm aware I can be immature, but I believe life is too short to take everything so seriously. Might as well shoot your shot.

I'm taking a risk tonight that will likely piss Winter off, but it was the only thing I could come up with at the time. She is a stubborn-ass woman. I've tried everything else I can think of to show her I'm fully committed to her and the boys, but Winter will not back down.

I know she's worried I'll hurt her or the kids the way her ex did. I can't say I know what it's like to have my heart broken, but I can say I would never hurt hers. Here's a little truth about me: being a twenty-seven-year-old virgin wasn't something I intended. There just hasn't been a woman who ignites that fire in me… until Winnie.

Don't get me wrong, I've dated and fooled around some, and I've watched a shit ton of porn. For learning purposes, of course. I want to make sure I know what the fuck I'm doing and what women like when I finally do it.

After parking outside the Hideaway, I take a deep breath before I get out of the car. With Journey and Briggs in tow, we walk inside.

Angela's face lights up when she sees us and gets Journey set up. I scan the room, searching for Winter, then I see her sitting in the corner at one of the tables.

She is pure, angelic beauty in her white dress, jean jacket, and sandals. Her hair is down, and just a splash of makeup sprinkles her face. She doesn't look impressed or entertained as she stares out the window, watching people and cars pass by. I wait out of her view until Angela announces the rules and dings the bell.

Ding. Ding. Ding.

That's my cue. Putting on my cocky persona, I strut to Winnie's table, glaring at the men who are looking at her like she's the last slice of pizza, and everyone is still hungry.

Not today fuckers.

I slide the chair out at her table, take a seat, and watch the surprise flush her cheeks before she quickly masks it and raises her defenses.

"What are you doing here, Baylor?" she huffs.

"I think it's called speed dating. What are you doing here, Winnie?" I say coolly, relaxing back into the chair.

She narrows her eyes at me in the most adorable way. "I think you know the answer to that. You can't just show up here, Bay. I'm pretty sure they have rules or something."

"Do they? Huh, I didn't know that. Anyway, I have a question for you."

"What?"

"Every year, we have a firefighter charity ball. I'd like you to be my date. It's in a few weeks." I did it. I shot my first shot.

Winter lets out an exasperated breath and droops her shoulders. "Bay, I've told you we can't date. I don't want to ruin our friendship."

She's denying me, but I can see a light twinkle in her eyes. Why does she have to fight this so hard? Our chemistry is off the charts, and she knows it. I'll improvise to get her to agree.

"As friends, then. Come on, it would help me out."

Winter eyes me wearily. "Fine. Now go away."

I figured that might work.

"Oh, yeah, I can't do that. Tonight is our first unofficial friend's date," I say with a big-ass grin, pointing to Ny, who is signing a photo.

"What did you do? Briggs is going to kill you, Baylor," Winter says, her mouth agape and eyes wide.

"Nah, he just wants my left nut, but it's okay. I can still reproduce with the right one," I tell her, giving her my best cheeky grin and a wink. As suspected, she's unimpressed.

She rubs her temples and looks at me with a hint of a smile. "God, what is wrong with you?"

"I know what I want, and I'm willing to pimp out my sister-in-law to get it."

"Wow. Your persistence is impressive and annoying."

"I heard impressive. Let's go get a real drink, or we could take a walk and get ice cream." I suggest.

"Bay, seriously, the whole you and me thing is a bad idea," she says, wiggling a finger between us.

I grunt at her remark. I know she's just scared to feel for someone again. I might be goofy, but I'm a decent human. Winter will be mine. I don't care how long it takes to get her.

"Whatever you have to tell yourself, Angel," I lean in closer to her and whisper. "I could almost smell you the other night while I was touching you. You want me, Winnie. I'm just not sure why you keep fighting it."

Winnie's eyes bulge as her mouth opens and closes a few times. "There is no way you could smell me," she hisses, and her face flames with embarrassment. Winnie sits back, refusing to make eye contact with me. She knows I'm right.

"Hm, you couldn't be more wrong, but I'll let it go for now. How do you like the new hoodie?"

She gives me a warning, "Bay," but I'm not backing down.

"Did you sleep in it last night? Let me know when you need my scent freshened. I'm already breaking in a new one for you." I keep pressing, smiling.

"Baylor," she whispers, squirming a little.

She is so damn sexy, acting all innocent and aggravated, with her pink cheeks and nibbling on her bottom lip. But I can tell she's turned on.

My face breaks into a cocky grin. "You didn't answer my question."

"You know I did. You threw my other one away." She glowers at me.

I lift a shoulder. "It was garbage. Ever been told you're adorable when you're all pissed off?"

"No. You're not giving up, are you?"

"Not a chance."

Winnie rests her arms on the table and leans in. "Fine. You're right. I find you extremely attractive. I think about you often, but I'm telling you, it's a terrible idea. I can't let the boys get hurt when our attraction eventually fades, and we realize that's all we had in common. You like me because I'm the new shiny toy in town. That's it." When she finishes, she leans back and folds her hands in her lap.

What the fuck?

"I'm not sure what made you think that, but you couldn't be more wrong. Are you hot? Hell yeah, but you're more than that. If I only wanted to fuck you, I wouldn't try so hard. Winnie, please take a chance on me. Let me show you. I will always be here. I would never do anything to hurt you or the boys. I won't let you down." I plead my case, hoping she'll see rationality.

Before we can say more, some jerk swaggers over to our table, acting like he doesn't notice that she and I are engrossed in conversation, my gaze flicks to Winter, and I see her watching the man in his sleek suit and well-groomed hair. Maybe she's interested in a rich-looking, handsome guy—that's definitely not me.

“Excuse me, Ma’am. I had to come over here and tell you how beautiful you are,” he says with a smile. I know it's a fake as fuck act, but Winnie blushes and tucks her hair behind her ear.

Seriously? She’d rather talk to this dipstick?

“Thank you.” She responds in a sweet voice.

“I was wondering if you’d like to get a drink?” His voice is as smooth as brandy; she doesn’t know it's the cheapest on the market, and it burns like Drano going down.

Clearing my throat, I glower at the man. He smirks before turning his attention back to Winter. This son of a bitch knows his fake-ass charm and masked rotten smile work. I’ve seen his type. He’s the kind of man Winter should be worried about.

“He’s just a friend. A drink sounds wonderful.” Winter purrs. She fucking PURRS.

My jaw tightens, and my fists clench. I should stop chasing her. Her action is a clear sign, but damn it, I can’t let her go.

My gut twists as Winnie gets up and sways her perfect ass past the prick, walking away from our table and putting an end to my pursuit. It’s safe to say my cock-blocking plan failed.

Fantastic

When I glance at Ny, I see her frown as she looks from me to Winter. Yeah, that slap in the face just happened, and it hurt like a bitch.

My skin feels like it's burning as I watch her sit with the man and order a glass of wine. The longer I stare, the more pissed off I get. I’d rather stand in a burning building, naked, covered in gasoline, than be here right now.

I shouldn't be this pissed. We're not a couple, but we've been dancing around each other for months. Have I not proven myself by now? People interested only in sex don't stick around for months. Or maybe they do. I'm not that kind of man, so I wouldn't know.

"I've decided to let you keep your nut," Briggs says, sitting opposite me. "She just left with the right one, and you'll need the left one to give me nieces and nephews. Come on. Ney is finished, and we're heading somewhere else to drink."

"You don't have to do that."

"I know, but I'm going to anyway. I'm tired of watching women hurt my brothers," Briggs says with a stretch and gets to his feet.

I stand, give Winter one last look, and see her laughing as our eyes meet. She looks so beautiful, but not mine. Her face falls when I look away, turn, and follow Briggs out the door, leaving my heart at the table where she shredded it.

Rejection is a bitter pill I refuse to swallow again. Winter wants to be friends. Fine, friends, it is. I'll help with her sister's room and keep my distance from her, but I won't distance myself from the twins. They depend on me to be there for them.

CHAPTER 6
WINTER

What is wrong with me? I didn't want to come over here and have a drink with this man. He's barely said a word since we sat down.

I just screwed everything up with Bay. He'll stop chasing me now. That's what I was hoping for, or what I thought I should hope for. The pain and hurt on his face when he left made my heart ache. I was worried about him hurting us, but I'm the one who hurt him instead.

If Bay and I tried dating and it didn't work, we wouldn't be able to go back to what we have now. The comfort and company of each other would be lost. What if he stops being there for Dyl and Dan? I don't want to risk that.

Every time Troy disappeared after making promises, I watched their disappointed faces, and it tore me up. I never want to see those faces again.

If Bay walks away, it would destroy them. It wouldn't be just sad faces; it would be shattered hearts. I'm not sure they would recover. They look up to him in a way I never could have imagined.

"Tell me a little about yourself. Do you live around here? Did you grow up here? I'm all ears, princess," Edwards says in a smooth voice.

Crap, I didn't hear a word he said.

"I'm sorry. I made a mistake. I'm going to go. It was nice meeting you, Edward," I blurt out.

Edward chuckles and points to my drink. "You didn't even take a sip of the drink I bought. I thought we were having a lovely conversation."

I refrain from rolling my eyes. Edward is one of those guys who points out everything they do, letting you know they think you don't appreciate it or expect something in return.

"I'm not much of a drinker," I say, skipping past the conversation since he's the only one talking.

I reach into my purse, pull out some money, and set it on the bar. That way, he won't think I owe him anything. I don't miss his jaw lock as I set the money down.

"Have a good night," I tell him, standing and grabbing my purse. I need to find Baylor.

Edward gives me a dangerous glare. The kind that makes your body tremble, and your hair rise. "Sit, Winter Anderson." His voice shifts to a dark, intimidating tone.

"I don't think that's a good idea," I answer warily.

As I turn to walk away, I see the woman from the bookstore. She still looks scary. Oh, God, this isn't good. My hands start to shake from the panic-induced adrenaline coursing through my veins.

"This isn't a debate. Sit. Now," Edwards demands.

Heart hammering against my chest, I retake the stool. What on earth is happening?

Edward's dark eyes meet mine, and he twirls a finger around the rim of his glass. "Troy has something that belongs to me. I want it back, and you're going to get it."

Of course, this is about Troy.

"I haven't talked to him since he got arrested. Before that, it had been years. I don't know what he took, but he'll never tell me," I say in a shaky whisper.

"You'll figure it out, or your boyfriend will pay the price first," he threatens, sipping his drink.

The words are a dagger piercing my chest.

"Being a firefighter is a dangerous job, after all."

My heart drops to the pit of my stomach when he threatens Baylor. It's as if all the stale air has been pulled from the room. My lungs are gasping for breath. I can't let Bay get involved in whatever Troy did. I was right to start pushing him away. I would never forgive myself if anything happened to him.

"I know what you're thinking. Don't. If you cut him out, he'll suspect something. You can't hide the undeniable spark in his eyes when he looks at you. I know a jealous man when I see one," Edward says as he swallows the harsh liquid.

"I-I…" My mouth sputters, unable to form a sentence.

Edward doesn't let me try before he holds his hand up to silence me. "I don't need him or his cop brother looking into me. And that's what will happen if you push him away. What you're going to do is bring him closer. Date him. Fuck him. I don't care how you do it. The reality is, I will kill him first, either way. Might as well enjoy him first."

Edward looks at me with his cold, dead glare and pinched lips. "If I don't get my items back, I'll move to your twins. I'm not a fan of hurting children, but I do what's necessary."

I swallow the sob lodged in my throat and hold back the tears that make my eyes feel like molten lava. Fucking Troy. I didn't think I could hate him as much as I do right now.

My babies. How could he do something that would put us in this situation? It shows he didn't care. We meant nothing to him.

"What is it he had?" I ask weakly.

Edward laughs without humor. "What I want back is priceless, but we'll start with the money. He stole $60K."

My throat constricts, and my anxiety spikes. How the hell am I going to get that kind of money? I own a small bookstore that my friend bought for me. I can ask Journey, but what would I tell her it's for?

"Oh, and don't ask your friends for the money. It'll tip them off."

"But Troy's in prison. They have cameras. I can't talk to him about this there." I argue.

"No excuses. I will be in town until I get what's mine back. The longer you take, the higher the stakes for people getting hurt. Better get started, Rabbit."

Without another word, he gets up, finishes his drink, and walks off with the woman, leaving me in shocked silence, staring into space.

When I start walking out of the bar, I realize Tink was my ride, and she isn't here. No one is. With my phone in hand, I order an Uber and wait outside for it to arrive.

Ny didn't even stick around. I saw the disappointment on her face when I walked away. I shouldn't have left Baylor. Not like it mattered. Edward already knew who I was. The woman with him had already scoped me out. He would have found a way to get me alone another time if I turned him down earlier.

Exhaling, I get into the Uber that shows up and ride in silence while I hold back the waterfall of tears that looms, waiting to be released.

With my keys in hand, I look at the house next door. The lights are off, making the night feel eerie. Great, he went to drink with Briggs and could end up bringing some other woman home with him, and he has no idea the danger he is in.

I let out a heavy sigh and unlock my door. Inside, I shower, put on Bay's hoodie, and crawl into bed. I bring the sweater's collar to my nose, inhaling his lingering scent, then cry until I run out of tears. With heavy, dry eyes, I close my lids and drift off.

Loud knocking on the door has me groaning. When I open my eyes, light blasts them like a laser beam, and I quickly squeeze them shut. I crawl across the bed, grab my phone, and check the time.

Damn, it's almost ten. I haven't slept that long in years. Then again, I released years of heartache and a new fear last night. It took more out of me than I thought. Now I have to figure out how to keep Baylor safe.

Edward won't harm the kids. At least not yet, but he will hurt Bay. I believe that. I need to keep him close without letting him know what's going on.

When I roll out of bed, I stretch, then walk into the living room. It's probably Ny here to yell at me. Tugging at the bottom of the hoodie, I pause at the door. With an exhale, I turn the knob.

Bay, standing in my doorway with two coffees, catches me off guard. He looks utterly delicious, and of course, I'm wearing his hoodie. A wave of sadness washes over me when he doesn't give me his usual lingering look—or his smartass flirtation.

No, today he looks me in the eyes instead. I have to fix this. I need him with me.

"Hi," I squeak. Geez, I just sounded like a child.

"Hey, figured I'd get that wall done today. I go back on shift tomorrow. I also told the boys we'd hang out once they got home today."

Something unfurls deep in my soul when he says he still plans to spend time with the boys. I was a total ass, and he's still thinking about them. I want to cry at how wrong I've been this entire time, and I could lose him if I'm not careful.

"Oh, right." I shake off the shock and step aside. Bay hands me a coffee as he steps inside.

"I'll change so I can help."

Bay nods and walks past me without a word. He brought me coffee, so he can't hate me that much. Right? Coffee is the equivalent of a dozen roses to me. I'd rather be hipped up on caffeine than watch flowers wither for days.

In my room, I change into a white shirt and baggy, ripped overalls. I refuse to ruin good clothes while doing home repairs. On the upside, I've learned a lot about building a wall in the process.

Back in the den, I start helping Bay measure and cut the remaining drywall. We fall into a groove with no conversation. I'm not sure what to say about last night.

I can't say, 'Oh, hey, by the way, your life is in danger if I push you away. So imma need you to stay close. Mm K'. This entire situation is going to be a dumpster fire.

Don't say fire.

The uncomfortable silence has me stepping away, and the raging emotions swirling through me have me staring at the walls. I remember Summer's favorite color used to be teal, so that's what I got.

I pick up the paint bucket and frown. Is it still her favorite, or is it a childish color? I look at Bay to ask his opinion, but he isn't paying attention. His focus is on plastering the wall. My chest constricts and aches. I miss our back-and-forth, his flirting, and my telling him no.

"What's the matter, Winnie?" His whisky voice flows through the room.

So much. I hold back the retort.

Is he that in tune with me that he knows when something is bothering me?

"I think I need a natural color. A green, tan, or white."

The comforting scent of sage and cinnamon wafts to my senses. Bay's closeness and the radiating body heat are warm against my back. His presence is like finding peace.

"What color do you have?"

"Teal, but I think I should do white. She's thirty-one, not sixteen."

"You could leave the color you have in here. The light yellow is relaxing." Bay's answer is simple.

"I guess."

"It'll be fine. Don't overthink it."

When his phone chimes, I glance behind me and see him smiling at something before he types back and slips it away.

Jealousy I've never known burns through my veins. I know he went out after he left Hideaway last night. Before I can do anything stupid, Journey's voice carries through the house.

"Winter Anderson, you're my best friend, but what the hell is wrong with you?" she yells.

Bay says nothing as Ny, unaware he's here, continues her rant.

"You and I both know Baylor is the best freaking thing that's ever happened to you and those boys. I can't believe you had the gall to walk away from him. All to entertain some unappealing, likely little-dicked pick? He looked like a fake-ass billionaire and about as interesting as a cheese sandwich. I'm just saying, if Baylor resembles his brother, wowza… Big, Winter. BIG."

I glance at Bay, who is holding back his laughter and not making his presence known so he can hear what else she's about to word vomit.

"Not only is he a good man, but think about the hot sex you two could have. I bet he's a palm necklace kind of guy. Dominating and demanding yet gentle. Don't tell Briggs I said that."

"Journey," I shout, then try to move, but Baylor blocks me.

"Oh, no, Angel. I want to hear this," he whispers, stepping closer. He locks his lake-green eyes on mine.

An amused grin spreads across his face. Heat spreads from my cheeks to the tips of my ears. The embarrassment is almost unbearable. Jumper cables on my nipples would be more pleasant than this moment.

"No. You and I both know you want to bounce on that pogo stick. Stop being so damn stubborn. All the Banks have the same persistence and fierceness. You really think he's going to let you walk away?" Journey's chuckles grow closer. "Don't count on it, twinkle tits. Baylor has big-dick stalker energy. That man wants you."

"Oh my god, Ny, shut up."

"Say it. Say you want to fuck him, and I'll stop." She halts abruptly when she sees Bay standing with me, but her grin doesn't fade.

"Well, crap. I didn't know you were here, Fritos. It's fine. I'm not embarrassed. Winter looks like she might pass out, though."

"She might," I grumble. "I can't believe that just happened."

Baylor finally cracks, bursting into laughter. "Winnie, that was the best ice breaker I've ever had," he laughs harder and steps away.

"I don't like that you two are friends." I point between him and Journey, who has joined his laughter.

"Thanks for the assist, Doritos. I've decided to give Winter her space."

"What?" I ask, whipping my head to the side and staring at the serious look on his face.

No. Edward will think I pushed him away. I can't let him give up.

"Don't worry. We're still just friends, like you want. I won't let the boys down like you assume I will," Bay says, lifting a shoulder. "Are the kids at your place?" he asks Ny, as if he didn't just cause the world around me to turn to rubble.

Ny shakes her head. "My parents are dropping them off later."

Fear can be a nasty bitch. It can stop you from living your life or force you to do things you never would to protect the ones you care about.

"No." I rush out the words, and both of them look at me with round eyes. "A date." I fumble the words and blink rapidly because I've never asked a man out before. "I mean, will you go on a date… with me? Next weekend, any weekend or day." I lift a shoulder, hold out my hands, and meet his green gaze.

There's a questioning glint in his eyes. Anxiety moves through me like a sandworm.

"What changed your mind?" Bay gives me a skeptical look.

I walk up to him and hug his waist. With my eyes closed, I rest my cheek against his firm, defined chest.

His comforting embrace helps calm my racing heart. Bay cups the nape of my neck with one hand and holds my back with the other. Dang, I've never felt a hug like this. It's all-consuming. I never want to let him go.

My ears perk as I listen to the thundering of his heart, beating erratically. The rhythm of his matches mine; both are equally chaotic.

"I fucked up last night. I realized what I want. If you can forgive me, I'll take a chance on you. Please." I murmur.

"Look at me, Angel." He whispers.

I lift my head and take in his beauty. It's like staring at a masterpiece. Bay frames my face with both his hands and studies me. His eyes search mine for a lie.

I pray he doesn't see how terrified I am, not just about Edward but about crossing this line.

"Are you sure about this?"

Am I? Not really, but also yes. It's ridiculous. I'm pulling him closer instead of pushing him away from the threat. I'm convincing myself he would prefer it this way if he knew. Baylor will lose his shit when he finds out.

"If you are. If you can promise that no matter what happens, it won't change anything with the kids, and we take it slow."

"Nothing was ever going to change with them."

"Damn, I thought it was my speech about big-dick energy." Journey's raspy voice cuts through the air, reminding us she's still here.

Glancing around, I see her perched on the back of the sofa, a grin so big it touches her eyes.

"I forgot you were here."

"Uh, like I was going to walk away from this moment? Hell no. It was like watching the romantic scene I've been waiting for in a movie." Ny wiggles her finger between Bay and me. "Now, kiss."

Groaning, I let go of the hot firefighter and take a step back. "Why are we friends?"

"Um, because I'm awesome."

"Right now, you're not." I retort.

"Oh shit. I'm cock blocking. I'll go." She says, jumping off the back of the sofa.

"You heard me say slow, right? I'm not going from a truth-or-dare kiss to getting naked." My eyes grow wide as I look at the tall, serious giant. "That's okay, right?"

"That's completely unacceptable. In the bedroom. Now. I want you undressed and bent over the bed in the next five minutes." Baylor tells me firmly. He takes a step back, crosses his arms over his chest, and plants a scowl on his face.

My heart is stuck upside down on a roller coaster right now. It feels like the room is spinning. I'm out of air and completely speechless. I swear I'm not going to survive this.

"B-but," my voice is barely a whisper. Not that I don't want him. I do, but I'm not ready for sex.

A handsome, playful gleam sparkles in his eyes before he bursts out laughing so hard he has to hold his stomach.

Fucking prick

"I'm sorry. I had to mess with you, Winnie. You deserved it after last night."

All the air whooshes out of me, and I steady myself against the new wall. "You're an asshole."

Baylor wraps his large arms around me, still laughing. "Aw, come on, Angel. You know I would never make you do anything you're not ready for. I can wait."

Ugh, the past twenty-four hours have left me exhausted. On Monday, I have to figure out how to get thousands of dollars.

CHAPTER 7
BAYLOR

"So, let's get this straight. I want to make sure I'm understanding." Beau says across the kitchen table. "The woman you've been chasing for months finally agrees to date you, and you think something's wrong?"

"Yes. There was panic and fear in her eyes when she asked me out. But it wasn't because she was asking me. I think the guy she had a drink with last night may have said or done something to scare her." I say, leaning forward and running my hand through my hair.

Beau sits back in his seat and gives me a bewildered look, like I have a third fucking eye. I know he's gauging how serious I am about this. I'd stake both nuts on this. That's how confident I am.

I know Winter, and she's scared. When I left her house, I damn near had to pry her off me. I told her I had to get snacks and drinks for the kids, but I came to talk to Beau first. Winter is chewing her lip raw and is jittery. She's never like this.

It's great she feels safe with me, but I don't like that she's scared in the first place and is using me instead of just telling me what the hell happened.

"You're sure? I don't make it a habit to run around flashing my badge and watching video footage to stalk my brother's girlfriend. I need to know you're concerned, not jealous. I already had my ass handed to me by Gemma for looking up the sister's name without cause."

I shake my head. "Am I jealous? Of course, but that's not it. I know her. She's spooked."

Beau sighs and gets to his feet. "Alright. We'll see if Red will let us have a look, but I won't lie, Baylor."

"You don't have to. I'll be honest and tell him what I told you."

"Alright,"

I follow close behind him, staring at my feet, and crash into his back when he stops at the open door.

Beau looks over his shoulder with a lifted brow, giving me the *'really'* look. It wasn't my fault. His big ass is the one that stopped.

"Where are you two going?"

I step aside and see Baxter standing in the doorway, without his baby in his arms.

"Where's Sprout?"

"Mom has him. She told me I needed a break and that I looked like shit. I don't know what to do when I'm not fussing over him." Bax says with a huff.

"You can come with us," Beau tells him, then walks past him.

"Where?"

"Apparently, to stalk Baylor's girlfriend."

Baxter furrows his brows and looks at me.

I roll my eyes and step past him. "We're not stalking anyone. I'll tell you in the car."

With all of us in the truck, I explain everything to Baxter while we drive to Hideaway. They think I'm crazy, but I know I'm right. I'm just not sure what kind of evidence we'll get from the cameras.

"Have you heard anything more about her sister?" Beau asks.

"No. I tried to ask when she was coming, but Winter isn't sure. Last Winnie heard, Summer, was still tying up loose ends. Whatever that means."

"Wait, she has a sister? I thought she didn't have any family. Damn, what have I missed?" Bax asks.

"Her sister is coming to live with her. Should be here eventually. I had Beau check her out so I knew if Winter and the boys were in any trouble, but nothing came up."

"That's a good thing, then, isn't it?"

"Depends. She could have been living an uneventful life, or one where she never got caught doing anything. I don't know. Winter told me they grew up in a religious cult. What if she went to another one and brought her ideology here?" I point out. It's an honest observation on my part.

"Huh. When did you get so suspicious of everything?" Bax asks.

"I want to make sure the kids are always safe. And I get suspicious when someone's norm takes a U-turn."

At the bar, we walk to the back door. I knock loudly enough and wait. Red should be here. He's kept the same schedule for as long as I can remember.

It's not long before the tall, slinky man opens the door.

"Hiya, boys. What brings you back here on this fine afternoon?"

Beau looks at me. He was not kidding about not lying.

“This is going to sound like a weird request,” I start, and Red listens as I explain everything again.

“You can have a look, but there’s no sound,” Red says.

“I just want to see the body language.”

“Alright.”

Red gestures for us to come in, and we follow him into a cramped office. The small space has a desk covered in papers and a chair. I notice cases of alcohol lining the wall.

Our three big asses crowd behind him and watch. Red sits and pulls up the footage from the time I gave him. We all keep our eyes on the screen as the interaction unfolds.

When Winter comes into the frame, I notice the man says something through tight lips. Winter looks at a woman and goes ramrod straight.

“Pause it real quick,” I tell Red.

Red pauses, and I see the woman's face. I dig my phone out, pull up the photo of the woman from the bookstore, and compare it to the image.

“Who is that?” Beau asks, leaning closer now.

Ha, now he believes me.

“She was in the bookstore on Thursday. She kept asking Winnie personal questions. Where she lives, if she has family here, and how long she’s owned the bookstore. Shit like that. Scared her pretty good. I think it's the same person,” I tell Beau and continue comparing the photos.

“It is. The forehead and nose are the same,” Bax says, leaning closer. “Can you play it, Red?”

Red nods and resumes the footage. We can all see Winnie’s body stiffen more before she sits back down.

“Zoom in on her face and play it,” Beau tells him.

Fear, panic, and anxiety are written all over Winnie's face. Her lip wobbles, and I can tell she's holding back tears. I was right. The guy fucking scared her.

Now, to find out who he is and what he wanted or said to her.

"Pause," Beau tells him when the man looks into the camera. We both snap photos of the guy.

"Red, could you call Beau or me if you see this guy or the woman come in again? Whatever he said to her shook her." I ask.

"Sure thing."

After saying goodbye to Red, we all get back in the truck.

"Sorry, I doubted you, Bay. Seems your hunch was right. I can get with Gemma. I'll let her know he was threatening someone. We'll run his image to see if we can get a hit."

"Thanks. Now I'm worried about what I'm going to do while I'm at the firehouse for three days at a time." The thought is starting to stress me out.

"Are you going to tell her you know something is wrong?" Baxter asks.

"Not until I know who he or she is and what we're dealing with."

"Well, we can take turns checking in on her this week. You said the sister should be here soon. She might be able to watch out for them once she gets here," Bax says, trying to help ease my anxiety.

It helps a little, but I don't know anything about Summer. What if she's a threat? Is it a bit coincidental that she called before this guy showed up? She also keeps pushing back when she'll be here.

"Winter is doing the right thing by pulling you closer instead of pushing you away," Beau says.

"Yeah," I think about it for a minute. "I don't know. All I know for sure is I won't let anything happen to them."

"We know that. On the upside, we know you're not a stalker." Beau laughs.

"Ha Ha. You're a real joker. Wait. Does looking into her window with binoculars and jerking off count as stalking?" I joke, but only Bax and I laugh.

"I'm kidding, fuckface. Don't be so serious all the time," I tell Beau, who is unimpressed.

"You say that, but I half believe you've done it."

He's an idiot. I jerk off thinking about her in the shower like a normal person, not while watching her through the window.

Shit. Maybe I am a stalker.

After parking in front of Beaus, we all get out.

"The twins are coming over to play video games. If you want to hang out, Bax."

"I might. I'm going to see if Mom will give me my child back." Bax waves and walks back to his truck.

"He's a helicopter dad. He'll get used to it once Everett gets older. I'll let you know what I get from the pictures."

"Thanks."

Getting in the driver's seat, I head to the store and pick up the shit I told Winter I'd get.

I may not be an investigator, but I knew my hunch was right. Winnie won't admit what's going on, and I need solid proof before confronting her. Is she only dating me because she's scared? Winter has to know she can trust me.

The annoyance and aggravation running through me have me on edge. My muscles are tight, my skin is hot, and I can't seem to focus. Maybe Summer isn't a bad person and can somehow help protect them. I assume she should be here by next weekend if she doesn't push it again.

Tomorrow morning, I will be on shift for three days. Hopefully, Winter won't get suspicious about my brothers randomly checking on her. I know Bax will make up an excuse about advice for Everett. Briggs will show up with Ny, and Beau is like a chameleon. She won't even notice him watching.

I just made that sound creepy.

With the car parked in the driveway, both boys sprint out of their house, each carrying a bag, when they hear my car. They're always eager to come over. Their presence eases all my tension.

"Audrey and Sul took us to get this for you," Daniel holds out a bag as soon as my car door opens.

Chuckling, I ruffle his hair. "We'll look when we get inside. Help me unload the groceries."

"Ok," they say, then start grabbing stuff from the trunk.

Inside, we begin putting everything away.

"Mom told us our Aunt Summer is coming to stay with us. I'm excited to meet her," Dylan tells me.

"I'm sure you'll like her. Your mom said she was a great sister."

"Yeah. Will you open the gifts now?"

"Sure," I say, putting away the last of the items and sitting on a stool. Dylan goes first and hands me a small bag. Opening it, I pull out a BFF keychain and a pair of sunglasses.

"I have the one that goes with it in my backpack."

"It's awesome. Thank you."

"My turn," Daniel says, shoving his bag at me. I pull out another keychain like Dylan's and a hoodie with the firefighter flag and my last name on it.

"Thank you, Daniel. It's great."

When they don't stop staring, I put on the hoodie, set the glasses on my head, and attach both keychains to my keyring.

Once they see me wearing the gift, they hug me and dash to the living room.

As soon as I make snacks, the boys glue themselves to their games. While I watch them, I have to mediate when they can't agree. Sundays usually go like this: me sitting on my ass eating shit food, watching the kids laugh, fight, and argue.

A knock at the door has me getting to my feet and opening it. I'm surprised to see Baxter, still childless, with a scowl on his face. With a laugh, I step aside and let him in.

"Why do I 'need' a break? I told mom I'm fine and Everett is fine." He grumps.

"She worries, you know that. Remember how overwhelmed Birdie would get sometimes? She is a fantastic mother, but parents need their time." I shrug and flop back down on the couch.

Baxter flops down next to me and stabs his fingers through his overgrown hair before scratching his newfound beard.

"I don't like it. He isn't even a month old. He should be with me since," Bax trails off. You can hear the pain in his voice, and his eyes show how much he's hurting.

"I know, man. But you have to get past that. It's not worth your time and energy."

Bax sighs and tilts his head back. "I know. It should be easy. Why isn't it, though?"

"Hm, the big L, I assume. Did you big L the B(aby)M(ama)? I think you were into the fact that BM needed help. Personally, I think she wanted B(riggs)." I try to speak in riddles so the boys don't hear us talking shit about Baxter's egg donor.

Hopefully, he's catching what I'm saying.

"I thought I did, but I think you're onto something with your assessment. To change the subject, I got bored and curious." Bax says, digging his phone from his pocket.

"Yeah. What did you do while you were bored and curious?" I lift a questioning brow at him.

Baxter taps on his phone a few times before handing it to me. As I take it, I stare at a woman with a slightly rounded, freckle-covered face and unruly copper hair. I can tell who she is. The cheekbones, lips, nose, and blue eyes give her away.

"Is that?"

Baxter grunts, takes the phone back, and looks at it. "Possibly. Social media is private. I could only find this one picture. But you're right. There's no other information on her. I got the name from Beau." Bax says, then locks the phone screen.

"Uh-huh. What do you think?" I ask with a smile.

"I think she's not my type, and I have a newborn to worry about." He grunts.

She is definitely his type. Bax has always had a thing for redheads: ergo, his crush on Anna. The only difference is that Anna dyed her hair red. Winter's sister's hair looks natural.

"Sure. That's why you got her name and had to show me."

Baxter lifts his shoulder unapologetically. "I told you I got curious. I was most curious about her life and whether she's going to have trouble following her."

"We'll find out soon enough. What did you do with your time before Everett?"

"Up until she left, I helped her with shit when I wasn't working. Now I lie around on my fat ass."

"Those are curse words, Uncle Baxter," Dylan says without looking away from the TV, making us chuckle. My heart swells every time they call one of my brothers' uncles, and when they call my parents, their grandparents.

"You're right, kid. Sorry about that."

"It's okay," Dylan says.

I'm not sure why he felt the need to point it out and then say it's okay, but he did. Winter curses in front of them, so they're used to it.

Bax and I joke around while the kids play the game. After dinner, Baxter has had all he can take and heads to our parents' to force our mother to return his child.

I gather the boys and the new hoodie, then walk them next door. Winnie comes to the door with her signature grin. When I hand her the hoodie, my lips curve up as she brings it to her nose and inhales.

When she looks back at me, she reaches out and adjusts the necklace she gave me, then rubs my pecs. Her touch is like being tickled with a feather. Soft and barely there, her fingers whisper to my flesh, making sweet promises of what to expect.

My hand goes to her hip, holding her while she keeps touching me.

"I'll give the other one back to be freshened up tomorrow. Does Saturday work for you?" She has such a sweet voice.

"It does, but I figured I'd be the one to plan it."

"I figured I would since I asked. You go on shift tomorrow?"

She knows I do.

"Yeah,"

"Be careful and make sure you text me after any fires. Keep wearing your pendant—promise," she says, chewing on her bottom lip. I reach out and remove it from between her teeth.

"I am always careful, Angel. I promise. Don't worry about me. I'll come see you at the bookstore as soon as my shift ends."

Winter nods, hugs me, and walks back inside her house. I really wish I knew what that prick said to her. It's been months, and this is the first time she's been this concerned about my job. Sighing, I walk back home and prepare for a long three days.

The bell ringing pulls everyone in the firehouse from their lounging. We rush through the building, gear up, and jump into the engine. Cap tells us there's an old warehouse fire.

We come to a stop in front of the building and jump out. The screams from a woman saying her sister is still inside travel through the air. It's an abandoned building. There shouldn't be anyone inside.

Rome and Derk pull the hose and begin tackling the fire on the building's east side.

"She was sleeping when I left. She isn't answering her phone. Please, she has to still be in there." She insisted.

Henry walks up to her and rests a hand on her shoulder. "Ma'am, where is she inside?"

My stomach drops when she points to the east side. Fuck, it's possible her sister didn't make it out of there.

"Banks and Harris, you're with me. Derk, Rome, and Zander, keep the hoses aimed at the east side. Backup is on the way."

With adrenaline surging, we slip on our masks, and Karson grabs the hose as we plunge into the inferno. As Henry crashes through the door, a wave of fire and smoke surges toward us, curling ominously along the ceiling. Karson springs into action, battling the flames as we race through the chaotic haze. My heart pounds as we search for the girl trapped inside.

When we move down the hall away from the flames, the smoke reduces our visibility. I look up and see the inferno creeping toward us along the ceiling. Time is running out to find this girl.

"CCFD," Henry yells.

Henry clicks his radio and gives orders to the men outside. "Zander, Rome, aim at the far-right corner window. Derk, front windows."

We burst through the door to a room where flames flare and surge outward as they meet the air. All of us step back as the blaze whips and lashes at us.

"We need more water," Karson shouts, running to the emergency hose. He unravels it and turns it on. Thank fuck it has water.

Flames consume the entire room, making entry impossible; anyone trying to check inside would be burned to a crisp. If anyone was inside the room, it's too late.

"Check the other rooms," Henry shouts again as two others join us in the search. Karson and I move together. He is extinguishing while I open each room. The fire continues to roar and chase us.

As we inch through the hall, I call out for the woman. We work together, checking every space we can reach. In the last room, I busted the door open and moved around the space.

"We need to pull out. The roof is starting to collapse," Henry shouts.

I can feel the floors squishing under my feet. They're about to collapse as well. Then I spot the woman in the corner, curled in a ball, not moving.

"Banks, Harris, move out," Henry yells.

"Karson, in here. I found her." I call out to Karson.

Karson moves the filing cabinets and junk out of the way, then blasts the flames as I make my way to her. I fling her limp body over my shoulder, and we all haul ass out the front doors just as the roof comes crashing down and fire engulfs the rest of the place.

I lay the woman down in the grass and step back so the paramedics can get to work. She isn't breathing, and I can see the burns on her clothes and skin.

I could never watch this part. I've had two people not make it while I was on shift. I turn away and help the team extinguish the fire just as our backup arrives. I don't look back at the woman when I hear the sister's painful wails. We all know those cries. It's a gruesome reminder of what we can encounter on the job.

By the time the fire is out, we all load up and head back to the firehouse in somber silence. The woman, now known to be Jane, shouldn't have been there. That fire shouldn't have taken a life. I understand not having anywhere to go. A roof over your head is just that, and when you need one, you'll take it wherever you can get it.

Tomorrow morning, my shift ends, and all I want is Winnie and the kids. It's always hard when there's a life we can't save, a life we were too late for. It reminds us that we're human and that our lives aren't guaranteed to last into old age.

If it were me, would my family's wails pierce the air like the sisters did tonight? How long would they grieve? Would Winter and the kids miss me? These are the thoughts that come after the chaos. The thoughts you don't have in the heat of the moment. They come once there's silence and no danger.

When we exit the engine, Henry claps me on the shoulder before we all head to the showers to wash the smoke, soot, and grief off.

I'm not sure how long I stared at the ceiling before my phone ringing pulled me back. When I see Winnie's name on the screen, I answer the call.

"Hey, Angel," I answer somberly.

"I heard there was a destructive fire at the old warehouse. Are you okay?" she asks in a worried voice, and I hate it.

"I'm fine, babe. Are you okay?"

Fuck, I forgot she made me promise to text her after we finish the call. Tonight was a bad one, and the gossip around this town spreads like wildfire now that we have the new InTheKnow website for Cedar Creek.

"Yeah, I am. When you didn't text…" She trails off.

"I'm sorry. By the time we got back to the firehouse, I had forgotten." I tell her. I hate that she's this scared.

"Promise you're, ok? Will I see you tomorrow?"

"Don't you always? I promise I'm ok. See you tomorrow, beautiful,"

"Tomorrow, goodnight, hotshot."

"Goodnight,"

I wish I could talk to her more, but I need sleep. I want to clear my mind of tonight's events.

CHAPTER 8
WINTER

My phone's chime makes me dig it out of my pocket. I've been applying for loans, so I don't even bother checking the number.

"Hello,"

An automated message starts. "You have a collect call from inmate Troy Mathews."

My stomach sinks when I hear his voice. I don't even listen to the rest of the message before hanging up. It's been a fucking year. The last time I talked to him was hell. Not to mention the bullshit he's gotten me into. I can't speak to him right now. I need to sort out the money.

I hate him. I hate him so much that I'm glad he's in prison. If he weren't, I'd have murdered him by now. When my phone rings again, I hang up. I want to cry and scream, but I can't. I need to stay strong for Bay and the boys.

It's been six days since Edward demanded his money. Over the course of this week, five banks refused to lend that amount unless I used the bookstore as collateral and added a cosigner.

The cold sweat prickled my skin as I imagined the crushing weight of repaying 60k. A silent scream formed in my throat, but I held it back. It's a crushing blow I have to take.

I considered selling the house. I would get about forty more than I paid for it, since we've put so much work into it, and it is now a four-bedroom instead of three, but then I would have to explain why I'm selling it.

Even if I get the money, I'm not sure how to deliver it to Edward without raising suspicion. If I try to withdraw that much, there will be questions. All of this is going to give me an ulcer. Hell, I don't even know how long I have before Edward comes to collect.

As I entered the bookstore, I switched on the lights and took in the cozy atmosphere. The vibe gives me the same warm, fuzzy feeling I get when I have my first pumpkin spice latte in the fall.

I'm expecting my new employee to arrive this morning. I'll need someone at the store while I deal with the uncertainties.

Then, I'm meeting with a small credit union here in town. Fingers crossed, they asked me to come in because they have good news.

I head to my office to drop off my purse, then return to unlock the front door. The scent of old paper and ink wafts through the air as I begin arranging the discounted books.

When I heard about the warehouse fire last night, I wanted to scream and cry. Then, when I heard there was a fatality, it made it even worse. I waited a couple of hours before finally breaking down and calling Baylor. I couldn't sleep until I knew he was safe. Every fire, every emergency call he goes on, leaves me in a constant state of dread.

I planned a simple date for Baylor and me this Saturday. I'm hoping it's a memorable time. I've never been to a drive-in theater, but I've always wanted to go. I thought that would be fun for us. It's open and public. I'm afraid that if we're alone, I will jump on him. I'm not ready for sex yet.

In the back of my mind, I wonder how many women he's been with and whether I will be enough. My experiences are limited to Troy, and they were simple, involving just the act itself with little or no build-up.

Over the past few days, I've been thinking about everything. I realized that Bay and I have been basically dating this whole time. It was just easier to fight and ignore what I already knew deep down.

The bell on the door makes me glance up to see the young woman with black hair and brown eyes step in, two coffees in hand, and look around with a smile. When she sees me, her smile widens, and she strides toward me.

"Good morning, Winter. I got you coffee. It's still warm. I asked Nyx what you usually order. I hope it's right." She eagerly hands me my coffee.

"Good morning, Ellie. You didn't have to do that, but I appreciate it. I was running late and didn't get a chance to stop this morning. It's on me next time. Are you ready to start?"

"Yes, Ma'am."

As we walk through the store, I watch the fluorescent lights reflect in her eyes as she nods to each instruction. Ellie remains fully focused on what I am saying. She's only eighteen and taking a gap year to figure out what she wants to do.

At the register, I observe her interacting with customers as they start flooding in. It's excellent that she has customer service experience and knows her stuff. I didn't have to explain everything over and over.

By lunchtime, Ellie is confident she can handle the store, so I can attend a quick meeting.

As I walk into the bank, nausea churns and curdles in my stomach. Not even the bright spring day and fresh air help. I'm not sure what I'll do if I'm denied again. Selling my home will be the next option, but even then, it wouldn't close for thirty days. I'm not sure Edward will wait that long.

When I step up to the counter, I let the teller know I have an appointment and wait, feeling even more anxious. Glancing around, I watch people laugh and joke at the counter as if they don't have a care in the world. Sometimes I watch people and wonder what their lives are like.

"Winter Anderson," the polite older man says. I get to my feet and head to his office.

"I'm Mr. Kittle. Make yourself comfortable and take a seat," he offers with a smile and gestures for me to sit.

"Thank you," I say, and take the seat.

Mr. Kittle takes his seat and shuffles through the papers in front of him. "I've reviewed your application, and because of your bankruptcy six years ago, we're unable to approve the loan without a cosigner and collateral."

All the hope I had drained away, like water seeping into the earth. I had been optimistic that his invitation was an approval.

"Okay, I'll have to see if I can get a cosigner."

Mr. Kittle nods. "We can do a smaller loan for fifteen thousand. You wouldn't need a co-signer and could use your car instead of the bookstore as collateral. At the current interest rate, you will pay around $10,000 in interest by the end of the loan."

Fuck me. Almost double what I'm borrowing.

"Okay, um, I'd like to think about it. I'm trying to renovate the store, and that isn't much to work with. Thank you for trying." I lie.

"I wish we could've done more; I am sorry. I have a few other companies in mind that could be a good match for you."

Mr. Kittle pulls out a list and hands it to me. I take it before I leave the bank.

Outside, it takes all my strength to keep my composure and not burst into the world's ugliest cry. Glancing at the list, I see three of the ten are companies I've already tried. Honestly, what did I expect? I couldn't get the business loan without a co-signer. Why did I think this would be different? Multiple small loans would kill me financially.

The phone's frantic ringing makes me reach for it. Without a glance at the ID, I end the call with a definitive click.

Each step felt heavy as I walked downtown. As I stopped out front of the café, its vibrant life felt like a cruel contrast to the hollowness inside me.

When I look through the window, I see him. My jaw clenches as fiery rage ignites. Baylor is sitting with a woman, and their laughter fuels my fury.

What the fuck?

Seriously? He agreed to date me. Is this because of the Edward thing? It doesn't matter. I've already decided Baylor is mine. If he's still pissed, he needs to get over it.

I yank the door open, the scent of fresh coffee beans hitting my nose as I stomp into the cafe. As I push through the boisterous crowd, I do the most impulsive thing I've ever done.

Before Baylor can register it's me, I grip his chin, lean down, and slam my lips to his. When his lips part, my tongue intrudes into his mouth. Baylor's tongue responds, warm and smooth, clashing with mine.

Was it a beautiful way to start a first kiss? Hell no, but I'm captivated by the heated battle, unable to pull away from the action. He doesn't silence his groan, even as it echoes off the walls. Instead, his hand lifts to cradle the back of my head.

I feel weightless, suspended in the cosmic void. The world around me is gone. My heart should be frantic, yet it beats with a calm rhythm, a newfound serenity. I should be ashamed, but I don't care. All I care about is Bay and this moment. It's all that matters.

Our tongues dance and twirl together. When Bay's hand moves to my neck, and he squeezes, liquid heat pools between my thighs, and I know he's won.

Breathlessly, I wrench my mouth from his and press my forehead to his.

"Is this payback? I said I'm sorry. Make no mistake, Baylor Levi, you are mine," I whisper to him.

Baylor's beaming green eyes meet mine, and a smirk spreads across his face. "I don't know what you're talking about, Angel, but please tell me whatever I did to get you to kiss me like that and call me yours so I can do it again."

My eyes flick to the wide-eyed bitch on the other side of the table, and Bay chuckles before tucking my hair behind my ear.

"Stand up, Winnie, and I'll introduce you."

Huffing, I glare at the woman and stand. Baylor rises next to me, wraps an arm around my waist, and squeezes my hip.

Good. Show this hussy you're mine.

"Winter, this is Hazel. She works at the animal rescue. I had to barter with Angela to get you out of the speed dating. The guys at the firehouse and I will be helping them with their next adoption event. Hazel and I were discussing the details. Hazel, this is my girlfriend, Winter." Bay introduces us.

Girlfriend?

Not important right now. I realize I just made an ass of myself.

"Oh god," I groan in embarrassment, dropping my arms and squeezing my eyes shut.

I am such an idiot. I just went full-on crazy, jealous girlfriend. Now that I've publicly declared him mine, that's what I am, right?

"Girl, do not be embarrassed. That was the sweetest and most assertive way to let everyone know he's off the market," she giggles.

"I am definitely not complaining." Bay chuckles and kisses my temple. Of course he's not. I'm pretty sure I just granted half his wishes.

"I'm so sorry. Please let me know if you need any help, and I'll see what I can do. Oh, I have some dog training books I can donate," I say, snapping my fingers.

"That would be amazing, but I don't think you have to because of this. Really, it's okay. If I saw my boyfriend sitting with a strange woman, I would have done the same damn thing. After I punched the bitch." Hazel winks.

Thank fuck she's being cool about the situation.

"Mm, I like the sound of that—boyfriend," Bay whispers.

I elbow him in the gut, making him grunt and laugh.

"I would love to. I probably have other dog books I can donate. I'll gather them up and send them to the rescue with this puppy," I say, thumbing at Baylor, who's still rumbling with silent laughter.

"That sounds great," Hazel says, getting to her feet. "Baylor, can you get me the number of volunteers?"

"Will do. Thanks."

Hazel smiles at each of us and walks off.

Baylor takes my hand in his warm, rough mitt and guides us out of the cafe. "So that's how jealous Winnie gets. I like it, and fuck me if I don't want to kiss you again already."

Bay spins me, then pulls me into his arms and captures my lips in a brief, wet kiss. God, it's too short. I want more. A lot more.

Breaking apart, he kisses my nose, then lets me go.

"How was your week?" he asks as we walk back to the bookstore.

"Good. Baxter came by a couple of times. He needed help with Everett. Then Ny, Briggs, and the kids came over for dinner one night. Summer called twice. She should be here anytime, and I hired someone at the store to help out."

Come to think of it, everyone showed up more than usual this past week. There's no way Bay or anyone else could know something is going on. Right? Nah, no one was at Hideaway by the time Edward threatened me. No, they were there for help or company. That's all.

"Sounds like a good week."

I want to ask how he's doing after losing someone to a fire, but I don't want to upset him, so I keep my trap shut.

"It was. I can't wait to see Summer. The kids are staying with Ny on Saturday." I blurt out that little detail.

"Ah, our date night. Plan to tell me what we're doing?" he asks, tugging me into his side like an overprotective hound dog.

"A surprise, and I'm hoping you like it. If not, you'd better lie and say you do."

"Noted, but I'm sure I won't have to. Did you mean it, or was it a heat-of-jealousy claim?" he asks.

I stop in my tracks and catch his nervous gaze.

Did I mean it? Yes. Did I mean to admit it so soon? No. Was it the heat of jealousy? Also yes.

"I meant it. But it was the moment that made me admit it." I confess, because, lord knows, I'm already hiding a big enough secret.

A broad, brilliant smile spreads across his face. "Yeah? So it's cool if I've been telling everyone you're my girlfriend already?"

"You have not. And I think we have to actually go on a date first before you declare our relationship status." I roll my eyes and pull him along as we walk. It's comical to see a petite 5'6" woman dragging a buff 6'3" man behind her.

"I have been. All the time we've spent together should count," Bay argues. He really is a man-child.

Entering the store, I find everything quiet, and Ellie is behind the counter, reading the employee manual I gave her.

"Hey, Ellie."

She looks up and smiles. Then she gawks at Baylor. My jealousy is off the charts today. I won't let anyone take Baylor or my kids from me.

Bay must sense the anger rolling off me like a fucking shadow. He pulls me back into his vibrating chest and wraps his arm around my waist.

"I'm Baylor. Winnie's boyfriend." He tells her for me.

Sweet whisky voice. He needs to stop, but also not stop. I need to stop. I'm spiraling.

"Oh, it's nice to meet you," she says sheepishly.

Turning in his arms, I rest my forehead against his chest. "I don't know what's gotten into me today," I whisper, shaking my head.

"I like whatever it is."

"I'm sure you do, but I don't. I've never felt like this before, and it's becoming irrational."

"Hey," Baylor leads me to one of the aisles.

The scent of fresh books fills my nostrils, making my heart swell. I love this place.

Bay takes my neck in both hands, places his thumbs under my chin, and tilts my head up to look at him.

"Let me enjoy this for today. I've waited months for this. We can start thinking rationally tomorrow," he squints for a second. "After Saturday. I'm looking forward to our date. Or maybe after the firefighters' ball. I'm looking forward to that, too." His eyes twinkle with amusement.

"So never? We'll think and act irrationally about each other, always." Since I've let myself explore this with Baylor, I feel like he's my first real crush. My brain doesn't think rationally around him.

"I mean, I don't hate that idea. Briggs had to stop me from killing that man last weekend." He shrugs.

"I'm so sorry, hotshot. I wish I could take it back. Nothing happened, I swear."

"I know, Angel. Full transparency, if you try to back out, I'll be forced to stalk you. After the kiss we shared, I won't be able to let you go. Not ever. It was the best kiss I've ever had."

That comment earns him a smile from me. I've been worried I might not be enough for him, but maybe I will be.

"Yeah?"

My eyes flick to his tongue as it darts out and moistens his soft lips.

"Mm hm. We should practice. I plan on kissing you as much as you'll let me." He tugs me closer, but I press my fingers to his mouth, keeping him from sucking me into his trap.

"Oh no. You have to wait until this weekend."

Bay pouts like a child. "You're killing me. It's like giving a child candy and then snatching it back."

"You're so dramatic. You'll live, you big baby. I have to get back to work for a few hours. See you tonight?"

"Don't you always?"

"Mm. I do." Standing on my tiptoes, I brush my lips against his, quick and light, then pull away before he can start another tongue war.

Bay growls and squeezes my hip. "Tease."

"You like it." I laugh and rub his biceps.

"I do, Angel. I'll pick the boys up today."

"Damn it, Baylor."

That's all I say before starting a war with his mouth. He tastes like candy and smoke. The warm strokes of his tongue against mine are one of the best feelings I've ever had.

I'd be lying if I said I didn't want him inside me right this minute. I want him to pick me up and fuck me against these shelves.

Bay's hand dives into my hair and tangles his fingers in it. Pushing his luck, the other hand palms and squeezes my ass tightly.

We both groan as the fire ignites between us. Neither of us relents; instead, we deepen our kiss and our bodies meld together, finally finding their rightful place. I almost climb him when he presses his growing shaft into me.

Holy hardness

Journey was not kidding about the size.

Huge

My pesky fingers move of their own accord, up and into his shirt. His searing flesh is a gift to my chilled hands. My hips roll against his thigh, now firmly between my legs.

Realizing I'm dry-humping him, I stop moving and tear my lips from his.

"Fuck, babe. I could die kissing you and be happy," he rasps.

My heart leaps, and my body heats when he calls me babe. I'm used to Angel, but babe feels so intimate.

"Me too. I didn't know kissing could be so good," I admit breathlessly, then giggle when I realize we're making out in a book aisle like two horny teenagers. Bay chuckles with me and looks around, clearly thinking the same thing.

He releases my hair, presses his brow to mine, and sighs.

"I have to go, or I'm going to keep doing it and eventually fuck you against all these books."

"God, that sounds hot," I whisper, arching into him again.

"Oh, it's going to happen eventually, but not today. Our first time will not be a frenzied fuck in a book aisle." His voice comes out gruff, like he's struggling to keep control.

My cheeks flush, and heat spreads up my neck when he says our first time.

Huffing out a breath, I stroke his back under his shirt. "Go. Before things escalate."

"See you soon, beautiful." He gives me one more open kiss, adjusts himself, and walks off.

I'm silently kicking myself in the ass for waiting this long. I do not doubt he will own me. I need birth control, ASAP.

CHAPTER 9
BAYLOR

At the kids' school, I get out of the car. We're nearing the end of the school year, and this morning is breakfast with Dad. Dyl and Dan said, 'We know you're not our dad, but will you come?' Who could say no to that? I feel like their dad most of the time, and even if I didn't, I would still show up.

Outside the car, I stretch before I see two of my other brothers. Beau and Briggs must have the same breakfast. It's Dyl and Dan's last year of elementary school, and the last time I'll run into these two idiots for a couple of years.

Both my brothers give me a questioning look when they notice me.

"The boys asked if I'd come," I tell them, grabbing the breakfast I picked up.

"Daddy, Baylor, how cute," Briggs says, messing up my hair.

"Stop. It's not cool to do that when we're somewhere I can't tell you to F off at." I grumble.

"I'm just giving you a hard time. I'm sure Winter and the boys appreciate it. Ny told me you two have your date tomorrow night. Finally going to swipe that v-card, little brother?" Briggs teases. He's a fucking asshole.

I growl and punch Briggs' arm. I'm not ashamed I've waited, but I won't let him disrespect Winter like that. "I wouldn't tell you. Winter deserves more respect than that."

"Good man," Beau says next to me.

"I was kidding. You should know I wouldn't want to know that answer. Don't count on Ney not bugging both of you, though."

"Same with Birdie. I've been meaning to text you about the photo."

That piques my interest. "Do you have a hit?"

"What picture?" Briggs asks.

"The guy Winnie had a drink with. It's a thing. I'll tell you about it later."

"Not yet, but we know her ex was into some shit. There has to be a reason Troy went to Winter after years to steal anything worth a damn. I have a feeling our guy is connected to him. I left a message for a detective in Atlanta."

"You think he led the guy right to her and the kids?" My jaw ticks and tightens. What a piece of shit. He chose to put them in danger rather than own up to his own shit.

"I'm not eliminating anything yet," Beau says.

"Why do I feel like there's a pattern to our love lives?" Briggs asks, pressing the buzzer to the front door of the school.

"It does seem to be our thing," Beau laughs.

Briggs opens the door, and we shuffle inside. Poor Baxter is just starting, but Everett will be close to Blue when he starts school.

When I enter the packed cafeteria, wall-to-wall kids and parents fill the room. A mixture of breakfast foods wafts to my nose.

My eyes scan the room until they finally land on my two favorite kids. I assume they get a lot of their looks from their father, with their taller, slinkier bodies, curly brown hair, and hazel eyes.

They look like they're expecting the letdown of me not showing up. Their father never fucking did. It breaks my heart to see their frowning faces. I'll show them they can always count on me.

Walking past everyone, I sneak up behind the two of them and bend over to whisper. "Hey, kids. I happen to have not one but three pancake breakfasts. You wouldn't happen to know someone who'd want to share them with me, do you?"

They both turn and look at me with big eyes, their smiles stretching their faces.

"Bay, you came," they both say, hugging me at the same time.

I hug them back, then wiggle between them. "I will always be here if I can, and I'll never promise if I think I can't. Are you hungry?"

"Yeah. We told you he'd be here, Russell," Dylan says, glaring at a little redheaded kid with a shocked expression.

Sitting between them, I hand out their food. I have a feeling Russell is a bit of a bully. He'd better be glad it's highly frowned upon to yell at someone else's child.

"What was that about, Dyl?"

Dylan huffs and takes a bite of his food. "Russell makes fun of us. He says we don't have a real dad, but we told him we have you, and you're better than a real dad."

"He didn't believe you'd come," Daniel finishes for Dylan.

"He's a jackass," Dyl snarls.

I choke on my food when he uses the curse word.

"I understand, but you can't say that here. Now Russell knows I'll always show up, and I'm way cooler than his dad." I say loud enough for the kid to hear, then glare at him.

Ok, silently threatening a child may also be frowned upon, but I will not allow anyone to bully my boys.

"Can you ask if we can stay with Nana and Papa?" Dyl asks. My heart flutters every time they call my parents that.

"Sure. I'll ask." I tell them while we joke and finish our breakfast.

At the sound of the bell, we pack up our trash and head to the doors.

"I'll pick you guys up this afternoon."

"Thank you for coming," Daniel says, hugging me. Dylan does the same, and they take off to class.

When I leave the school, I decide to shop. I have two spare rooms at my place, so there's no reason the kids have to sleep on the couch when they come to stay.

When I park at the Bed Bath store and look up at the place. My house currently has the bare minimum. I'd like to make it feel a bit more comfortable for Winnie and the boys.

Inside the store, I grab a cart and start walking down every aisle, picking up things I think the kids will like. Should I do the bathroom too?

Shit, I'm in deep.

As I wander down the aisle, I look at the kids' displays for ideas and try to think about how Ny and Briggs set up Ox and Lux's rooms. Then I see comforters with their favorite video game. Finally, I'm getting somewhere. I haven't noticed them playing with toys, but then I see the Nerf guns. Hell, I want to play with the damned things.

In the cart they go.

Two carts later, I'm checking out. It makes my heart warm to know they'll have their own space at my house.

I pack everything into my car, then get into the driver's seat. I groan when I check the time. I still have a few hours to kill. Guess I'll see if I can drag out redoing the rooms.

I can't help but drive past the bookstore and stop. With any luck, maybe I can steal a kiss from Winnie.

When I walk into the building, I see Ellie, then my queen, checking out the last customer. She usually has a breathtaking smile, but over the past few days, it hasn't been as bright.

When she sees me, her eyes twinkle, and she steps out from behind the counter and saunters up to me.

Unable to control myself, I wrap my arms around her waist, lift her off her feet, and kiss her so fiercely that I forget where we are. I needed this. I need to feel and touch her. She has no idea what she unlocked when she kissed me the other day. I was a starving animal that caught a whiff of my favorite meal. I won't starve again. I release her and set her back on her feet.

"I thought we could watch a movie and hang out tonight: you, me, and the kids. I'll cook meatloaf. I know it's your favorite," Winter says, while both her hands caress my pecs.

"I like the sound of that, but I went to the boys' breakfast this morning, and they asked to stay with mom and dad. I'm dropping them off after school. I also picked up some stuff for my place for them," I tell her.

"Breakfast with dad? What stuff did you get?" Winter stares at me with her crystal blue eyes.

So many things pass through her eyes that I can't tell what she's feeling. In hindsight, I should have checked with her about breakfast. I went because the kids asked, and I didn't think to check with Winter first.

"They asked if I would go. I didn't think to check with you first. I have two spare rooms at my place, and they stay over a lot." Shrugging, I tuck a strand of hair behind her ear and inhale her lavender-and-vanilla scent. "Figured I'd give them their own space there."

Winter shakes her head, grabs my hand, and tugs me to her office. Crap, I overstepped, and she's pissed.

As soon as the door closes behind us, Winter turns me, pushes my back to the door, and latches her mouth to mine as her hands roam under my shirt.

Her warm, silken mouth tastes like innocence. I know she's not, but it feels like she is. Our last few kisses were a frenzied battle. This kiss is slow and passionate.

Reaching out, I plunge my fingers into her hair and tighten my grip, while my other hand squeezes and kneads her perfectly plush hip.

Winter's hands trail to my belt buckle. Her fingers move with fevered purpose. My heart thunders and booms inside me with anticipation of what she might do.

Pulling my lips from hers, I rest my back against the door. "Winnie," I rasp as she starts unbuckling my jeans and lowers my zipper.

"I want to do this." Her tone is thick with desperation and eagerness.

That's all she says before she drops to her knees. Winter looks up at me through her thick-blond lashes as she releases my throbbing cock.

Holy shit.

When I look down, I watch her mouth form an O, and her eyes glaze over as she takes me in.

"Damn," she whispers.

I chuckle before my hips jerk as her petite hands wrap around my shaft and she strokes. Should I tell her this is my first time letting someone do this?

"Fuck. Winnie, babe," the words sputter from my lips. I can't tell her a damn thing right now. My cock has siphoned all the blood from my brain, and I'm only thinking about her on her knees. It's a glorious sight.

She doesn't let me say anything else before her lips wrap around the crown of my cock. Definitely not telling her. I don't want to risk her stopping because she thinks I'm some delicate flower.

Winter's mouth is gentle and soft. Her hot tongue twirls and teases while her hand strokes in rhythm. She paces herself, taking me into her sweet mouth inch by inch.

My hand grips her hair tightly, and my hips thrust as she takes me deeper. Glancing down, I see her smiling around me. Oh, she likes it when I do that. Let's try dirty talk.

"You want me to fuck that pretty mouth of yours, Angel? Can you handle that?" I groan as she sucks harder and bobs her head.

"Mm, good girl."

Recently, I've read a few smut books and know that dirty talk is something a majority of women enjoy, apparently. I'm not sure if I'm doing it right, but fuck it, she seems to like it. I'll give her what she wants.

I tighten my grip on her and pump into her mouth, hitting the back of her throat and making her gag. I move hard and fast until tears leak from her eyes. Winter moans and rubs her thighs together.

I'm not going to be able to hold on. I can feel the promise of release about to implode. I've done pretty well holding back, considering I wanted to unload as soon as her hand touched me.

"I'm going to cum down your gorgeous throat. Are you ready, beautiful?" My voice strains, the words labored by my heavy breathing.

Winnie answers with the sexiest moan I've ever heard. With both hands in her hair, I fuck her mouth faster.

"Angel," I groan.

One last slam in. I hold her head in place as streams of my warm seed coat her throat. My vision darkens as sparks flare into flame, setting me ablaze. The tantalizing orgasm is so intense that my legs almost give out. If this is what her mouth feels like, I can't wait to have her pussy. I hope she enjoyed it as much as I did.

Winnie greedily accepts the salty liquid. I knew she'd be good at everything. I watch her thighs rub once more, then her body twitches, and she moans around me. Mm, the dirty minx just got herself off while sucking my cock.

Fuck, that's hot.

Once my hips stop jerking, she sucks and licks me clean, pulls my pants up, and puts me away. I help her to her feet; she presses her body against mine, slips her cool hand under my shirt, and gently caresses my side. I should recuperate. It's the polite thing to do.

"Did you make yourself cum, baby?" I whisper to her.

Winter's cheeks turn pink, but she gives me a light shake of her head.

"That was the hottest thing I've ever felt or watched." I hug and pull her into me. My lips find hers, but she stops me before I can deepen the kiss.

"That was just for you. I want you to know I want you."

"Babe, you did not have to do that for me to know you want me."

“I wanted to. I’ve never tried it. Have you had many, um, never mind.” Winter's face flushes, and she sucks in her cheeks.

I hate that she’s so insecure about this.

“It was the first time for both of us. You're the only person I’ve let do that, Winter.” I confess.

Her shoulders sag with relief. “Sorry. I know we both have a past; it wasn't a fair question, but really? No one.” She eyes me skeptically.

“You can ask me anything, and I’ll be honest.” I sigh and thumb her cheek. Maybe if she knows I’m not a man-whore, it’ll make all of this easier on her. “Winnie, at the risk of sounding like a loser, I’ll admit I’ve never slept around. Ever, with anyone.”

Winnie's brows shoot up, and her jaw drops. “Never? Like, as in never been with anyone?”

I shake my head and palm her plump ass. “I’ve been to third base a couple of times, but that’s it. No one ever felt right, and I didn’t want to be one of those guys or carry that reputation. I knew I would know when I found the right person.”

In my soul, I know I’m falling in love with Winter. I’m past warm feelings. Just thinking about her or being near her sends a flock of moths into flight in my stomach. My heart never rests when she’s close, and my brain never stops thinking about her. And my soul longs for hers.

“But you seemed pretty experienced a few minutes ago.” She giggles.

“I’ve been watching porn since I was thirteen, and I may have read some books. Being a virgin doesn’t mean I won’t know what I’m doing. Does it weird you out?” I ask nervously. Most men like the idea of a virgin girlfriend, but is it the same for women? We’re about to find out.

"Not at all. I think it's sweet, but are you sure you want to start wasting your firsts on me?"

"It's not a waste. I plan on you being my first and only, Angel."

Damn, I'm starting to sound like a lovesick loser. I need to fix that. I hook a finger under her chin and tilt her head up to look at me. Her glazed crystal orbs lock onto mine. She is a stunning piece of art.

"I have to go, but I will see you when you get home. Don't overthink what I told you. We're taking the chance together."

Dipping my head down, I kiss her nose before letting go.

"Together," she whispers with a smile.

Good, she understands. I open the door, kiss her goodbye, and walk out of the store. I hate leaving her after what just happened. It feels wrong to walk away after an orgasm that shook my foundation. I know I'll see her tonight, but it's not soon enough.

CHAPTER 10
BAYLOR

Today is date night, and I'm a nervous wreck. All I can think about is having Winnie forever. She makes me feel complete. It's like floating lazily on a lake on a hot summer day. It's the best feeling in the world.

Next weekend, I have the dog adoption I agreed to help with. The following weekend, Winnie and I are going to the charity ball together. Things would be aligning perfectly if it weren't for the mystery man and woman looming over our heads. Beau still isn't any closer to finding out who they are, which is concerning.

Showered and ready, I grab my wallet and keys, lock up, and walk over to Winters. I'm planning to try to convince her to stay at my place tonight, not for sex. I want to know what it feels like to have her lying next to me.

I feel my heart skip a beat when Winnie opens the door before I have a chance to knock. She's gorgeous in her ripped mom jeans, a shirt that fits her curves perfectly, and sandals.

Her hair is in a messy bun, with strands falling into her face, and she wears wide-framed glasses. How the hell did I not know she wore glasses? Her entire being has my dick twitching. I mean, come on, everyone has a girl-with-glasses fantasy. A thrill runs through me knowing we're about to go on an official date.

"You wear glasses?" I ask.

"Don't judge. I lost my contact lens in the shower, and I need to order more. I usually only wear these when I have to, and I'll need them where we are going. You look very handsome and smell fantastic," she says, changing the subject from her glasses.

"I think you look hot as fuck with them on. You should wear them more often. Like every day. Thank you. You look gorgeous and smell like heaven," I tell her.

Winnie gives me a questioning look, as if I just told her the biggest lie. I hate that she can't see how beautiful she is. I've noticed her silently judging herself on multiple occasions.

"You're messing with me. I'm pretty sure no one thinks glasses are attractive," she says, laughing nervously.

"I would never lie about how beautiful you are." I grip the nape of her neck, making her gasp. "Angel, men fantasize about the girl next door. And I'm lucky enough to be dating one." I kiss her briefly, then let her go and guide her out the door before she can argue with me.

"It's not a fancy date, but I thought it would be fun," she says while she locks her door.

"I'm sure I'll enjoy whatever it is."

With her hand in mine, we walk to her car. I get to be a passenger princess today. I can't say a woman has ever taken me out on a date before.

As we drive through the lot, Winnie gives me a brilliant grin. "I've always wanted to go to the drive-in movies. I thought it would be nice, and we could get food from here. If you don't like it, we can go somewhere else."

"No. This is perfect. I like the drive-ins. We used to come here with our parents when we were kids."

Winnie pulls into a spot, parks, and we step out of the car. I bring my arm around her back, resting my hand at the base of her bouncy ass, and she lets me. I don't know what's gotten into her lately, but I like it.

"We still have about an hour and a half before the movie starts," she tells me. I like that she picked something low-key.

"What are we watching?" I ask, giving her ass a little tap.

She glances back at the massive screen we'll be watching the movie on and does a little hip shake with a cheesy grin on her face. "A scary movie."

I bark out a laugh at her little jig. I know how tonight will go, and fuck, I like seeing her this happy. She is so damn excited.

"Does that mean you'd be willing to stay with me tonight? I know you like scary movies, but I also know they genuinely scare you, and you eventually freak yourself out."

She stops her happy dance and huffs. "I know they do, but I can't help it. And yes, I'll stay with you tonight."

Victory surges through me when she agrees to stay with me. I didn't even have to argue with her about it.

"Don't worry. I'll keep you safe from the invisible monsters."

Her arms fly around my waist as I turn her into me. My hands reach around and pat her ass. She's so soft and fits my body perfectly.

"My giant protector," she jokes, grabbing a handful of my ass, making my dick twitch.

"Yup, you will always be safe with me, my sexy, delicious girlfriend."

Winnie hums and rests her chin on my chest. When she locks eyes with mine, my lips curve as I take in her excitement.

"Is that what we are, hotshot?"

"Fuck yes." I declare.

"I guess I can allow it since we're officially dating now," she giggles. My stomach dips when I take in her beauty.

"It's possible I'm enjoying the glasses too much. You're stunning." I watch the blush creep across her cheeks.

Winter tucks her head to hide her face, but I stop her. I hook a finger under her chin and bring her eyes back to mine.

"You never have to hide from me."

"Thank you." She whispers the words bashfully.

It's strange seeing this side of her. Tonight, she's let go and is more relaxed than I have ever seen her, but she also has a new shyness.

Once we're back at the SUV, she opens the back and pulls out the two-person camping chair, where we sit and eat. My eyes roam the area, taking in the parked cars and people milling about. Kids are running around, adults are converging, and the concession stands are full of teenagers. Glancing back at Winnie, I see her brows pinch together and her cheek twitch as she thinks. She's got something she wants to say. When she finishes her food, she finally works up her nerve.

"Do you want kids one day?" she blurts out nervously, catching me off guard, but I recover quickly.

"I'd like to, but I'd be okay if you didn't," I answer honestly. I mean, I want to see Winter's stomach swollen with my child, but I'd be okay if she didn't want that.

She visibly relaxes and shakes her head. “Until you, I never allowed myself to think about having more. It felt like it was out of the realm of possibilities for me.”

“I’m sorry, Angel. I’ll give you all the babies you want when you're ready.” I grab her knees, twist her body, and drape her legs over mine.

“You should know that twins run on my side of the family. My mom has a twin sister, and my uncles are twins. Summer was a twin, but the second embryo didn’t make it. Be careful what you wish for, hotshot.” She winks and tosses popcorn into her mouth.

Leaning in, I grip the side of her neck, squeezing just enough to make my point without hurting her. My eyes meet her glittering crystal orbs. Let’s see how much of the dirty talk she likes. Who knows, maybe I’m not wrong about what I’m going to say.

“Mm, I think you might be asking me to breed you, Winnie. If that’s what you want, I will fill you repeatedly until we have multiple sets of twins,” I tell her. Winnie's lips part as hunger and need flash across her irises like shooting stars.

“Damn, that shouldn’t have turned me on,” she gasps.

I move in closer to her, trail my nose up her neck, and bite her earlobe. “Do you want my babies, Winnie? Does the thought of my cum filling you turn you on? We can make that happen,” I taunt her with my filthy talk.

I know we are not ready for more children, but talking about it has her thighs rubbing together, reminding me of her making herself come while sucking my cock. Or maybe it’s the act itself that has her scorching hot right now.

And now I have a raging hard-on.

"Holy dirty mouth, hotshot. You almost have me saying yes," she whispers, stifling a moan as I massage the top of her thigh and work my way down to her calf.

"Almost?" I ask in my best seductive voice.

"Yes. If we weren't here, we might be in trouble. Oh my god, I didn't know that could feel so good," she says with a low moan as I keep massaging her leg. I dip my head to her neck and drag my teeth along it.

It's like she has never really been touched before. No man has ever worshipped this woman. I like the idea of being the only one to do it.

I don't finish the dirty conversation because if I do, I'm going to erupt in my pants. Instead, I focus on massaging her legs. When I start to remove her sandal, her foot jerks, but I keep my grip.

"Ew, are you going to touch my feet?" she gaped at me.

I hold back a smile at her dismayed look. "I am."

"But what if they're dirty from the sand?" Winnie scrunches her nose and wiggles her foot to get away from me, making me laugh.

It's like trying to catch a flopping fish out of the water, but I succeed. I lift her foot, turn on my phone's flashlight, and inspect it.

"They're not dirty. The movie is starting soon. Relax and let me take care of you. You've been tense, and your muscles need to release that tension."

"Uh-huh. If you say so, but just in case, here." Leaning over, she digs in her purse and hands me a tiny bottle of hand sanitizer.

As the movie starts, I keep working her muscles. When Winter finally lets go, she looks so content until thirty minutes into the film, when she screams and damn near falls out of the chair during a jump scare. My body shakes with silent laughter. After the second jump scare, she sits up and hugs my arm as she watches intently.

My heart is racing, fueled by the adrenaline her closeness is causing. Her warmth is comforting, but I feel like I just drank ten espresso shots. Near the end of the movie, she's in my lap, clinging to me as if I'm the anchor keeping her from being snatched away. I soak up the fact that she's comfortable enough to hold me like this. I feel like a teenage boy who took his first girlfriend to her first scary movie so she would hold onto him.

Once the movie ends, the lights come on, and everyone gathers their belongings. But instead of moving, Winter looks at me bashfully.

"Sorry. It was a good movie, and I might have gotten a bit scared."

Laughing, I brush a strand of hair from her face. "I think it's more than possible, Angel. I didn't mind one bit. In fact," I whisper, "You can sit on my lap anytime you want to."

"I think I should move before I do something that will embarrass both of us," she whispers back.

"Nothing you do would ever embarrass me."

Her chest rises and falls rapidly as she drinks me in. "Oh, I think if I did what I'm thinking right now in front of all these people, it would."

Groaning, I shift her and stand. She's thinking dirty right now. It has me hard enough to cut a fucking diamond because I know it.

"If you told me to take you right here, I would," I say, kissing and lightly licking her neck, making her back arch into me.

I need to stop before I go too far. I kiss her forehead, load our stuff into the car, and we head to my house.

During the drive, my heart pounds against my chest. I don't know why I'm so nervous, but I am. Even though I teased about breeding, neither of us is ready for that. I would like to make Winnie feel good.

As we pull into the drive, every video and book I've ever seen starts playing in my head, showing me what to do. I want this to be special and pleasurable for her, not inexperienced and sloppy.

Inside the house, we head to my room, and I give her a shirt and a pair of sweats that are going to be way too big for her. While she changes in my bathroom, I change in the other one.

As I pull the covers back, Winter steps out wearing only my shirt. It's an instant turn-on to see her in my clothes. I want them on her all the time. The CCFD shirt I gave her is more like a dress on her short frame.

"I hope this is okay. The pants were way too big," she says, rubbing her hands together in front of her.

"Perfect," I say, my voice hoarse.

In bed, we face each other. I reach out and tuck her hair behind her ear. Winter is a goddess I must worship.

I bring my mouth to hers and kiss her gently. Winnie moans and arches her soft body into mine. My hand slowly glides up her thigh. I want to give her time to tell me no. I hope she doesn't, but I will stop if she tells me to.

My heart quickens as I feel her soft stomach under my palm, and I give it a gentle squeeze before my fingers trace every well-earned groove, every stripe that deserves attention.

Winter breaks our kiss when I thumb under her breast.

"Bay," she whispers, then rolls onto her back. Her body arches as my hand covers her perfect, taught breast.

"Spread those gorgeous thighs for me, baby."

As soon as she does, I kneel between them and pull her into a sitting position. "I want to make you feel good. No sex. We'll save that for another time. If you don't want it, Winnie, you need to tell me because I have zero plans to stop." I tell her, then pull the shirt up and over her head to reveal her perfect, symmetrical breasts.

"I want you to. God, I want you to," Winnie whispers breathlessly.

"Mm, if I do anything you don't like, tap my shoulder. If you want me to do anything differently, tell me."

"Ok," she says before her lips take mine in a heated, demanding kiss.

"Lie back, beautiful," I command, and fuck me if she isn't quick to obey.

Bracing my weight on one elbow, I bite and kiss my way down her slender neck. I can feel her heart racing.

My lips and tongue work their way down her body, and I meet her tight pink nipples. She hisses when I suck her stiff peak into my mouth, flicking and teasing each one while my hand slips between us. I'm in sweatpants, but my cock feels like it's in a metal cage.

Winter inhales sharply when I pull her panties to the side, and my fingers explore her soaked pussy. It's slick and smooth.

"Mm, so wet for me already, Angel?" I murmur into her breast.

Wet is an insult; she's drenched and ready for me to ease her aching pussy, ready to feel a release she's never experienced before. Let's hope I don't disappoint.

"Yes," she moans.

I trail my lips and tongue down her body while gently massaging her clit between my two fingers. Winter moans and rolls her hips.

As I kneel before her, I remind myself not to overthink this. When Winter lifts her ass, I remove her panties. Winnie rises to her elbows. I can't help the twisted smirk that spreads across my face.

"I want you to stay just like that so I can see every beautiful face you make." It's a command I know she'll obey.

She nods, watching my every move. Her insecurity gives way to burning curiosity and fascination.

My eyes take in the delicate view before me. Her bare pussy has my mouth watering and my cock straining against its fabric enclosure. She's fucking gorgeous, just as I knew she would be.

"Your body is breathtaking—every last inch of it. Spread your legs wider for me, beautiful," I rasp.

Winnie bashfully parts her knees more, but not wide enough. With both hands, I open her as far as her legs will part, then moan at the sight of her glistening wetness laid bare before me.

"Baylor," she whispers. Her hooded gaze meets mine through her thick, blonde lashes.

Gorgeous

I massage the inside of her thighs, then slip my fingers through her folds to her warm, soaked center. My finger circles her tight entrance. Her body stiffens at the touch. As if the intrusion is new, never felt before, and fuck, it probably is.

Nervous, I hurt her. My eyes meet hers to make sure she's okay. She may have had kids, but this is new for her. Her ex was a piece of shit who didn't care for her or give her this kind of attention. But I will for the rest of my goddamn life.

"Okay, babe?" I ask, hating the insecurity in my own damned voice.

Her hand smooths over my cheek like a soft breeze, and I lean into the reassuring touch. She is showing me I'm the only man she'll ever let this close again, which is good because I am.

I have fully staked my claim on this woman. No man will ever come near her again.

"I'm okay." There's an uncertainty in her tone, but I will show her she has nothing to fear with me.

"Relax and keep your eyes on me. I want you to see how a man should have treated you." I lean down, biting, kissing, and sucking the inside of her thighs, leaving as many marks as I can. Her body jerks as she moans, and one hand dives into my hair while the other clutches the sheet tightly beside her.

"Oh God," she says, and a moan breaks free.

"Hotshot," I tell her, making her giggle and groan as I work her swollen bud with my thumb and slip a finger into her tight canal. Shit, she's so damn tight. Winnie's hips roll, and her legs start to shake. Her hand digs into my hair, nails scraping my scalp, and she tugs, making me groan.

Adjusting my body, I lie between her legs, bringing my nose to her center and inhaling deeply, breathing in her sweet, succulent juices. Fuck, even her pussy smells like heaven.

A growl leaves me before my tongue lashes out, stroking her bud. "You taste like sweet innocence, Angel," I tell her in a muffled voice. "So good."

I flick, suck, and tease before slipping another finger halfway into her and working her slowly. I eat her pussy like it's the last thing I'll ever do on this earth. I've never tasted anything so good.

My hips move and grind into the mattress as I work her pink clit. The friction and the taste of her have me wanting to blow.

By her moans and movements, I must be doing it right, and she's feeling the same thing I am.

"Baylor, I've never. No one's ever," Her breathing increases, and her hips roll as she rides my face and fingers.

I pump and twist my fingers into her faster. While I work her, I take in the sexy faces she's making.

"I know, and from this moment on, I will be the only one who ever has or ever will."

Winnie's pupils dilate, her face flushes, and she bites her bottom lip. I watch her brows lift and her mouth part. She's about to cum, and I want to taste everything she offers. I dive back in, sucking and lapping at her pussy as her hips roll and rock faster. Her hand tightens in my hair, and she holds me where she wants me. Goddamn, I fucking love her.

"That's it, gorgeous, ride my face. Tell me you're mine, Winnie." I murmur into her pussy.

"I-I"

"Use your words, beautiful," I tell her, pumping my fingers faster, making her hips buck and her scream in bliss. My cock is aching to be inside her, but it's not time yet. He has to settle for self-pleasure for now.

"I'm yours, baby. All yours."

My pupils explode, and my eyes meet hers as she watches me eat the delectable treat before me. Releasing her clit, I swipe my tongue slowly. "Repeat it."

"W-what?" she asks in a pre-orgasmic haze.

"You know what," I growl as I latch onto her clit and suck hard.

"Baby," she screams. Yes. That's what I wanted to hear.

"Mm, good girl." I groan against her swollen clit, sending a vibration through her. As I give her another hard suck, I take mental pictures of the moment the dam breaks. Her walls tighten and her hips buck.

"Yes, I'm cumming, Bay." I watch her beautiful features as her pussy sucks my fingers and pulses around them while she cries out from the orgasm consuming her, and her body convulses.

Her taste and moans have imprinted themselves on the library of my brain. I love watching her come undone. I suck and lap at her relentlessly through her orgasm. My hips thrust and still as I groan and release my own climax.

Fuck. I didn't mean to do that.

I give her one last swipe before slipping my fingers from her and prowling up her body. Now hovering over her, I bring my fingers to my mouth and suck her juices from them, then brace myself on my elbows. Her eyes spark and light up as she watches me.

"Bay, that was. God, that was fucking amazing. Are you sure you've never done that before?" she says in a sleepy, breathless voice.

"Never. I'm glad you enjoyed it." I lean down and give her a brief kiss, then move off the bed and out from between her legs.

In the bathroom, I remove my cum-soaked boxer briefs, clean myself, and slip my sweats back on. I grab a warm washcloth and stroll back into the room.

Gathering her panties and the shirt, I clean her up, help her get dressed, and lie beside her. With her in my arms, I tangle our legs together and run my fingers through her smooth hair until she drifts off into a deep sleep.

This is where she should always be. Right here in my bed, in my arms.

CHAPTER 11
BAYLOR

"Good morning, gorgeous," I whisper into Winter's ear, brushing the hair from her face.

It's early, and her friends decided to ambush me at my place because she didn't answer her texts or the door to her house.

I can't help the smile that spreads across my face as I watch her stretch and roll onto her back—her white-blond hair fans out under her head. Even just waking up, she takes my breath away.

She's my sweet angel.

"What time is it?" she groans, covering her eyes with her arm.

"It's 10 AM. I made breakfast and coffee. Birdie and Journey are here," I tell her, kissing her soft shoulder.

Winter's arm lurches from her face, almost hitting me in mine, and her eyes fly open. She sits up, checks her phone, then falls back into bed.

"It's too early to deal with their questions. Tell them I died."

Chuckling, I kiss her collarbone. "I think that would raise a ton of questions, and if you don't go out there soon, they'll come in here. No offense to them, but you're the only woman I want in my room, Angel."

Winter gives me a soft smile and gently caresses my cheek. "You're too cute, Hotshot."

Taking her hand, I bring it to my lips and kiss each finger. "I'm not cute. I'm very manly," I tease.

"Sure you are, baby," she says, patting my cheek like I'm a child.

In a swift move, I straddle her and hover over her. I bring my face within inches of hers. "Repeat it," I tell her.

Rolling her eyes, she obliges. "Baby. My sweet, sexy man."

"That's my girl," I tell her, then start showering her face with kisses. I love hearing all those words. I'm a hopeless romantic at heart, but I'm still a man.

Winter giggles, pushes me off her, and tosses the covers back, revealing her perfect porcelain legs. There isn't a blemish on them except for my bite marks. My eyes trail up them until they land on her sweet juncture.

Goddamn, I can't wait to sink into her.

Groaning, I shuffle off the bed. Winnie gives me a wicked smile, then gets to her feet and locks her crystal gaze on mine as she stretches dramatically, letting me see her black panties.

"Really?"

"What? I have to wake up my muscles."

I met her gaze, letting my seductive stare linger just long enough for her breath to catch. My lips twitched with the smirk I was holding back as her thighs squeezed together. "Uh-huh. You're lucky two of my sisters-in-law are in the living room right now, or that whole breeding discussion we had last night would be a reality right now."

Tingles run down my spine as I see the spark ignite in her blue eyes. I'm starting to think my angel wants more babies.

"If you keep looking at me like that, I'll tackle you to this bed and make that little fantasy spinning through your mind right now a reality," I profess.

"W-what? I'm not thinking anything." She lies.

In three strides, I'm chest to chest with her, gripping the nape of her neck. "Liar," I whisper before giving her a greedy, ravenous kiss. Winnie returns it just as feverishly, trying to take more than I'm giving. Her sweet, gentle tongue battles mine.

So greedy

Releasing her lips, I press my forehead to hers. I can't get enough of this woman. I swear I'm so lost to her that if she asked me to jump off a bridge, I'd do it without hesitation. Winter has consumed my mind and soul. And soon she'll have all of my body, too.

"Get dressed, Angel. I put clothes in the bathroom for you."

"You went and got me clothes?"

"Yeah, I stole a pair of panties, too."

Winnie's face flames. She looks completely mortified. I have to say, I love teasing her. Most of the time, she doesn't know whether I'm serious or not.

"No. No, you did not," she protested, a look of dismay on her face.

I plaster on my best grin and start walking backward toward the door. "Guess you'll never know. I doubt you remember every pair you had in that overstuffed drawer, or maybe the hamper in the bathroom?" I joke. I didn't steal her underwear. If I had, Beau would be correct, and I really would be a creepy stalker.

"I swear to God, Baylor, if you stole a pair of my dirty panties, I will flick you in the sack."

"Ouch. All I heard was that the clean ones are fair game." Laughing hysterically, I back out the door just as she reaches over, grabs a pillow, and launches it at me, making me laugh even harder.

She really is too easy to rile up.

When I walk into the kitchen, Journey and Birdie give me a knowing look. I am unashamed that Winnie is at my house, in my bed.

"She's getting dressed," I tell them, and they both make woah noises before I grab my phone from the counter.

I swear they're children.

Glancing at it, I see a text from Beau saying everyone is at the park with the kids.

"I'm going to the park. Let Winter know I'll be back, and for fuck's sake, do not go into my room. Wait for her out here." I narrow my eyes at my nosy sisters-in-law.

"Damn, why are you so uptight about that? It's just a room. Oh, wait, is it a sex room in there? Do you have medieval sexual torture devices?" Journey asks playfully.

Rolling my eyes, I make a cup of coffee. "Really, baked potato? You need to quit reading dark mafia romances. See ya."

"I will do no such thing. Briggs and I like to recreate the dirty scenes," she says, wiggling her brows.

"Beau and I do too. It's hot."

I blanch at their admission. I do not want to know that.

"Gross," they both chuckle as I shake off the shudder.

I take a wide berth and move past them. I know they'll both try to fuck with me if I get too close. At this moment, I'm glad we didn't have sisters growing up. I can only imagine how that would have gone.

Winnie opens my bedroom door as I reach for the handle. She's gorgeous in the yellow sundress I grabbed for her.

"I'm going to meet everyone at the park and let you ladies talk."

"Okay. Have fun." Winnie kisses my cheek and gives me that precious smile.

My lips tilt up at her; she's trying to be discreet. I can't have that. Her friends want a show. I'll give them one.

What was it? Journey said, "palm necklace." I think, then smile internally.

I reach out and wrap my hand around the base of her throat, not hard but with just enough pressure, and tug her in while my other hand grabs as much of her ass as I can. Then I capture her lips, swallowing her gasp and moan.

The kiss isn't pretty; it's rough and demanding. Winnie moans and arches into me as her mouth and body surrender to mine. Her hand dives into my hair while the other digs into my back.

I'm starting to think my heart is in a permanent uptick. Its constant, out-of-rhythm beating can't be good for me, but fuck, she's worth the risk of it eventually giving out. Maybe the same goes for my brain and the lack of oxygen it's been getting lately.

Releasing her neck, I thumb the area and break our kiss. Her blue, flaming irises meet mine. She's barely holding on to her restraint. It's only a matter of time before we both break.

"YES," Journey shouts, making both of us laugh. "I fucking knew it."

I shake my head and watch Winnie's dress flow around her, her thick ass bouncing as she makes her way to her friends. That ass is all mine now. I feel smug as fuck knowing I finally have her.

As I come to a stop, I spot my three brothers and a slew of kids playing on the playground. We have all officially gone from Sunday-morning hangovers to Sunday-morning park visits.

When I exit the car, I inhale the spring air. It's probably my favorite season. As I stride over to everyone, I wave to Daniel when he calls my name and waves his arm erratically.

"Birdie and Journey kick you out?" Briggs laughs.

"I left on my own. I can't handle the shit they talk about. I swear every conversation involves a dick, and I learned way too much about you and Beau before I left." I do a shimmy to shake the disgust from my brain.

"What? What did they say?" Beau asks.

"Pfft, I am not repeating it," I gag. I did not need to know about their role-playing.

"They're worse than dudes," Briggs says, standing when he sees Tulip trip, but she laughs it off, gets to her feet, and starts chasing Harley again.

"Yup. Beau, have you heard anything back yet?" I ask, sitting at the picnic table.

"No. The detective in Atlanta called me back. I sent him the photos. He's going to call me once he looks into it."

"Have they shown back up?" Briggs asks.

"Not that I'm aware of, but I don't think she'd tell me if they did," I tell him.

"Maybe you should talk to her about it," Baxter offers, a suggestion I don't want.

"I know, but I wanted her to trust me enough to come to me on her own."

"She probably won't if she's scared," Bax says, adjusting Everett in his arms.

"I'll try to push harder for an answer, but unless he shows up again, my hands are tied," Beau says, bouncing his babbling daughter on his knee.

"Any news on the sister?" Baxter asks.

What is his angle? He's never this curious. Baxter has been anti-women since Anna left months ago.

"She called Winnie and let her know she was aiming for next weekend."

"Hm."

"What's with you? You got a hard-on for her or something?" I ask, looking at our eldest brother.

Baxter is broad and stacked. Right now, he seems like a mess. The black rings under his eyes tell me he's not sleeping. We can't blame Everett for that. Those are all Anna.

"Please. I'm just curious. It's hard to imagine there being no evidence of someone's life over the past thirteen years," Bax shrugs, completely denying his intense interest in the redheaded stranger.

"Uh-huh, we'll go with that. Anyway, let's play soccer," I tell them.

As I step away, I hear the three familiar voices. I look over my shoulder and see the three women I just left at my house. My brows furrow in confusion. In a few strides, I'm face-to-face with Winnie. The smile on her face makes my chest swell.

"What's going on?" I ask, reaching out to tuck her hair behind her ear.

"She wouldn't spill the tea, so we came here to watch the soccer lesson," Ny says with disappointment.

Winter lifts a shoulder at her friend. She's completely unbothered by Ny's reaction. I like that she wants to keep that part of our relationship private.

Since they're here, they can keep an eye on Everett so Baxter can join the game. Winter kisses my cheek and jogs over to the baby before the other women, which makes me laugh. The baby is a true ladies' man.

My brother and I gather with the kids on the grassy field. Beau gathers them into a circle. He explains that soccer isn't just about kicking a ball, then lays out the rules.

Briggs joins in and gives them a warm-up exercise. Even as they run up and down the field, each of their faces wears a broad smile. Laughter erupts when Ox, Daniel, and Lux trip each other.

When they get back to us, I pick up one of the balls and show them a few moves. All eyes are on me, watching intently. After I've shown them, we give three of them a ball.

First comes dribbling. I tell them to keep the ball close, as if it's glued to their feet. The three boys move the ball down the field and back. Second, they practice stopping the ball. Beau, Briggs, and Baxter roll the balls to each of them, and they trap each ball with the soles of their feet.

Their favorite part is shooting at me like I'm the goal. After the first three are done, we show the others. Before we know it, more kids have to join the game.

We set up the teams and guide each of them. Laughter and shrieks fill the park with happiness and joy. The moms' cheers and shouts push the kids to play harder.

Hours tick by like minutes, and before we know it, three hours have passed. The kids are sweating and dragging their feet. They will all sleep well tonight. As we approach our woman, I see Journey has the baby now.

Winter stands and spreads her arms wide to embrace the boys as they rush up to her. She pulls them close and praises them for how well they did. That is my family. When I approach, Winnie wraps her arm around my sweaty back and scrunches her nose.

"Ew, you need a shower." She giggles but doesn't move away.

A devilish smirk crosses my face. I draw her into me and lean down, rubbing my sweaty face against her neck.

"Gross," Winnie mutters, squirming away, but I hold her steady. The boys laugh, find it hilarious, and start rubbing their faces against her arms. Winnie suddenly bursts into laughter and playfully shouts at us.

"You three think you're funny, don't you?" she asks, wiping the laughter from the corner of her eyes.

"Yes," both kids reply in unison.

"I will find a way to get you back."

Winnie wraps her arms around the boys and tickles their sides. Today was a great day. Daniel is going to kill it during soccer season. With everyone tired out, we all load into our cars and head home.

CHAPTER 12
WINTER

Snuggled into Baylor's side, we sat on the couch in silence and watched the movie. Since our date, we have spent every night he isn't on shift together. Last night, we all stayed at his house. I snuck into his room after the boys went to sleep and woke up before them, so they thought I slept on the couch. I'm not ready to tell them that Bay and I are dating. Bay understands and won't push it.

There is still the little issue of Edward. He demanded his money two weeks ago, and since then, twenty loan applications have been denied. I'm sure he'll be visiting me soon.

It's Friday evening, and the boys are staying with Baxter to *'help'* with the baby. Even though he is exhausted, he never tells them no. When I tried, Baxter chastised me.

'My nephews can stay anytime they want,' he told me, and I relented. It's his exhaustion, not mine. Baylor's entire family has accepted us as family since the day we got here. I love that the kids have that.

Summer called to let me know she'd be here sometime this weekend. Things in Virginia took longer than she'd planned.

Bay and I have watched plenty of movies together, but never cuddled up like this. I have to say it's one of the best feelings I've ever had. Troy was never a cuddler. Every time I tried, he'd huff, push me away, and tell me I was smothering him.

But not the man beside me. For him, I can't get close enough. If I scoot away, he pulls me closer. If I get up, he pauses the movie. He brings me drinks, not the other way around. I wonder if it's because I was his first blowjob? Shit, how clingy will he be if we have sex? He's already acting like a lost puppy. I kind of like it. I like that there's no competition and that I have him entirely entrapped.

I want a clingy Baylor.

A knock on the door has us both getting up.

"I'll get it," Bay says, moving to the door before I can.

"I can get it. It's my house, you oversized chihuahua."

He laughs instead of arguing with me.

"Hey, what are you doing here? You just left an hour ago. Where are the boys?" Bay says.

"They forgot their games, and they're with mom and dad at the pizzeria. But maybe you should be asking the woman what she wants."

When Baxter says to ask the woman what she wants, I rush to the door. Moving past the guys, I see her—my sister.

My eyes take her in; she still has her beautiful, wild, curly, copper hair, bright blue eyes, fair skin, and dark freckles sprinkled across her face and neck. She has always been shorter than me. The poor thing is barely 5'2 and resembles our father, while I have our mother's blond hair and porcelain skin.

As my eyes roam, I notice the extensive tattoos on her arms. One arm features summer-themed artwork, and the other, winter-themed artwork. My chest swells because I know they're for us. Her right leg is covered in fantasy art. Then my heart drops to the ground when I see her left leg, a partial prosthetic from the mid-calf down.

"Oh my god," I run to her and take her into my arms as the sob breaks free.

Summer holds me tightly while I cry into her neck. Thirteen years of missing her. All the years of wondering where she is and what she's done with her life. I had wondered whether she was hurt and safe. What happened to her?

My body shakes and trembles as I hold onto her, as if letting go would make her disappear again.

"Shh, it's ok," she soothes.

"You're hurt. You were hurt," I tell her. Pulling back, I start lifting her shirt to see where else, and I notice a little scar. "Fuck, were you shot? Summer, were you shot?" My voice cracks.

Summer laughs and swats my hand away. Her voice is a magical song to my ears. I missed her tremendously. Now that she's here, I never want her to leave again.

"How about we go inside if you plan to strip me down? I don't think your neighbors are going to want to see my bare ass, and at the rate you're going, that's what might happen," she chuckles.

"Right, sorry."

I step aside to lead her into the house. Baylor and Baxter stand at the island, waiting. I notice both of them taking in the scars and the leg. Summer doesn't seem bothered by it, though. She is likely used to people staring.

In the kitchen, she looks at both men and points to Baxter, who is holding Everett. "Is that one yours?"

“What? God, no. No offense, Bax. That one is mine.” I tell her, pointing to Bay, who puffs out his chest with pride at my claim.

Damn it.

“Are you going to tell me how this happened? What have you been doing all this time?”

“Military. Now medically retired. For obvious reasons.” She says, gesturing to her body. I can now see the scar divot on her forearm and the burn scar on the left side of her neck. There’s a massive scar on the outside of her left thigh. Fuck, what happened? Wait, I don't think I want to know.

I watch Baxter and Baylor’s brows shoot for the stars. I lift her shirt and start looking at the scars, finding one more hole. I keep searching, looking for more scars. Summer squirms away from me, laughing.

“Damn it, woman. Stop undressing me. I like to get the guys' names at least before I get naked. I also prefer dinner first.” She jokes.

I snort with laughter. She’s right. I’m practically undressing her in front of two strange men. Pulling her shirt back down, I take in her beautiful face. She doesn’t look a day older than when I last saw her.

“Sorry. That's Baylor, and that's Baxter and his son Everett.”

“Pleasure to meet you both.”

“Likewise. How long do you plan on staying?” Bay asks.

I flick my eyes between the two standoffish brothers and glower at them.

“As long as she wants to,” I snap. I hate their overprotective egos sometimes.

Summer chuckles. “I’d like to stick around permanently. I’ll admit I made the mistake of choosing my career and not reaching out sooner, but I’d like to get to know my sister and nephews now. And don't worry, Bigfoot, all my enemies are halfway around the world. No harm will come to them."

"How long has it been since you two have seen each other?" Baxter asks, adjusting Everett.

"Thirteen years," she answers again.

"And you think you'll be able to pick up where you left off?"

"Baxter," I say in a clipped tone. "What the hell is wrong with you two?" I growl. "Keep it up, and you can both leave."

"It's okay. If Winter tells me to leave, I will, but make no mistake: Bigfoot and brother, Yeti, will not run me off. I don't think I need to tell you I've survived worse than you two pompous asses."

"You're not going anywhere. I want you here for as long as you want. Keep it up, Hotshot, and there will be no more dates." I threaten Baylor, and he clamps his mouth shut.

Summer whistles and shakes her hand. "I think I just cock-blocked you, dude."

"Really?" Bay groans. "She's as bad as Journey."

"She's always said and done what she wanted. I'm glad that hasn't changed."

Summer shrugs and looks at Everett. "Now, have we established I'm not a threat? I am dying to look at that baby."

Summer gets to her feet and walks over slowly, then looks up at Baxter, who rolls his eyes and shifts Everett. Summer leans in and beams at the baby like we all do when he's around.

"Oh, my clouds, he must look like his mother. He's too cute to look like you, Yeti," she jokes, and for a half a fraction of a second, Baxter almost looks like he might smile.

I use the distraction to get the kids' games from their bedrooms. Baxter has limits on how much socializing he's willing to do, and I have a feeling Summer will drive him crazy.

Back in the kitchen, I hand Baxter the video games.

"Thank you. Well, this has been eventful, but I should head back to get the kids. It was nice meeting you, Summer," Baxter says, then moves away from Summer. He nods once more before he leaves the house.

"Mm, I like 'em big and broody. Girlfriend?" Summer asks me, and I shake my head. Her grin grows. "I actually have a meeting. I wanted to stop here first. You two look like you want the evening alone. I got a room at the B&B when I got into town. I'll come by and see you tomorrow?"

"Yes. Of course," I tell her.

Summer smiles lightly and gives me another hug. "I missed you," she whispers, then leaves.

Once we're alone, I glance at Bay. He is a cocky son of a bitch. I want to smack the smug look off his face.

"What was that all about?" I ask, and his face drops.

"What?"

"You know how excited I've been to see her, then you and Baxter went all caveman."

"I'm sorry, Angel, but I meant what I said. You and the kids are mine. I need to make sure you're safe. Always. She seems like a nice woman, and I shouldn't have been so harsh. I'll do better."

Tears prick the back of my eyes. Not because of what he said, but because I can't stop thinking about what happened to my sister that caused all the damage to her body.

"Shit. Winnie,"

Two strides and he has me enveloped in his arms.

"I found two bullet scars, Bay. She doesn't have a fourth of her leg anymore. I can't stop thinking about what she went through, and then you and Baxter gave her the third degree. I don't want her to leave," I croak.

"I was out of line. I shouldn't have questioned her," Bay says in the softest, most apologetic voice I've ever heard.

"But you did, Baylor. Her being here is my decision, not yours."

"You're right. Let me make it up to you."

Bay dips his head and starts kissing down my neck, but I push him away.

"No. That's not something we'll do when one of us is upset, or when the conversation isn't something we want to hear. It's a cheap escape, and the issue will still be there. We need to be able to talk it out."

"I know." Bay takes my hand and leads me back to the couch.

Once we've both sat, he turns to me and places my legs in his lap. Do I have the right to be so upset? How is he going to react if he ever finds out about Edward and what I'm forced to do? Or that, in the beginning, I only asked him out because I had to? Or that Troy has tried to call me every day for the past two weeks?

"Talk to me, babe. Tell me what you're feeling," he says, and damn it, my brain goes in a different direction.

"I know what love is. What's it to you?" I sing because I have word vomit. Bay lifts a brow, giving me the 'really' look.

Bursting out with laughter, I cover my mouth. "I'm sorry. I couldn't help it. It popped into my head and was out of my mouth before I had time to think about it."

To my surprise, Bay gets up and yanks me to my feet. He places one hand on my lower back and takes my hand with the other, then starts singing the rest of the song and dancing me around the living room.

To my utter shock, he has the singing voice of a country king. I've never heard him sing, and damn it, I love it. He could serenade me anytime.

Our bodies move in harmony, hips and feet in perfect sync as we dance through the space. The air between us feels light and unburdened. I could easily become accustomed to this happiness. It's a romantic moment you hear about but never believe really happens. Yet here I am with the man of my dreams, dancing while he sings to me.

We finish the song with smiles on our faces, then Bay dips and kisses me.

At this moment, I understand why Briggs thought he was living his afterlife when he met Ny. I feel like I am living in a dream with Baylor.

CHAPTER 13
WINTER

After I pull into a parking spot behind the bookstore, I gather my belongings and get out of the car. I only came in to grab the book donation I promised Hazel.

The sun is high, with white clouds drifting in the wind. The breeze dances on my skin, making me smile. The sounds of traffic and businesses starting their days echo around me. With a deep inhale, I tip my head skyward and take in the blue hue of the morning. After I've soaked up the sun, I start my walk to the building.

When I stop at the back door, I hear a thumping noise behind me. My lungs freeze, and my heart skips a beat. When I hear the thump again, I squeeze my eyes shut.

"No, don't turn around, Winter. Do not do it. Open the door and go inside. It's nothing." I chastise myself, but I'm not one to listen to my own rational thinking, apparently.

I can do this. Slowly turning on my heels, I flinch when I hear the thud again. My eyes flick to the dumpster, and my heart starts to race. My brain finally starts to consider what the noise could be, and a thought hits me. Oh god, what if Gene fell in and hurt himself?

I drop my things and rush to the dumpster, pushing the lid open while fighting the wind.

"Gene," I say frantically, peering in.

A shriek slips out as the kitten jumps and meows. My hand flies to my chest, as if that will calm my racing heart. I can't let the poor thing stay in there. Glancing around, I look for something to help me get in and out to get the little thing.

Of course, there's nothing, but I know an eager firefighter. I dig my phone out of my pocket and call Baylor.

Bay answers with a rumble. "What did you forget?"

"Damn, nothing. Wait, I forgot my coffee, but that's not why I called. There's a kitten stuck in the dumpster behind the store. I'm not sure I'll be able to get it out if I go in after it."

"I'll bring your coffee and get the kitten. I'm on my way."

"Thank you." Hanging up, I stand on my tiptoes and look in at the little thing. "Help is coming. You'll be out of there in no time. My favorite firefighter is coming to save you," I tell the cat, as if it understands me.

"And who will save him?"

My body stiffens, and the air around me stills and cracks as I hear the sharp male voice behind me.

No, I need more time.

My heart pounds in my ears as I meet the devil's dark brown eyes. Edward stands before me, wearing a fitted all-black suit, a sinister grin spreading across his face. He looks even more menacing in the early-morning light. As he moves closer, I step back and press my body against the dumpster.

"You're a good listener. I half expected you to ignore my demand that the boyfriend stay close," Edwards says.

"I didn't do it for you," I hiss at the villain.

"Tell yourself what you want. Where's my money, Winter?"

"I need more time. I don't have those kinds of funds lying around. I've been applying for loans, but no one will approve me without a co-signer. Troy destroyed my credit." I try to explain, but his face tells me it's not the answer he wanted.

"I am not a patient man, and that sounds like an excuse. It would be a shame if your boyfriend were to encounter another fire and couldn't get out. It's unfortunate for the young woman trapped inside the last one." Edward clucks his tongue.

My breath refuses to leave my lungs as the realization hits.

"You?" I whisper, closing my eyes. "That girl didn't do anything to you."

Edward shrugs and flicks his hand. He inches another step closer, leaving half a foot between us. He's so close I can smell mint and cigarettes on his breath. My throat tightens, and my stomach churns at the scent.

"Collateral damage. Wrong place, wrong time. Your time has run out. I have my collection covered. I'll let you know when to visit Troy for the item he stole."

"What?"

"Hm. It's not time for that yet."

"What the fuck is going on?" I hear Baylor's whisky voice echo through the alley. My entire body wants to collapse at the sound of his voice.

My gaze shifts from Edward's, and I see Bay's tall, lean frame coming toward us, looking even more fierce and dangerous than the man in front of me. His muscles are tense and bulging, as if he's grown five sizes. Clenched fists hang at his sides, and the color of his tattooed arm looks darker.

Fuck me.

My breath stills when I see his green eyes are 20 shades darker, with flecks of gold flickering like a flame against the murkiness. Baylor doesn't take his glare off Edward as he stalks toward us.

Holy Hades, Zeus.

"It appears I miscalculated his timing," Edward says in a low, threatening tone, letting me know to keep my mouth shut.

"I asked you a question," Bay's voice comes out deep, dark, and aggressive, as if he were on the verge of a murderous rampage.

"My apologies. I saw a woman in distress and was offering to help." Edward's tone is calm and controlled.

When Bay steps up, he shoves Edward back and shields me. I hear Edward's dark chuckle and the shuffle of his feet on the gravel.

A gasp escapes me before I can think better of it. Bay has no idea who he's picking a fight with.

"Ah, the friend," Edward says coolly.

"Boyfriend, motherfucker. I don't think I need to warn you to stay away from my girl, but I'll say it anyway. I will not hesitate to put you in the ground if I see you within a hundred-foot radius of her." Bay growls.

"Hotshot," I whisper, clutching the back of his shirt. He has no idea who he's threatening.

"It's okay, Angel. Why don't you go inside while I and… what's his name, Winnie?"

Edward clears his throat, then answers Bay. "Edward, there's no need for threats or fighting. I'll be on my way. It was a pleasure talking to you again, Winter."

I peek around my protective barbarian just as Edward smirks, turns on his heels, and stalks away.

Baylor turns and frames my face with his large hands, gauging the fear rolling through me. The flare in his eyes is brighter now. His chest rises and falls rapidly. There's no denying he's barely holding back his fury.

"We're going to talk about this. Go inside while I get the cat," he tells me firmly, leaving no room for gentleness or argument.

He kisses my forehead roughly and ushers me to the door. Even when he's pissed off, he shows he cares. As I pick up my things, I find the keys and fumble through the ring until I find the right one. When the door is unlocked, I look back and notice Bays' tense muscles visible through the back of his shirt.

He's pissed

Anxiety has taken over my head and heart. He's angry with me. God, I hope he doesn't think I wanted Edward here. I wish I could tell him the truth, but I can't. If I tell him, he'll get Beau involved, and Edward will kill him.

Inside, I head straight to my office and shut the door. I swipe the tears away, steady my shaking hands, and work to control my breathing.

I hear a knock on the door and pull myself together. When I open it, I come face to face with Bay, holding the small gray cat.

"Who is he, Winter?" he asks, then walks me back into the office.

I avert my gaze before I answer. "I don't know what you mean. We met at the speed-dating thing, and I haven't seen him since." It's only a partial lie.

Guilt hits my gut like an axe, making nausea creep up my throat. I hate lying to him. Ten thoughts race through my mind like rapid gunfire. They're moving so quickly that I can't recover from one before the next hits.

"Bullshit. You were terrified, Winnie." He seethes, then closes his eyes and takes a deep breath.

"Well, yeah. I wasn't expecting some random guy to show up. I thought it was you at first," I say, petting the kitten and avoiding eye contact.

"Don't do that," he says.

My gaze lifts to his. His irises reflect his anger and frustration.

"Don't do what?" I ask innocently, though I'm anything but innocent at the moment.

"Lie to me. I know you better than you think."

"Bay, please let it go. I'm begging you."

"You know I can't. You're in trouble. Tell me what it is so I can help." His plea damn near breaks my heart.

"You can't help. Can we focus on the cat and the adoptions today?"

"I'm not sure I want you to go with me, Winter." He retorts, clenching his jaw.

My chest sinks and aches when he says that. I can't tell him everything. Can I? I can't lose him either.

"Why?' The question is barely a whisper.

Bay runs his hand through his hair and down his face before he looks at me again. "Because trust works both ways. You're lying to me. I have to trust you, just as you needed to trust me. It doesn't matter whether you tell me or not. I'll find out what's going on. I'm already looking into the guy."

"What?" He couldn't be. There's no way. I never gave him any hint that anything was going on.

Bay laughed bitterly and set the cat down. "Winnie, you fought me for months. Didn't you think I'd get suspicious when, all of a sudden, you wanted to date me? I'm not a complete idiot. I knew something was wrong. But I hoped you'd come to me rather than use me and hide it." Bay shook his head. "I wish you could have trusted that if you told me, I'd never do anything to make it worse. That I'd use everything in my arsenal to protect you and the kids."

He's right. Logically, he's right. I should have known my sudden change would make him question my motives. He's a Banks. Each of them was bred to be a protector.

"I'm sorry. You have to stay with me. I can't let you push me away." I plead with him, reaching out to take his hand. His fingers lace with mine.

"Then talk to me. Tell me who that guy is and why you're so fucking scared. Tell me why I have to stay with you." His voice rises an octave, then tightens as he works his jaw. Today is the first time I've seen a pissed-off Bay.

"It's you, Baylor," I snap at him in frustration. "He's threatening you. If I don't do what he says, he'll start with you and then the boys. The warehouse fire wasn't an accident. It was a threat to you, so I would know he's serious. He didn't even care that he killed an innocent woman." My voice cracks, and the tears I've been holding back break free.

"Why? What does he want, Winter?"

Sniffling, I wipe snot and tears from my face.

"Troy," I hiccup through a sob. "Troy fucked him over, and he's here to collect. I've been trying to get the first thing he asked for, but he's threatening you if I tell anyone or ask for help. Please, Baylor, please don't tell Beau. I can't lose you or the kids if he suspects I talked." I beg him.

Baylor reaches out, pulls me into him, and presses his lips to the top of my head.

"Nothing is going to happen to any of us, babe. You and the kids are always safe with me. What's the first thing?"

"60k. I've been trying to get the money for two weeks. When I told him, he said he'd take care of it because I was taking too long. I don't know what that means, but I assume it's not good." I hiccup.

"Fuck. I wish you had come to me sooner. I could have given you the money."

How the hell does he have that much money? Doesn't matter. Edward would have known I asked him for it.

"I couldn't ask anyone for it. He's watching us to make sure I didn't ask for it. I didn't know what to do."

Bay rubs my sides and exhales. "What else does he want?"

I bite my lip and close my eyes. "He won't tell me what the last thing he wants is, but Troy has a priceless item he wants back. I'm supposed to ask for it when Edwards tells me to."

Baylor chuckles dryly. He drops his hands from my sides, then steps back and rests his ass on the edge of the desk.

"Okay, so he's planning something to make sure he gets his money. Then you have to get God knows what else from your ex, who's in prison. And you were going to try to do this all on your own?" He grits his teeth. The bitterness in his tone leaves a sour taste in my stomach.

"I thought I was protecting you and the kids. I thought I could handle it. I never imagined Troy was this deep with someone. I hadn't seen him in years until he robbed us and showed up at my job like a raging lunatic, begging me for money last year." I say, flinging my hands in the air.

Bay sits quietly and thinks. After a few minutes, he finally speaks up. "Ok, we need to keep this between us while we figure all this shit out. We can't go to our family because he'll know. There's one person we can ask for help. I have a feeling she might have better resources." Bay finally says.

"Who?"

"Don't hate me. We're going to ask Summer. This guy likely won't pay any mind to a woman with half a leg. No one except

Baxter, and we know she's your sister, and she's already here. I have a feeling he'll see her as weak."

"But what if they're watching my house? She was there last night."

"And she showed up at the same time as Baxter and left at the same time. She could be an old friend of his that he introduced you to. I'll talk to Baxter and see if she can stay in his guest room to make it look more real."

"You want me to put her in danger? Were you not listening when I told you about the bullet scars? You were skeptical of her last night, and now you want to get her involved?" I argue.

This is all too much for me. My heart is beating so fast it's skipping beats. I knew Edward would be showing up soon. I guess I was secretly hoping he would give up.

"Yes. Call her, and I'll call Baxter. Ask her to come here."

"I can't."

"Winnie. We have to keep you and the boys safe without tipping him off while we figure out who he is and how to take him down. Call Summer," he says curtly. His tone isn't one I've heard before.

When I take in his features, I see he's barely holding his anger in. I've fucked this all up.

"We're supposed to be going to a pet adoption and dating, not planning how to take down a criminal. I'm supposed to be getting to know my sister again, not asking her to risk her life for me," I say, feeling completely defeated.

"I know, but this is where we are," he says in a lighter tone now.

The entire situation is a disaster. All because I can't keep my mouth shut, and I'm choosing him. Now my sister is getting involved. I haven't talked to her yet to get answers, but she looks like she's already been through enough.

"I'm going to let Ellie close the store today. I feel like I'm having a heart attack. I hate that this has been my life. When I'm finally happy and think I'm free from Troy's messes, this happens," I say as a tear streaks down my cheek.

"I'm sorry, Angel."

Bay hugs me to him and lets me sob into his neck. I wrap my arms around his waist and hold him tightly. I'm not sure what I'd do if I ever lost him. He means more to me than I've allowed myself to admit. No matter how much I fight it, I know I'm falling in love with Baylor.

I feel Bay shift and adjust me, but I refuse to let go. I can feel my phone slipping out of my back pocket. There's a moment of silence before his whiskey voice cuts through the air.

"Hey, Summer, it's Baylor. Can you meet Winter and me at the bookstore?"

"Sure. On my way."

She doesn't even ask why. She says yes and hangs up. Thirteen years later, she's still willing to drop everything for me. It shouldn't be that way. She just got here, and we can't even enjoy it. Instead, she's going to learn how shitty my life has been.

Just the thought of her finding out sends another sob ripping through me. She's going to be so disappointed in me. Summer always hated Troy. When I started dating him, she told me it was a mistake, but I didn't believe her. I should have listened.

Bay runs his fingers through my hair and holds me to him. Everything I've kept bottled up spills out.

When the kitten starts crying, I remember it's still here. Letting go of Bay, I bend down, pick up the cat, and cuddle it to me. It's more of a teenage cat than a kitten. It's cute, and I assume it's a stray since it was stuck in the dumpster. I wonder if I could keep it. The boys would love it.

Bay takes my hand and leads me out of the office to the front so I can let Ellie in and gather the donation books.

With all the books boxed, Baylor loads them into my SUV. I open the front door, let Ellie in, and tell her she'll be on her own today, then step out for fresh air.

I see Summer and Baxter walking up. Summer is in yoga shorts and a tight top. Her prosthetic looks like a hook at the bottom. She had a different type yesterday when I saw her.

She seems so happy, with a radiant smile, while Baxter wears loose jeans and a tight AF shirt that makes his thick, tattooed arms look even bigger, his signature scowl plastered on his face.

It must be the sunlight today because both of their tattoos look like they're glowing brightly, too.

I watch her say something to the grizzly man and laugh. He is not impressed with whatever she says.

Holding the door open, I wait for them, then follow behind to my office. I place a hand on my stomach as I try to keep the vomit from coming up.

"What's up, Bigfoot?" Summer asks, leaning against the desk and eyeing Baylor with squinted eyes. "Is that a book cat?"

"What's a book cat?" I ask, stepping in front of Baylor.

"Like one of those fat cats you see in bookstores in small towns."

Bay holds me from behind and rests his hand on my hip. I melt into this touch and the warm, chiseled body behind me as I seek his comfort. "We saved it from the dumpster. I know you just got here, but we could use your help. Both of you, actually." Bay tells her.

"Uh-huh. Help with what?" Baxter asks, folding his arms over his chest. He really is a broad man, and he looks intimidating standing like that.

“Can Summer stay in the guest room at your place temporarily? We need you to be ‘friends’. We don’t want anyone to know Summer is Winter's sister.”

“You want me to let a stranger live with my son and me? I don’t know anything about her,” Baxter says, glowering at Summer, who smirks at him.

“I thought we established I wasn’t a treat, Yeti,” she says with a wide, toothy grin.

“Troy,” I blurt out, meeting Summer's gaze.

I want Baxter to understand we would never ask this if there were another option. I watch his arms fall to his sides, and his glower shift into something unreadable.

“Ah. What has that shitsmear done now?” Summer snarls.

My brows shoot up as her face morphs into something I’ve never seen before. Sheeez, she can look scary.

“It’s complicated,” I whisper, rubbing my hands together nervously.

“Usually is. I assume Baylor didn’t bring the ex-military sister here to suggest I act like his brother's friend. How much trouble has he gotten you into?”

“Troy owes… a lot. Someone came to collect it. I only know him as Edward, and I know he will hurt Bay and the boys if I don’t do what he wants. He doesn’t know you're my sister, and Bay thinks that since no one knows who you are yet, you can act like Baxter's old friend and help figure out who the guy is and what we can do to take him down.” My voice sounds weak and pathetic. I hate it.

“I do have resources. But are you sure it's a good idea for Sky and the kids to be alone at her house? If I’m there, it would be better. I may have a peg leg, but I’m a hell of a shot and have fists of fury. There’s also the issue of Bay being at the firehouse for three days a week. Same for me. I'm the town's newest EMS lieutenant and will be on his shift," Summer points out.

My eyes fly to hers. She's serious about staying permanently. She's staying, and we can finally be a family again.

"Why are you calling her Sky?" Bax asks.

"Code name," Summer shrugs. She's ridiculous. From Baxter's eye roll, he thinks the same thing.

"I can check in those three days. I'll stay with Everett at Bays, so I'm close, and it will look like I need help with a newborn while my 'friend' is at work. I take it she and I aren't on the man's radar right now," Bax asks.

"No, and because you're a single dad, that scenario would be plausible. The friend came to help with the baby, but still needs to make a living. I'll stay with them, or they'll stay with me on my days off," Bay states, leaving no room for argument.

"It's believable. What resources do you need from me?" Summer asks.

"I have a photo of Edward and a woman he is with," Bay tells her.

Summer nods. "Ok. I can have a few friends. It's usually pretty quick. I assume you're not sure if these are the only two people watching you?"

"We're not. We know Edward and the woman are. I want to limit Beau or Briggs from getting involved," I say next.

"And they are?" Summer asks.

"Our brothers. Beau is on SWAT, and Briggs is married to Journey Preston," Bax answers, shifting on his feet.

Summer whistles because everyone knows who Journey is and who her parents are. "Got it. I say we do some recon while we wait for the suspects to be identified, then find the best plan of attack."

"Really?" Baxter looks at her with a lifted brow.

"What? That sounded badass, and you know it, grumpy. I'll go incognito tonight and survey your neighborhood to see if I notice any extra men. You both need to pay better attention to your surroundings," Summer points out.

"I'm so sorry, Summer. You coming here was supposed to be a good thing." I can't help the tears that fall.

"Hey, it's okay. I'm still here with you. If an IED and a few bullets can't take me out, I doubt some dumb crime boss can," Summer scoffs.

"Oh god." I sob harder, but Summer tips my chin up.

She's completely unfazed by what's happening. Instead, she walks up and tugs me into her arms. She's trained for tricky situations. I'm also sure she's trained to keep her emotions in check.

"It was my job, and I did it proudly. Just as I will proudly help protect you and my nephews. I'm even willing to put up with the Yeti shifter for you."

That makes me laugh. Baxter is more like a rabid grizzly.

"Feeling is mutual, gimp. Yeti shifter isn't even a thing."

"Hey, it's Sgt Foot. We may be strangers, but I'm sure you can come up with something better than that. In the fantasy world, everything is a thing." Summer's body vibrates with silent laughter. I wish I had her strength. I know she's trying to make me laugh and distract me.

Once I've cried everything out, Summer pulls back and wipes my face.

"We got this. Between the four of us, we'll figure it all out. The best thing to do right now is to act like you usually would. You can't let anyone see you spiral."

I nod and step back. "We have plans tonight. The kids will be at Ny and Briggs."

"Sounds good. Give Bay my number so he can send me the photos. I'll get Baxy's when we leave."

Summer hugs me once more, and she and Bax leave together. I can tell Baxter is already regretting it. Summer is the bright rays of sunlight, and Baxter is the night sky just before a meteor shower.

"Come on, we need to get this cat taken care of," Bay says.

With an exhale, I make sure Ellie knows everything before we leave the building and head home.

CHAPTER 14
BAYLOR

At home, I set up a space for the kitten. Winter is already attached to the cat and is in the kitchen, bathing it. I woke up this morning thinking about what tonight might hold. When Winter called me to rescue a cat, I thought it was adorable. Showing up for the rescue and seeing a man cornering my girlfriend made every cell in me burst into a fiery rage.

I'm still pissed. At Winnie, at the bastard threatening her, and at the piece of human trash ex. This is Troy's fault. It's frustrating to know Winter was going to do all of this alone. She wasn't going to tell me. I had to threaten to walk away if she didn't, and then she broke down.

I knew it would be bad, but not this bad. If she had come to me, I could have given her the money. I still have my inheritance from Gramps. I would have given her every dime.

I don't give a shit if someone is threatening my life. I'm confident in my skills to protect myself. What I do care about is someone harming her and the kids. Now here I am keeping a secret because I haven't told her that Beau is already looking into the guy. If I tell him to stop, he'll ask questions, and I'll have to explain all of this.

The truth is, Winter only asked me out because he threatened me if she pushed me away. How fucked up is it that this is how we're starting?

Sighing, I rake my hands through my hair. I guess it doesn't matter how it happened. All that's ever mattered to me is having Winnie and the kids in my life. Except now I have her sister and my brother involved. My brother is a single father to a one-month-old.

There's a strong sense that Summer is a bad bitch and won't let anything happen to her family or Everett. Even though I was skeptical at first, she seems like the type who doesn't need to know someone well to want to keep them safe.

While filling the food and water dishes, I set them out so everything is ready, then I head into the kitchen. When I enter the room, I see Winter wrestling with the feral cat, which is screaming to get away from the water.

Stepping up behind her, I reach around and grab the loose skin at the back of its neck to subdue it long enough for her to wash it.

"Thank you. I've never washed a cat before, and I hope I never have to again," she grumbles.

"It's not fun," I chuckle lightly.

"Have you done it before? I mean, obviously, you have. You knew what to do."

"We had barn cats growing up. Sometimes they would get into shit. Mom made us help clean them up."

"I can see Ivey doing that."

The silence lingers between us as she works. Neither of us knows what to say. I don't want us to break before we even have a chance. Right now, it feels like there's a crack in the relationship we're just beginning.

"I don't want to start our relationship with lies. I need to tell you something." I wait while she processes. Her body trembles as she takes a shaky breath.

"Ok," the words are barely audible. She doesn't look at me; instead, she stays focused on the animal.

"Beau already knows something's wrong. The day you asked me out, I went to Hideaway with him and Baxter and watched the video footage. We all noticed your body language change. He's already trying to figure out who Edward is. And Briggs knows I got suspicious, but he told me I was paranoid." I whisper the admission.

Why am I whispering it? I don't know. Winter cries softly. All I can do is step closer to her and hold her with my free arm.

"So, they all know. Why did you ask Summer to run the photos then?"

"She has better resources. Beau hasn't gotten a hit yet, and it's been two weeks." I lift a shoulder in a half shrug. "I figured it wouldn't hurt to have Summer run it, too. Winnie, you have to know we won't let anything happen. That I will always be here for you and the boys."

"I hate this. I hate that I was so stubborn. I wish I had never walked away from you that night. I should have finished our unofficial friends' date and left with you. I wish I had never settled for Troy. I should have left when the twins were born," she sniffed.

Turning off the water, she reaches over and bundles the cat in a towel as I let go of it.

"I am so sorry, Angel. Is this what you want now? Not because someone is threatening us. Don't think about that. Do you want to be with me? If you don't, that's okay. We can still make it look like we're dating." My chest tightens and aches as I wait for her response. I'm not sure what I'll do if she says no. Even though we have some shit to work out, I still want her.

Winter turns to face me. Her angelic features and eyes look like those of the most beautiful creature in heaven. "Of course I do. When I first asked, it was because of him, and I'm sorry about that. But I realize now I was fighting for no reason. We're great as friends, but it's always been more than that. We've only added titles and intimacy to what we have. Do you still want me?"

My heart slows, and the pulsing in my ears grows quiet. That's all I need to know. I needed to hear that she wasn't following through with this only because of him and that she wants me as much as I want her.

"Thank fuck. Absolutely. I do."

I bring my hand up and cup her neck, thumbing her jawline. She has the smoothest, warmest skin I've ever felt.

"No more lies. Full honesty from this moment on. You were right. We need to trust each other. Troy has been calling me from prison," Winter admits.

My posture stiffens at the news that the bastard has been calling her. "Agreed. Have you answered?" I ask. Winter shakes her head. That's a relief.

"Okay, don't until we get a little more information. I have to get ready for the adoption event. Do you still want to come with me?"

"I do."

After she answers, we spend the next couple of hours discussing and preparing for the event.

I want to point out that Hazel didn't mention anything about sexualizing us by making us shirtless in our fire pants and suspenders so she could take photos of us with the adoptable dogs for their website. After an hour of uncomfortable photos, we're sent to different areas.

We're set up in the heart of downtown. Outside, the sun is shining brightly, and people are bustling about. Hazel has a booth set up with pamphlets and the books from Winter. There are several pens with three dogs, and a couple that can only house one dog each. So far, four dogs have been adopted, and that makes it all worth it.

"Oh my god. This has made my day. Look at Journey's Dad." Winter, Journey, Birdie, and Astor are all here, laughing as they look through the photos.

"Damn, Ny. Henry looks like an age-gap Daddy," Astor says, and I almost gag. I hope Noah heard her perverted ass.

"Ew, please don't ever say that again." Ny blanches.

Good

Six of us, including Henry, volunteered today. Not only did they take a shirtless picture, but I feel like I can't move my arms in the tight-as-fuck shirt I'm in.

"So this is what firefighters do in small towns? Get half-naked and take pictures with cute puppies? I'm in." Summer's voice rings out to Henry, who shakes his head at her with a smile. Clearly, he likes her already.

My gaze flicks toward the voice. I see Summer staying close to Winter, but not too close. She's got a wild smirk on her face, and her eyes bounce between the men.

Minutes later, I see Baxter walking up quickly and alone, then stopping beside Summer. Holy shit, he actually let Mom take Everett. He's safer with our parents than with us. Bax looks like a giant next to her tiny stature. I watch as the two draw the other woman's attention.

"Baxter. Um, are you going to introduce us to your friend?" Birdie asks.

Panic starts to seep in, but I can't intervene, or it would look suspicious.

"Friend," Summer says at the same time Bax says "Nanny," then they flip it, "Nanny," "Friend."

They both scowl and growl at each other in a heated death stare before Summer gets a look of victory and tilts the corner of her lip up mischievously. Shit, this isn't going to go well. Summer turns to Baxter and trails a finger down his chest.

"We're fucking. I'm Rayn Cooper. Tell 'em, big boy."

I swear to Christ, Baxter looks like he's about to erupt and kill the woman. I don't think anyone's face has ever been as red as his is right now. Even through his beard, I can see his jaw working.

I'll give Summer credit. She's quick with her quips.

"Oh," Birdie says with surprise.

"Damn," Journey chuckles.

"Good for you," Astor commends.

Winter giggles nervously.

"Just a little tip, the big and broody ones fuck hard, angrily, and relentlessly. And OMG," Summer whistles, stretching her hands apart with wiggling brows. "So good."

“Rayn. They’ve heard enough. Let's go,” Baxter says through clenched teeth, grabs her by the bicep, and drags her away from the woman.

“But… puppy. Come on, Yeti, you said you would think about it. I did that thing you asked me to do with my leg. Remember?”

“Dear lord,” Baxter grumbles, then keeps walking her away.

Yeah, we may be searching for her body later tonight. I can see the fumes coming off Baxter.

I already texted Summer the photos, and she confirmed she’s working on it. I also let her know Beau was looking into it. All she did was give me a thumbs-up.

Today has felt like gut-wrenching, twisted lies. I have no idea what this Edward guy plans to do to get his money, but I have a feeling it's going to be bad.

Clearing my thoughts, I look at the dogs in front of me. I squat down and pet the dogs in the pen I’m standing guard over. The retriever mix comes over and stays right beside me, waiting for her turn. She’s a beautiful dog, golden with a sleek, thick coat.

I read her stats—her name is Nila, she is three years old, and she is good with kids, dogs, and cats. Hell, I’m thinking about adopting her. I’ve always wanted a dog, and the boys would love playing with her.

I know Winter wants to keep the cat we found today. I’m not sure whether the feral feline would despise a canine companion. We don’t know unless we try. The cat is a teen and learned to use the box right away. Maybe the previous owner had a dog, too.

“Baylor,” I hear my boys call my name before they rush through the crowd and over to me.

They come to a screeching halt and look at Nila.

"Hey, what are you two doing here?" I ask them.

"We were with Uncle Beau at the ice cream shop. We're going to the arcade, then we're getting a burger at Flaming Flavor. Can we pet the dog?" Dyl asks.

"Of course. Her name is Nila."

Both boys come over and start petting the attention-seeking dog.

"She's so cute. You should ask Mom if we can have her. We've never had a dog before."

Chuckling, I hug Daniel back as he wraps an arm around my shoulder. He's the more affectionate of the two.

"I'll see what I can do."

"Mom might say no to Baylor, too," Winter says from behind them.

"Busted," I mutter to Daniel, who giggles.

"But Mom, look at her?" Dylan says, then cups the dog's cheeks as she starts licking his face, making him laugh. "What if she lived at Bay's house and we could spend the night with her when we stay with him?"

He's got sound logic. Kinda. I intend for us to be a family one day, and that means all of us living together.

"That's up to Baylor," Winter tells them. I see the moment she falls for the dog. Nila closes her eyes and leans into Winter's hand.

Standing to my full height, I look around for Hazel. Once I locate her, I let them know I'll be right back. Striding over, I wait for Hazel to finish with the current family.

Once she's done, she smiles at me. "You want to ask about Nila. I saw you and your family with her."

"I do, but I have a question. We found a cat this morning, and I know Winnie wants to keep it. The cat seems like she's probably a teen. Do you think she would get used to Nila?"

"I think that would put her at about 5-6 months old, so yes. There's time for them to become acquainted. Do you want me to start the application?" she asks with a growing grin.

Glancing over, I look at Winnie and the boys. The smiles on their faces as they fuss over the dog are pure joy. In that fraction of a second, I see it all.

Winnie, with a ring on her finger, pregnant with twins, sitting on the couch petting the cat while the boys run with Nila in the backyard. I see a future I never imagined until they came into my life.

"Yeah, I think she belongs to my family." My chest swells with pride. It feels good to call them that.

"I have to agree. I'll have everything ready so you can take her home tonight."

"Thanks, Hazel."

I walk back over to where Birdie and Harley have joined in the petting.

"Are you getting her?" Dylan asks excitedly.

"I'm thinking about it." I want it to be a surprise when they come home tomorrow and see her.

"Can we play video games at your house when we come home tomorrow?" Daniel asks.

"It's our Sunday ritual."

"Yes. Maybe we can stay the night again, like we did the other day."

"We'll see," Winter answers for me. I know she'll stay.

"She is beautiful. Are you boys ready?" Birdie asks the boys.

"Yeah, come on," Harley says, bossing the boys.

I like that they never seem bothered by all the younger kids. That may change when they become teens, but for now, they all get along well.

"Bye, Mom. Bye, Bay. See you tomorrow," Dylan says before they each hug Winter and me and take off with Birdie.

"You're adopting her?" Winter asks, petting the dog again.

"Yeah. I asked Hazel about the cat, and she thinks it's young enough for them to get along."

"You have the best heart, hotshot. I'm lucky you're mine."

My heart and lungs stutter at her admission. It feels like my world is finally complete.

"I'm the lucky one, Angel." I step next to her, squat, and wrap my arm around her. "Are you staying with me tonight?"

Winnie bumps me with her shoulder. "You already know the answer."

"Just making sure. I have a couple more hours here. Then I have to stop and get stuff for the dog."

"Okay, I haven't seen Summer and Baxter again. Do you think he killed her?" she jokes.

"Oh, it's a real possibility. Never in my twenty-seven years have I seen him that embarrassed."

Winnie and I both burst out laughing, making the dog jump and eager to play. I lean down and start playing with her on the other side of her pen.

"I'm going to take off. Is it okay if I go to your place?"

"You never have to ask that. I'll be home soon." I kiss her cheek before she gets to her feet. Winnie squeezes my shoulder and takes off. I know her sister is watching her, and she'll be safe.

CHAPTER 15
BAYLOR

As I unload all the stuff I was talked into buying, Winter rushes outside to help, but stops me before I can walk inside the house.

I lift a brow at the glint of mischief and the nerves that cross her face. "Angel, what don't you want me to see in there?" I ask with a teasing smile.

"It's a surprise. Set everything down and close your eyes. I'll guide you to the bathroom. I already put clothes in there."

Setting the bag and food down, Nila waits patiently beside me. She is a good dog so far.

I step into Winnie's space, lean down, and whisper in her ear. "I'm pretty sure I'm the one who's supposed to be blindfolding you and telling you to trust me right before I plunge my tongue inside of you. You know how I did the other night when I tied your hands behind your back and ate your delicious pussy until you came three times."

Winnie bites her lip and arches into me. The dirty talk gets her fired up. I bet she's fucking soaked.

"Please," she whispers back.

Damn it, that soft plea and her bright eyes staring up at me have me folding. I reach out and cup her smooth cheek.

"You know I'd do anything for you, don't you?" The statement is half fact, half question.

"I do, baby. And I would do anything for you."

Groaning, I pull her into me. I love how her body fits mine, as if she were always meant to be there. "You know what that name does to me."

Winnie giggles and rubs my sides. "I know. That's why I said it. Trust me, hotshot."

"Always."

I give her a brief kiss on her soft, sweet lips, then stand straight. I hand her Nila's leash and close my eyes.

"I'm all yours, beautiful. Do with me what you will. If you plan to kill me, make it quick," I tease, smiling.

"So theatrical." She teases back.

Winnie takes my hand and slowly guides me through the house to the bathroom, not my room. When I hear the door click shut, I open my eyes and see she's left a pair of jeans and a T-shirt here, but no boxers. Commando, it is.

As I pull my shirt off, I catch a whiff of the dog smell that's clung to me all day. Stepping over, I turn on the water and let it heat while I finish undressing.

After this morning, it was a good day. Winnie and I now share a dog and a cat. The boys are going to be so damn excited about Nila.

I let the water pelt me before I start washing off. I'm curious what her surprise could be. The more my thoughts wander, the faster I try to get this shower over with. I want her in my arms, her mouth on mine. With that thought, I turn off the water, towel off, get dressed, and leave the bathroom.

In the living room, I see she has set up a few things. A smile plays on my lips. On the island, she has two tabletop easels set up with watercolors. At the kitchen table are a pizza and two beers. The stove has uniced cupcakes on it. The coffee table is set with checkers, and pillows and blankets are scattered on the floor. Winnie is standing in the middle of the room, barefoot, in a short white sundress, with a gorgeous smile on her face.

"What is all this, Angel?" I chuckle and keep looking around.

Winnie steps up to me, takes both my hands, and twines our fingers together.

"I'm ready to take the next step, and I hope you are, too. The night I lost my virginity, I was drunk. I don't remember it, and I ended up pregnant. Tonight, I want this to be special for both of us because I am giving myself to you just as much as you are to me. I want this to be one of our best memories together. I have four dates set up, and with each one, we'll take the next step." She says lightly.

My heart skyrockets. The adrenaline I feel is at a level I didn't know existed. It's not the thought of sex that's doing it. It's knowing she's ready to go all in.

"I love this idea, babe. It's perfect." I lean down and press my forehead to hers. Winnie's giggle is a musical whisper in the wind.

"Good. We'll have dinner first." Winnie guides me to the table. I pull out her seat, and she sits.

Once we're settled, Winnie leans into me and takes a selfie. Sitting up straight, she starts small talk.

"What's your favorite thing to do on your day off?"

"I like to read. There's a bookstore downtown I like to visit. You should check it out. The owner is amazing." I tell her, sipping my beer. "What about you?"

"I like to hang out with my kids and sometimes my neighbor." Her lip twitches as she holds back a smile.

"Sounds like a good way to spend your days off. Tell me about this neighbor."

"Well, he's a firefighter. He's funny, kind, and probably the most gorgeous man I've ever met. He's fiercely protective of the boys and me. His possessiveness should be scary, but it sends a thrill through me knowing he wants me so badly. You may have to watch out for him. He might kick your ass."

"Hm, I think I could take him. I can understand his obsession with you."

Once we finish eating, Winnie hums, gets to her feet, and holds out her hand. I take it and follow her to the stove, where she pulls out two butterknives and the icing for the cupcakes. I take one from her, and she takes another photo of us together before we start decorating our desserts.

As we spread the icing on the cupcakes, Winter follows our routine. "Tell me about the bookstore owner," she asks, licking the icing from her knife.

"She's stubborn as hell, which makes the chase more interesting. She has two wonderful, amazing boys. Gorgeous doesn't begin to describe her. I'm pretty sure she's an angel sent from heaven. She's funny, shy, kind, and hardworking. I fear she has the same possessiveness toward me that your firefighter has toward you."

"I'm not scared of her. I can be scary when I find something I want to keep, and I'm starting to think I want to keep you."

When I glance at her, I see raw desire burning in her eyes. I watch as she dips a finger in the icing, reaches over, and touches my lips with it.

My heart thunders as I wrap my arm around her waist and pull her to me. Winnie's small, cool hand grips my neck. She stands on her tiptoes, her tongue darting out to lick the icing from my lips.

Closing my eyes, I savor the sensation of her seduction. When her tongue traces the seam of my closed lips, I part them, giving her the access she seeks.

Winnie moans into my mouth as I tighten my arms around her and kiss her back, slowly, lazily, as if we have all the time in the world. Because for tonight, we do.

I let my hand fall from her waist, down her thigh, and slip under her dress. My hand stops, and I grab as much of her ass as I can. I groan at the feeling. Fuck, her ass is perfect.

When she breaks the kiss, I growl in protest. I want more. I want all of her, all the time. I can't get enough.

Winnie giggles and places her palms on my chest.

"Patience. Time for the next date. Take your shirt off and sit right there." She points to a stool in front of one of the easels.

I raise a brow but do as I'm told. Winnie's eyes rake over my body once my shirt is off, and her thighs squeeze together. A smirk stretches my face, and I take my seat so I'm facing her.

"What are we painting?"

"Each other."

The pesky organ that is my heart leaps and flips when she slowly lifts her dress and slips it off, revealing her white lace bra and panties and her tiger tummy that I could cum over seeing. She sashays over, sits on the stool in front of me, and crosses her legs. Lifting her brush, she dips it and flicks her eyes from me to the canvas.

"Fuck, babe, you're going to kill me. I don't think I can sit here without touching you." I groan and adjust my junk.

Winnie giggles. "Then you'd better paint quickly."

I'm no artist. Not even a little. I wonder if I can get away with splashing random colors on the damn canvas so we can end this early and get my hands on her.

Before I know it, the brush is moving. By the time we're done, we show each other our paintings and laugh at the blobs we both made.

"I love them," she says with such enthusiasm.

"Me too," I tell her, then get to my feet.

I walk over to her and uncross her legs. I move between her thighs, and her eyes glow up at me. Her slender hands grip my hips and squeeze, making my body jerk.

"Second base, hotshot. Keep it above the waist," she teases.

I capture her lips with mine. My hands play with her stomach before roaming to her round breasts. I flick and tease her nipple through her bra. I'd prefer them in my mouth, but this is good, too. My cock throbs and twitches to be released from the jean barrier it's in.

Winnie's tap on my shoulder tells me it's time to stop. I release her and breathe heavily, working to pull myself together.

"You're perfect, Angel. Everything about you mesmerizes me. You'll always be mine."

"And you'll always be mine. Ready for the next one."

"Yeah,"

Taking a step back, I help her from the stool, and we move over to the blankets on the floor where the checkers are set up.

"I should have asked this, but you distracted me. Where are the dog and the cat?" I ask.

Winnie chuckles and moves a checker. "They are happily cuddled together in Dylan's room."

"That was quick," I chuckle, moving my piece.

"Where do you see yourself in five years, Baylor? Do you have dreams or goals?" she asks, moving her piece.

I look back at the board before answering. "I see myself married with two teenage boys. I see my boys giving their mom a hard time for being pregnant. I see twin toddlers running around. I see a dog and a fat, lazy book cat. Where do you see yourself in five years, Winter?"

When I finally muster the courage to look back at her, I reach out and catch the stray tears rolling down her cheek with my thumb. God, I hope I didn't just screw that up.

"I saw myself with you and the twins. I like your vision better. Will you share it with me?" she asks.

"Everything of mine is yours, beautiful. My heart, my body, and my soul are yours. My hopes and dreams all include you, Dylan, and Daniel. This house and everything in it are yours as much as they are mine. Everything, Winnie."

She doesn't respond. I watch her rise and hold out her hand. I take it, rise, and let her lead me to the bedroom door.

"Close your eyes one last time."

With my eyes closed, she leads me into the room.

Winnie releases my hand, and I hear the door click. "Keep them closed until I tell you to, and trust me."

"Always."

There's silence before her fingers feather lightly down my chest and land on the button of my jeans.

Winnie flicks the button on my jeans and unzips me. I continue to trust her. I never thought a man's first time had to be romantic. We don't really care, but the way she set everything up made it just as special for her, which made me fall even more in love with her than I already was.

With my jeans off, I jerk when she trails her fingernails up my thighs. Mother of God, that felt amazing.

Winter places her hands on my hips and turns me. Her fingers roam and touch. My poor cock is weeping to be inside her, and my eyes strain against my lids to see her.

"I like that you want a life with me. I like that you take care of my kids as if they were your own. I like that you want to have more babies with me. I like that you see us as your future, and I like that you were so patient, waiting until I was ready. You are a better man than my imagination could ever have created. Everything of mine is also yours: my heart, my body, and my soul. I like everything about you, Baylor. Everything." She whispers her proclamations.

Once she's done talking, cold air fills the space she occupied. With each use of the word like, my heart thumps harder, faster. She's telling me she loves me without saying the word. I'll take what she can give until she's ready to say it.

"Open your eyes."

Peeling my lids open, I take in the dark room lit with a soft glow. Gently, candlelight flickers and dances. It's everywhere.

The world around us feels distant and unimportant; all that matters is Winter in the middle of the bed, in all her naked glory, with her knees up and spread.

The flickering light dances across her porcelain skin. Her face, softly illuminated in the dim glow, takes my breath away. She's stunning.

At this moment, I'm sure I made the right decision to wait. I know Winter Anderson is, and always will be, exclusively mine, and this act will belong only to her.

When her crystal eyes meet mine, she wiggles a finger, beckoning me to her. Crawling up the bed slowly, I position myself over her, nestling comfortably between her thighs, and stare down.

This is it.

Do not

I repeat

Do not fuck this up.

This needs to be just as good for her.

Resting on an elbow, I lean in and take her mouth hostage again. Her tongue flicks and teases mine. What starts slow and passionate becomes erratic and urgent.

My hand moves between us, I slip my fingers through her slickened folds, and massage her swollen bud.

She's dripping.

I groan into her mouth, slip a finger inside her, and work her tight canal. She may have children, but she's hardly ever been touched.

Her hips grind and rock as I slip another finger in and use my palm to keep massaging her.

Winnie rips her lips from mine and moans loudly.

"Condom," I rasp.

"Pill. I want you like this. I want to feel you cum in me," she says, biting down on that pouty lip of hers.

Ah, fuck. Why does that make my cock harder? When she looks up at me through her thick blonde lashes with those big, longing eyes, the moths in my stomach flutter, and I know I will not refuse her. How could I when she looks at me like I am the only man in the world?

"Are you sure you're ready?" I whisper, removing my fingers. I line my cock up. Hell, I already want to cum, and my dick hasn't even touched her yet.

Amateur

Winter reaches up, cups my cheeks, and locks her legs around my waist. Her eyes scream nervousness and vulnerability. "I'm positive. I like you, Bay. I like you more than I thought possible. I want everything with you."

My hips move, and the tip of me begins to enter her. "I like you, Winter. There will never be anyone but you," I tell her, slipping deeper into her tightness.

Winter loves dirty talk, but tonight is too intimate, too important. She needs soft words and love, not a filthy mouth and a quick fuck. I want to savor every move, every moan, every face she makes.

Gripping her hip, I push in slowly with a groan, giving her time to adjust with each inch. God, it's like a tight, warm blanket wrapping around me and suctioning to my thick length. Winter feels incredible. I'm barely halfway in, and it's already better than I ever thought it would be.

My eyes roll back as I slide in, and Winnie lets out a whimper. Shit. My pleasure is hurting her.

"I'm sorry, beautiful. I'm trying to go slow. Are you ok?" I whisper, peppering her face with kisses.

"Yeah, baby, I'm ok. I just. I haven't done this often, and it's been many, many years," she says with a shuddering breath.

My lips claim hers in a desperate, dominating kiss. Winnie's fingers find their way into my hair, and with one swift roll of her hips, she takes me to the hilt, making me groan.

Our bodies go still, and she cries out into my mouth. Yanking my lips from hers, I bury my face in her neck and think of anything else but the feel of her. I'm about to blow.

Her breathing quickens, and she digs her claws into my back; with us fully connected, an overwhelming wave of emotion rocks through me.

"Are you okay, baby?"

"Yeah. Just need a minute, or this is going to end embarrassingly fast," I murmur against her skin.

Winnie giggles and runs her fingers through my hair, sending a shiver down my spine and raising goosebumps. Her gentle touch isn't helping me regain control.

Once I finally pull myself together, I draw back and meet her hooded, glittering gaze. The need to protect, possess, claim, and care for her courses through me, taking over my entire being.

Fuck, I'm not in control anymore. Instead of fighting to hold back, I surrender to the need that's taken me hostage.

Winter rolls her hips and moves. I can't imagine anything ever feeling as good as this, as good as she does. Fuck, she feels good. Too good. Being inside her is euphoric and intoxicating. Winnie is my everything. She's the sun and stars. She's my world. There will never be another moment when we don't exist together as one.

She holds my back with one arm, then brings the other up to cup my cheek as we move together. I don't rush. Instead, I take my time and draw this out as long as I can, slow and easy. I never want to stop being inside her.

"It's too much," she groans, clenching her walls around me. She's so damn tight, so warm and right.

"It's not, baby. You're doing so good. You take my cock so well. We were made for each other, Winnie." I praise her because she is. I nuzzle my nose against her neck and breathe in the scent of candles and our sex—the smell of us.

Winnie moans as her eyes flutter shut, her head tips back, and her back arches. Perky, taught nipples scrape my chest, almost sending me over the edge, but I keep my hold and drag this out just a little longer for both of us.

"Eyes on me, babe," I command. Her eyes fly open and lock onto mine. I watch her lips part as she sucks in a breath. I hope she sees how much I want and need her in my eyes.

Rocking my hips, I move in and out of her warmth in smooth strokes. As my pace picks up, she meets each of my thrusts perfectly. I'm going to cum. I can't hold back anymore. I'm lucky I made it this long.

"I need you to cum for me, beautiful," I rasp, pressing my forehead to hers.

Reaching between us, I rub her clit, making her cry out as I fuck her faster. I need her to go over the ledge with me.

"Baylor." She cries out. I can feel her starting to clamp down around me. I watch the orgasm begin to consume her entire being, and it's the most beautiful thing I've ever seen.

"Let go, Angel,"

Winnie screams my name again, responding to my command, and unravels before me. My own climax takes over as I feel her pulsing around my throbbing cock.

"Winter, my Angel." I groan, locking my lips with hers in an urgent, sloppy kiss and holding her tightly to me as I push in once more, burying myself to the hilt inside her and beginning to release my seed.

My stomach tenses, and my balls tighten as I cum. Hard. Flames fan out and explode behind my eyes. Not that I have anything to compare it to, but I can't imagine sex being that mind-blowing with anyone but her.

Our bodies rock and jerk as we ride the high of the consummation that solidified us. Drawing back, I press my forehead to hers and run my hand up and down her moist side while we try to catch our breath.

"You're gorgeous when you cum for me. I like watching you," I murmur to her. Winter looks at me and gives me the best fucking tired, satisfied smile I've ever seen.

I hook my arm around her waist, rolling us onto our sides. I lift her leg and rest it over my hip. My hand roams, massaging her soft, warm body wherever it can.

"How was it for your first time, Winnie?" I whisper, pushing her wet hair from her face and taking in the beauty before me. She looks like a queen.

"Perfect. Absolutely perfect, baby. Once I'm not sore anymore and catch my breath, I want to do it again." She giggles, and I laugh.

"We have time. I'll be right back." I kiss her quickly, roll off the bed, go to the bathroom, warm a washcloth, and come back to clean her.

After I toss the cloth into the hamper, I put on joggers. "Sorry, babe, we need to let the animals out of the room now, but I promise to snuggle you as soon as I'm done. I like you."

I take "I like you" to mean she loves me but can't say the words yet. So, I will use 'like' until she's ready.

"That's probably a good idea. I like you, too. I named the cat Stormy. We should finish our checkers game."

Hovering over her, I kiss her forehead, chuckling because I can't contain how fucking happy I am. This woman makes my heart feel so full that I need a larger chest cavity to hold it all in.

"We can do that."

"Can we watch a scary movie, too?"

I stand and raise my brow because I know how that goes, but I will not say no to her.

"Of course, Angel. We can do anything you want."

With a bigger smile on her face, she gets to her feet and gets dressed while I get Nila and Stormy.

CHAPTER 16
WINTER

There's a weight on my chest. A weight that shouldn't be there, I reach up to rub the heaviness away. Sleepy confusion hits me when my fingers slide into soft, silken hair. Wait, hair? My fingers bury deeper, and I feel soft fur. Why is there heavy fur on me? I don't have any animals.

Oh god!

My eyes fly open when I realize there's something on me that shouldn't be. Panic jumps into the driver's seat and hits the gas full throttle. I let out a blood-curdling scream and fling myself upright, my arms and legs flailing to get the fur-covered demon off me. Baylor's weight shifts quickly next to me before I hear a loud thump and a groan. Then the light comes on, illuminating the room while I'm still freaking out.

"What is it? Winter, what's wrong?" he asks as he kneels on the bed in front of me and tries to stop the chaos. Nila's nails click on the floor as she comes running into the room, barking. She searches the room, looking for the invisible threat.

“There was something on me,” I yell. I’m pretty sure I’m having a heart attack now. “It was big and fuzzy.” I shriek in a high-pitched voice. I move the covers, trying to find what it is.

“Where did it go?”

Jumping out of bed stark naked, I start moving in circles, checking myself like it was a roach and not a large animal. Baylor jumps out of bed, his dick flopping every which way, stops me, and I swear to all the gods that have ever been created, when he bursts out laughing, I could have killed him.

“It isn’t funny, you assclown. I’m serious. There was something on me, and it wasn’t Nila.” I yell at him and try to shove him away, but he’s built like a statue and doesn’t budge. I’m pissed he’s making fun of me. He thinks I was dreaming, but I know what I felt.

“Angel, it was the cat. You know the one we rescued yesterday? Nila, it's ok.” He tells the dog while he pets her head. Nila stops barking and trots back to the living room.

Freezing in place, I blink rapidly as I try to make sense of what he’s telling me. When my brain catches up, tears burn the backs of my eyes with anger, fear, and complete embarrassment.

“Fucking cat,” I say, barely holding back the waterworks.

“Oh, come here, Angel,” Baylor laughs again and hugs me to him. “This is why you shouldn’t watch scary movies before bed.” He pokes fun at me.

“Get away from me, you big orc. I forgot the damn thing was here.” I growl and shove him again.

“I know. I’m sorry I laughed.” I wrap my arms around him and hold his warm body as if my life depended on it. I bury my face in his bare chest and breathe in his soothing scent. I swear this man is a walking sculpture.

"Do you think the cat is okay? I think I scared it as much as it scared me," I ask in a muffled voice, not ready to move and face this man again.

"I'm sure it's fine. Are you calming down now?"

"I'll be fine now that I know it wasn't a hellhound coming for my soul."

Baylor holds it in, but his rumbling body betrays that he's dying to crack up again.

"Winter, Baylor, open the fucking door," she screams, slamming into the door.

BOOM, crack

BOOM, crack

Both our bodies stiffen before we realize what's happening. We rush to put on clothes and run to the front door.

Violent, sharp cracking grows louder, then a loud pop fills the air, and the door flies open. Summer stands there, looking larger than usual. Copper-red hair floats around her face from the wind and the force she used to bust the door open. I see a flash of bravery mixed with fear on her face.

Summer rushes toward us like a damn linebacker, arms out at stomach level. "Down," she screams, catching us both off balance and tackling us to the ground just as the explosion rings through the air.

The boom vibrates the house. Windows burst and shatter. My scream rips through the air while Summer shields me as best she can with her body. I can feel Bay roll, covering us both with his body. Nila yelps and barks out of control.

The ringing in my ears makes me cover them and open my eyes. Glass and light debris glisten in the air. Through the empty window, I can see the night lit up in red.

Fire. The sky is on fire. What was that? Summer groans, and Baylor rolls off of us.

"Winter, call 911," Baylor shouts, then gets to his feet and runs out the front door. Moaning, I roll to my side, cough, and slowly rise. I reach over and check on Summer. Shock and horror have my voice stuck in a void. I can't speak, can't think. I can hear, but the ringing is overpowering; everything sounds underwater.

"I'm fine. Here, I'm going to help Baylor." Summer hands me her phone, then rolls and stands on shaky legs. "Tell them there was an explosion." Summer holds my shocked-in-place face. "Give them your address, Winter. It was your house." Her voice is muffled. Her words don't register until she smacks me across the face to bring me back. Summer shakes my shoulders, and my eyes meet her blue orbs.

"There you are. I know you're scared, but I need you to call 911, Sky. Now."

"Ok," I whisper. Summer nods and runs out the door. She's braver than I could ever be. There's no hesitation in her.

With shaky hands, I do as I'm told. A sob, I've never released before, tears from my throat as I tell the operator my house exploded.

When I hear the sirens, I step out of Baylor's house and see that half of mine is gone, with flames devouring the remaining half.

The view around me doesn't seem real. It's like watching a scene from a war movie. Red and yellow make the night sky look bright. Floating embers look like fireflies, leaving destruction in their wake. Ash rains down, and smoke blocks out the moon's glow.

Baylor and Summer both have hoses and are dousing his house and the grass around it to keep burning debris from igniting it. I watch them work together to make sure they cover everything.

I clutch the phone to my chest, and my breath lodges in my lungs. I drop to my knees as I watch the horror of the fire, and the engines come to a stop. I see the firefighters jump into action to put out the flames.

When large, hot arms wrap around my shoulders, my wail pierces the air. My body starts to shake violently. Fear, pain, anger, rage, and complete disbelief run a marathon inside me.

My kids.

My babies.

Baylor.

We could have been in there.

We could have died.

I know this was Edward. This is what he meant when he said he was already taking care of things. This was about more than his precious money.

I am convinced this is about the one thing he wants most. Whatever the priceless item is, I will use it to take him down. I don't care if I have to kill him myself.

Leaning back against Bay, I sob harder as his arms tighten around me, trying to keep me grounded, trying to keep me from losing it. Tears and snot leak from my eyes and nose, but I don't care. Edward will take everything from me. He's making sure I know that.

"Shh, I got you, babe. It's going to be ok," he says in his usual soothing voice.

"It's not. It was him, Bay. I know it was him." I cry harder. The ringing in my ears has eased, but my cries are deafening.

I'm not sure how long he holds me while I rock until I have nothing left. When I finally open my eyes again, I see the fire is almost out, and then I notice Summer in the distance talking to Henry. Why is he here? He usually works on Bay's shift. Guess they would have to call him in for something like this.

Not taking my eyes off them, I watch them turn and look at us. The sorrow on their faces makes me want to weep, but I have nothing left. I just lost everything I managed to salvage and rebuild over the years.

It was material things. I should be grateful we weren't in the house when it happened. The twins are going to be so upset to start over again, and this time it's still their father's fault.

Henry and Summer make their way to the porch. Henry steps up and squats. "I'm sorry, honey. It looks like a gas line explosion. It was an accident. Why don't we go inside? There's nothing we can do now."

Accident, my ass. Edward is a professional. I do not doubt he knew exactly what to do.

Wait, how did Summer know to warn us? I'm so confused.

Nodding at Henry Bay helps me get to my feet. I walk inside, and Bay dusts off the couch so I can sit. As I look around his house, I see several windows missing their glass. Nila comes up beside me and rests her head on my knee. My hand darts out and mindlessly pets her.

"I'm sorry, Bay." My voice cracks, and my head drops.

Baylor kneels in front of me and frames my face with his large mitts. He lifts my head so my eyes meet his. "Hey, don't be. Windows can be replaced. All that matters is that you and the kids weren't in there when it happened." His voice is thick with emotion, as if he's trying to keep himself together.

I place my palm on his chest and feel his heart pounding erratically.

"There will be a formal investigation. I'm sure your insurance will send an adjuster out as well. Do you remember if you left anything on? Is it possible the stove was left on?" Henry asks, watching Summer pick up the cat. "When did you get all these animals?"

Summer is decked out in all black and stands like a soldier, feet together, back straight. How the hell did she manage to kick down a door? When I focus, I notice the bandages on her arms. My eyes burn again. She was hurt shielding me.

"Not that I know of, and today. We saved the kitten and adopted Nila. We're supposed to be starting our family," I sob.

"We are, Angel. This won't stop that. I like you," Bay soothes me.

"I like you," I whisper, wrapping my arms around his neck and pressing my forehead to his.

"Okay, how's the ringing in your ears? Is it okay if I check them real quick?"

I nod. "It's not as bad as it was."

Henry uses his little gadget to check one ear, then the other.

"They look okay. If you experience pressure, pain, hearing loss, or dizziness, I want you to go to the ER. Baylor, I called in a few guys to bring some plywood to board these windows up until we can replace them," Henry says.

"Got it. I'll be right outside," Bay tells me before he kisses me softly and gets to his feet.

Glancing up, I watch him and Henry walk out of the house together. I feel so small that they look like giants.

Once they are out of the house, I look to Summer, who is petting Stormy lazily.

"How?" That's all I get out before she places a finger over her mouth and pulls something from her pocket.

Summer walks through the living room, checking different areas. I sit and wait until she comes back from checking the rest of the house.

"He needs cameras, and you need to keep this," she says, handing me the device. I furrow my brows and look at it. I'm not sure what the hell it is.

“It’s to check for bugs. I wouldn’t put it past this guy. Bay needs to do random sweeps of the place.”

Holy shit, my sister is a badass.

“I told you I was doing some recon tonight. I saw a man go into the house, but he wasn’t in there long. I was hiding when he walked past me, and I heard him say it was ready. I knew I had roughly one to three minutes. I figured the guy wouldn’t want any evidence of a bomb. The gas line explosion made sense and gave me more time to warn you when I saw the light over here come on. If done correctly, no one but us will know it wasn’t an accident.” She says in a professional tone.

“You were hurt.” I barely manage to say.

“Pfft, this is nothing. I’m fine. I’m just glad you're ok. How was your night before this?”

I know she’s trying to distract me, and I appreciate it.

“Good. I pushed him away for the longest time, but he is so patient and persistent at the same time.” I chuckle and sniffle. “Tonight we kind of said, 'I love you.’ I’m not ready to say love, so we keep saying like. And now we have animals together.”

“That’s good, though. Right?”

Sighing, I lean back. “It should be, but nothing about us coming together is romantic. I mean, look at what happened afterward. I just lost everything, Summer,” I barely manage to get the words out.

“You lost things. You still have what matters most. You have your kids and a man who loves you. That is what matters most.” She says softly.

We sit in silence, listening to drills screwing wood into the broken windows. My brain tries to wrap around everything that’s happening. I get to my feet, walk to Baylor's room, grab my phone from the nightstand, and return to the living room.

"I have no idea what the kids and I are going to do now. I don't want to move back into Journey and Briggs' guest suite."

"You're not. You and the boys will live here with me," Baylor says through the blank window.

My gaze flicks to his, and I see that possessive determination in his eyes. I know there's no arguing with him, and honestly, I'm too damn tired to argue.

"I'm working on figuring out who he is," Summer says, brushing off the seat next to me. She wraps her arms around my shoulders and holds me tightly as I start crying again.

I want to curl into a ball and hide.

"I got her," Bay tells Summer. Seconds later, I feel her petite arm lift and her move off the couch.

"I'll be back in a few hours," Summer says, kissing my head.

Bay brings one arm around my back and the other under my knees. He moves to one of the kids' rooms and lays me on the bed. Pulling the covers back, Bay gets in next to me and cocoons around my body.

Tomorrow, I have to figure out how to tell the boys we lost everything again.

CHAPTER 17
BAYLOR

My eyes cross the longer I stare at the glass mug, so I smack it across the room. I'm pissed. This son of a bitch blew up her house. They could have been in it. My girl and my boys could have been in there when it happened. I could have lost them, and I wouldn't have been able to stop it.

How the hell do I protect them from this bastard? I'll have to ask Henry for some time off until this is over. I can't leave them. I need to be at the store with Winnie and at school with the kids. I need to be anywhere and everywhere they are.

Fuck.

With a deep inhale, I try to tame the fury rioting inside me. I want Edwards' blood for threatening my family. Bending down, I pick up the broken cup and toss it in the trash.

I pour a cup of coffee into a metal travel mug and put the lid on. I couldn't fall back to sleep last night. When daylight hit, I decided I needed to go to the store and get what I could of what Winter and the kids had lost.

Nila went to bed with Winnie once I let her back in from her potty trip, and Stormy stayed curled up next to her head. They know she needs their comfort.

My gaze shifts to the busted door. I still can't figure out how a tiny woman with a prosthetic leg managed to kick the fucking thing in.

I laugh dryly to myself, picturing it. Her sister saved us last night because I didn't know there was a threat. I thought we didn't have to worry yet.

I will never regret the night Winnie and I shared. Not ever. My only regret is not being cautious enough or anticipating a move like this.

Walking to the door, I swing it open and come face to face with my parents, brothers, and Ny.

Great

"Back up," I hissed at them, moving past everyone and ushering them away from the house.

"What the hell happened?" Dad asked in a hushed tone.

"Gas line," I said. When my eyes met my brothers, I knew they knew this was no accident.

Before anyone could move, Summers' red Range Rover pulled into my driveway. She parked, got out, went to the trunk, and pulled out a huge-ass army bag.

When she looked at us, her eyes landed on Baxter, and she gave him that smirk I was sure he hated. I'm starting to think it's a torture tactic she's using on him.

"Yeti," she said cheerfully. I'm not sure anything phases this woman.

Summer jogged over to Baxter, jumped, and threw her arms around his neck, making him growl. He caught her on reflex. You'd think her gait would be off with the prosthetic, but she moves with it fluently.

My eyes flick to Beau when I see the top of her weapon sticking out of the back of her shorts. Beau's eyes zero in on it, too. Just what we needed. They're going to think she's the bad guy.

Good god. We needed a leisurely morning, but it will be anything but that.

"Kill me," Bax grumbles under his breath.

"Don't be so dramatic," Summer says, kissing his cheek, then letting go and looking at everyone. "You're in your thirties and have a son. I'm sure they all know you." Summer whistles, poking a finger through the O, the other fingers formed.

"Who are you?" Briggs and Beau ask in unison.

"Oh, I thought I just told you who I am. Baxy and I have been riding the bang train through Pound Town together." Summer winks. "Bay, I have some things for you and Winter. I'm going to take them inside."

"Yeah. No, you're not. Who are you, and what happened to your arm?" Beau asks again, crossing his arms over his puffed-out chest.

"Beau," I warn. I have a feeling Summer could take us all out without getting a scratch on her if she wanted to.

"Aw," Summer pouts her lip out. "Let me guess. The cop and the tattoo artist. I see all you boys share the pompous-ass gene." She doesn't answer Beau. Instead, she throws her head back and laughs, walks back to her car, grabs the bag, and heads inside the house.

Beau stomps off and follows her inside. "Hey, I asked you a question. How do you know who we are?"

"Damn it," I grumble, jogging back to the house. I can hear the crowd following me.

Inside, I see Beau and Summer locked in a staring contest.

"Answer me," Beau barks.

Summer wiggles a finger at Beau in an air scratch. “You’re too cute. Like the abominable snowman. I mean, not as cute as my Yeti. Broody is more my type. I don’t have to tell you who I am. Obviously, Baylor is fine with me being here.”

“Or he could be nervous about telling us who you are,” Beau retorts.

“I think he just called you a pussy, Bay. Insinuating you’re scared of a five-foot-two woman with a prosthetic leg.” Summer smirks at Beau, making his face turn redder.

“You’re carrying, and we all know Baxter isn’t hooking up with anyone.”

“Oh yeah? He tells you about all his fuckering around? I think he just called you pathetic, Baxy. Keep going. Who else can you unintentionally insult?” Summer's smile widens.

She is enjoying this too much. Anyone else would have caved by now.

“I didn’t insult anyone. If you’re not a threat, it shouldn’t be so hard to give us your name and explain the bandage on your arm.” Beau continues to argue.

“I mean, you kinda did. Ugh, ok, I’ll tell you. I come from the land of pixies. My parents were simple plum fairies. The berries are always juicy and lucrative because of their hard work. My fairy name was once Niamh Raindrop.”

I cover my mouth to keep from laughing as she tells this little story. It shouldn’t be, but it’s funny. My family is pissed, but she isn’t giving up.

“Can you take anything seriously?” Baxter asks.

“I prefer not to give in to intimidation. Humor is my shield. I was supposed to follow in my parents' footsteps and live a simple fairy life, but I had a big dream of becoming a fairy warrior in the human realm. I had to make a deal with a warlock.”

"Young lady, you realize a member of our family's home exploded last night, right? This is no joking matter." Dad cuts in, watching Summer, whose face has turned scary as fuck. It's like watching a thunderstorm roll in at high speed.

Shit

"I am fully aware, Sir. But like I told your son, I don't give in to intimidation tactics. Baylor, I think it's best to get Winter up before I lose all my humor." Summer's tone has my brows rising.

"Is that a threat?" Beau asks gruffly, shifting his stance and resting a hand on his weapon.

"Oh, no, you oversized dildo, it's a promise. I don't need my gun to drop your ass. But if you're looking for a duel, well then, I'm your huckleberry."

The twinkle in Summer's eyes is as unsettling and terrifying as the twisted smile spreading across her face. Her fingers twitch at her sides as if she's itching for him to accept the challenge. I let this go too far. It was fun watching them banter, but she might kill him.

"That's enough. Tell them who you are." Winter's soft voice comes before she steps into view.

Holy hot mama, Winnie, in her glasses with a messy bun, wearing a pair of my boxers and my t-shirt, is sexy as hell, and everyone in this room knows she is mine.

"I want to point out that he started it," Summer says, pointing at a pissed-off Beau.

"You started it when you refused to answer my questions," Beau husks back like a second grader. I'm pretty sure the twins are more mature than these two right now.

Winter chuckles lightly, walks over to me, and hugs my waist. I wrap my arms around her, kiss the top of her head, and hold her close.

When Nila comes out, she trots up to Summer and sits next to her as if reporting for duty.

"It doesn't matter who started it. My house blew up, and they're all naturally suspicious men. The other two will find out eventually," Winter tells her sister.

"What the hell does that mean?" Briggs asks now.

"Fine, but can I still act like I'm banging the Yeti shifter? It's funny watching how pissed he gets."

"Sure."

"You're still mine, Baxy," Summer says, waving her fingers at Baxter.

"I hate you, Baylor," Baxter grumbles.

I can't help but laugh silently. Summer steps up like she owns the space, taking her proper military stance. When she speaks, her voice is strong and demands respect. All humor has been replaced with authority.

"I am Retired Sergeant First Class Summer Anderson. I served 11 years on active duty in the U.S. Army Special Forces as an 18D. You may have a big body, but I'm not too sure about that brain of yours. Raise your hand if you know what that means."

When no one moves, she continues. "I didn't think so. The 18D, Special Forces Medical Sergeant. The scratch on my arm came from tackling your brother and my sister to the ground right before last night's explosion while I was on recon." Summer steps into Beau's space. She doesn't flinch or falter. "I am not scared, nor am I impressed by how you have conducted yourself or how you reacted to my presence. I have faced scarier men. Now, there is one thing you should always remember."

In a flash, Summer strikes her palm into Beau's nose. Simultaneously, her prosthetic leg sweeps his leg out from under him, knocking him off balance. She drives to the side, forcing him to the ground. Beau lands hard on his back with a grunt.

"Damn," the rest of us say at the same time.

Summer chuckles and squats down. "Never let your guard down. I just won the dick-measuring contest. Make no mistake, officer, I know what I'm doing, and I fucking do it well. You, on the other hand, let me keep you distracted with talk of fairies and ended up on your ass because of it. You need to work on that. The nose isn't broken. You'll be fine." She says, then pats his cheek.

Summer stands straight and holds out a hand to Beau. He takes it, and she helps him to his feet. She walks over to her bag and pulls out something. Standing in front of Beau, she gestures for him to lean down, then pops a nasal plug into each nostril. Wiping her hands on a wet wipe, she tosses it onto the coffee table.

"Those will stop the bleeding."

"If you weren't retired, would you have reached out to Winter?" Journey asks.

I'm curious about that, too. Winter's arms tighten as she waits. I hate that this is happening.

"Maybe we should wait. Winter has enough to think about," I interject.

"I want to know," Winter whispers. Summer frowns, then straightens.

"The honest answer is no. Sometimes not knowing is better than knowing. I have heard the screams and cries of mothers, fathers, siblings, wives, husbands, and friends. They knew the danger their loved one was in and lived every day in fear that ultimately became their reality. It breaks a piece of you. That was a burden I would never put on her."

"You thought it was easier for her if you stayed away, but do you have any idea what she's been through?" Journey presses.

"I think that is a conversation she and I should have alone," Summer says. It's as if no one in this room understands that she is built to hold secrets.

"It's ok. Ny has been a big part of my life for the past nine years."

Summer rolls her shoulders and neck, then tightens her jaw. "Fine. Yes. It was simpler for her not to know. Sky was spared the phone call about me nearly dying. She was spared the details of the loss of part of my leg and the metal rods holding my bones together to heal. She didn't have to know I was shot and that my flesh was burned."

The sharp intakes of breath fill the silent space in the room.

"Gruesome, isn't it? She didn't spend the last thirteen years waiting for the visit to announce my death. Winter believed I was traveling the world, and I was, but not the way she thought. I protected her from that pain. From that knock on her door. Do not look at me like I did her a disservice by staying away. Her not knowing gave her hope that I was safe and happy. I shielded her from my life."

Summer flicks her gaze to Mom and Dad. "Your son was undercover for five years. Was it better for you not to know where he was? Not to know the danger he faced daily?"

"Yes," Dad says without hesitation.

"How do you know that?" Beau asks.

"I told you I do my job well." Summer turns and looks at Winter. "I always kept up with your life. I'm the reason Troy was able to get you an apartment when you got pregnant, and the reason it was paid until you turned twenty-one. I'm also the reason he disappeared."

"What? What do you mean?" Winter asks, stepping up.

Summer inhales deeply. “I would check on you randomly. You didn't know I was there. I paid the bills for you and him because I knew Mom and Dad would shun you, and Troy was, well, Troy. I went to him and told him I would pay, but he couldn’t tell you it was me. I did what I could from a distance.”

Summer steps closer and takes Winter’s hands. “I couldn’t handle the thought of you suffering any more than you already were, so I did what little I could.”

“You did that?” Winter asks.

“I did. But it wasn’t enough. All I did was pay the bills. I didn’t protect you from him or from all the bullshit he brought home. Leaving you is one of my greatest failures.”

Winter shakes her head. “It’s not.”

“It is. Six years ago, I came to check on you, and you were flourishing without him. The night before I left, I saw Troy yelling at you outside your apartment. When he left, I followed him into the alley, beat his ass, put the barrel of my gun down his throat, and told him that if I found out he came back, I would blow his head off, and no one would ever find his body. I quit paying the bills after that so you wouldn’t get suspicious.”

“You threatened to kill him?”

“No, Sky. I swore it. I would have done it that night, but I decided to give him the benefit of the doubt. Over the years, I kept checking on you, and when I couldn’t, I hired a PI to do it for me to make sure Troy listened.”

“And what if the PI caught him? Troy would periodically show up at my work,” Winter asks, and Summer sighs.

“He understood the assignment and what had to be done if he found Troy there. The fucker got lucky; he was never caught.” Summer growled.

“You hired a hitman. Is that what you really mean?”

"Pfft, you say hitman, I say trusted ally. With that out of the way, I have to tell you what I've found out."

"It's been less than twenty-four hours," I say now. We just told her about all of this. It's wild that she already has information.

"Why does everyone keep doubting me?" Summer says, throwing her hands in the air. She has a point; everyone keeps questioning her and her abilities.

"Edwards' name is Tony Lopez. He leads the Atlanta Kings. The woman is his sister, Liz Lopez, and she is more ruthless than he is. Tony doesn't care about the money Troy stole. That's literally pennies to him. Tony is wanted for a ton of shit. You name it, he's wanted for it, but there's never enough evidence, and he has good attorneys."

Summer purses her lips. "What he wants is a flash drive worth millions. It contains all the evidence of his activities. The FBI has been searching for that drive for years. It has everything they need to put him away for good, along with all his acquaintances."

"All of this is on the flash drive?" Briggs asks.

"Did you not hear why it's so important?" Summer asks, looking at him like he's a brainless minion. "It's mostly that, but it's also about betrayal. Troy worked for one of Tony's men, peddling drugs. Low-level shit. Then he met Tony's wife, Jasmine. They had an affair and had two kids together. Over the years, she told Troy all of Tony's secrets. She wanted out, so Troy broke into Tony's home, stole the money and the flash drive. He gave the money to Jasmine. She and the kids used it to hide from Tony."

Winter looks like her entire world has just been tilted upside down. I hold her closer, trying to give her comfort.

"He had other kids? While we were together? He's actively protecting them while he lets this happen to ours," she whispers. Summer gives her a sorrowful nod.

"How the hell did you get all of that so quickly?" Beau asks.

"Bay asked me to use my resources. I know someone in the same prison as Troy. You can use your imagination to figure out how he got the info."

Summer is a mountain of information. Beau has had the photo of Tony for weeks and hasn't gotten anywhere with it. It took her one fucking day.

"Once the facial recognition search you ran pings, this town will be crawling with law enforcement of every kind. He never does the dirty work himself. Since he's the one doing this, that alone tells you how important the flash drive is. I noticed at least ten men with him, but I'd double that." Summer tells everyone.

"Oh my god. What am I going to do? He's a serious bad guy. He's going to kill us." Winter starts to panic and cry.

I wrap my arm around her middle and step closer. Winnie's breathing is quick as she tries to control the panic. "We'll figure this out, babe. I'll make sure you and the kids are safe." I try to soothe her, but she shakes her head vigorously.

"We need to, I don't know. What do we do now?"

"I have it taken care of. Baylor, walk to that window." Summer points.

Reluctantly, I release Winnie and walk to the window. Two seconds later, I have two lasers pointed at my chest.

"What the hell?" I shout, moving out of the way. I was right. She can take us all out without a scratch on her.

"Tony has his men, and I have mine. I called them yesterday when I left the bookstore. More guys are coming in any minute. We'll set up cameras. They'll be watching around the clock.

You may not see them, but you can guarantee someone will be watching you and the kids at all times."

"But what if they get hurt? I can't let more people get involved. What if this guy finds out I talked? I wasn't supposed to talk." Winter starts to sob. Within two quick strides, I have her in my arms again.

"You're not letting us. This is what we're trained to do, and we do it well. The man blew up the house of a woman whose boyfriend is a firefighter, whose brother-in-law is a cop, and whose friend's parents have more resources and money than God. He knew something would be coming. He just isn't going to expect ex-military assistance. I will still annoy Baxter, and my name will be Rayn Cooper."

"Damn it. I thought I would get out of this since everyone knows."

"Not a chance, Baxy. I'm starting to like you a little. You're so cute and angry. It really gets my dick hard."

"Jesus," Baxter grumbles.

"I prefer honeyplum, sugar, babydoll, kitten, kitty, snuggle bottoms, buttercup, lovebug, princess, bunny, baby… I can keep going."

"Are you sure she's your sister?"

Winter finally laughs and shakes her head. She told me she loved that her sister spoke her mind, and, man, does she. She's a chaotic mess.

Summer looks at Winnie with a big grin. "I think he loves me already. When's the wedding, Daddy?"

"I'm done. She's fucking crazy."

He's going to kill her, not marry her.

"Only a tiny bit. It's fine. Crazy is keeping you all safe. I put a detail on all of you."

"How many people are here?" Beau asks.

"I don't know. Enough." Summer shrugs.

"Briggs and I will cover any costs," Journey tells her without hesitation.

"We will too," Dad says next.

"That's not necessary. I'm only covering air B&Bs and living expenses."

"We'll cover those then," Journey tells her.

"We'll split it. And don't you argue with us. You brought a fucking army to protect not just your sister and nephews but also our son and his entire family. This is the least we could do."

"Agreed," Briggs says.

"It's honestly not a big deal." Summer glances at her watch and smiles. "The rest of the cavalry has arrived."

CHAPTER 18
WINTER

As we stand on Baylor's porch, we watch three trucks park and their doors open. Men and women step out in black jeans and T-shirts. Each looks just as badass as the next. I can't believe she did all this for us. She didn't waste a second after she found out I was in trouble.

"Shit," Bay whispers.

"Power Puff," the silver fox shouts at my sister. When I say silver fox, I mean 'Yes, Master Sergeant.' I don't know if that's a real title, but DAMN. The man is a lean giant with salt-and-pepper hair, green eyes, a strong jaw, and an ironman, robotic-looking arm. Most of the people have just as many tattoos as Summer and Briggs.

Summer squeals, jogs over, and jumps into the older man's arms. My eyes widen when he pats her ass with a laugh. Alrighty then. Looks like she really is just fucking with Baxter.

I watch as he sets her on her feet, and she makes her rounds. They all shake hands, dance, or sing. Then they form a group and shout "Hooah" before breaking apart.

“Do you think they act like that because this situation is normal for them?” Ivey asks.

“Yeah,” Beau answers. “Even undercover, what I saw was nothing compared to what those men and women have. They’re trained to be serious when it matters.”

Once Summer is done goofing off, she walks back to us with the man.

“Colburn, I’d like you to meet my sister, Winter Anderson.”

Colburn reaches out and shakes my hand firmly. “Pleasure. If you’re ready, we can set up the cameras. I’m sure Summer mentioned you won’t notice we’re here.”

“She did. Thank you for coming.”

“If Summer calls, I answer.”

“Col and I are besties. Been together since I got to my first station. Don’t worry, Yeti, it's not like that with us. I’m saving all my lovin' for you.” Summer winks and blows a kiss to Baxter.

“Why? Why does God hate me?” Baxter grumbles, tilting his head back.

Col bursts out laughing. “Summer's dazzling personality takes some getting used to, but once you do, you’ll have a friend for life. She’s gotten me through some tough times.”

“She’s gotten all of us through some shit. I have never seen anyone have more fun than she did in the hospital after she lost part of her leg. She would go to the kids' ward and tell them she was a treasure-hunting fairy and that a crocodile had bitten her foot off while she was trying to escape with the jewels. Then she’d have them come close to look at it and shake it, making them scream and laugh. Are the cameras inside?” another guy asks, laughing behind them.

“Yup. Green bag, and the kids loved it.” Summer chuckles.

The guys nod and go inside. Of course, Beau and Bay follow them.

A sadness I can't explain runs through me. I know she wanted to protect me, but I hate that I don't know her the way these men and women do. I hate feeling like a stranger. I want to know all about her. I want to hear the treasure story. What if something happens to her and I don't get to hear it?

"Hey. Don't do that, Sky."

"Do what?"

"You know what. It may have been thirteen years, but I still remember that face. I'm not going anywhere. I'm like a cat, and so far I've only used three of my nine lives," she jokes.

I snort a laugh and roll my eyes. "How do you do it?"

Summer lifts a questioning brow.

"How do you stay positive and breezy about everything? Even with all this going on, you can laugh and joke."

"Life is full of darkness, fear, and pain, my dear sweet baby sister. I find it best to see the bright side. I laugh, smile, and joke because it feels good. If you let this life drag you down into the pits, it's a hard place to dig yourself out of. Don't let what's happening take your sunshine."

"Why do you call her Sky?" Ivey asks.

Summer smiles at Ivey. "Winter Sky and Summer Rayn. She hates her middle name and tells people she doesn't have one. I've called her that since we were kids because I knew it pissed her off."

A bubble of laughter rips through me when I think about all the fighting and hair-pulling we used to do to each other because she called me that.

"It did piss me off, but I kind of like it now."

"Good. I wasn't going to stop calling you that. I'm going to help set up. Baxy, in all seriousness, can I crash on your couch?

I promise not to try to touch your wiener." Summer half-asks, half-teases. Briggs loses it for a second and tries to mask his laugh with a fake cough.

Baxter exhales loudly and rolls his neck. "Fine, but I'm locking my door at night. I have zero trust in that promise."

Summer beams at him. "Big, broody, and smart. Yummy. He keeps getting better. I was totally going to try to touch it." Turning, she looks at Ivey and Bryce. "You two outdid yourselves creating all these godly monsters. But, like, you could have held the pompous-ass gene back or maybe only given it to one of them. I'm just saying," Summer says, holding her hands up and walking into the house.

This time, Ivey finally loses it over Summer's mouthy shenanigans and cracks up laughing.

"She's a mouthy one." Bryce chuckles.

"It's worse now, but she always said what was on her mind."

"I think that's a good thing, Honey. I can see how much she loves you, and I can also see her sorrow when she looks at you," Ivey says, hugging me to her.

When she releases me, I step off my porch and start walking toward my home, now a pile of ash and burnt wood. As I take another step, a hand grips my shoulder, and I turn to see Bryce.

"It might not be a good idea to go walking around in there. You and Bay are going to have your hands full. I already talked to Henry; he has Bay's shift covered, and Birdie agreed to help at the bookstore while you're away. Your sister has everything else taken care of. I'll do my best to stop Baxter from killing her," Bryce says with a smile.

"All of this is too much, Bryce." Sniffling, I stare at the charred wood in front of me.

"Not just what everyone is doing for me, but what Troy has done. I feel broken. It hurts to know we meant nothing to him.

He protected his other family and stole from us. Why are her kids more important than mine? Why did they get the good version of him? Look at our home. He doesn't care that this is the danger he put his firstborn children in." My voice cracks, and tears flow when Bryce wraps his arm around my shoulders.

I won't tell them I fully intend to see Troy. I want answers. I want to know why it's okay for him not to care that our children could get hurt. I need to know why he never cared. If Summer hadn't paid for the apartment, would he have left me when I found out I was pregnant?

"Sweetheart, those are questions you'll never have the answers to. What I can tell you is that you have a man who would lay down his life to protect you and those boys. Bay may not be their father, but he loves them as if he were. If he had a child, his love for that child would be the same as it is for Dylan and Daniel. All might seem lost and overwhelming right now, but you still have the only things that matter."

"You're right. I can replace the material things. I should start with clothes. I can't exactly keep walking around in my boyfriend's underwear."

Bryce lets out a low chuckle and rubs my upper arm. "No, I don't think you can. Let's go see what we can get taken care of."

Using the sleeve of my shirt, I wipe the snot and tears from my face. I know it's gross, but compared to everything else going on, being gross is the least of my worries. I'll wash the damn shirt.

As we get closer to the house, I notice half the people who were here are nowhere to be seen, but all the trucks are still parked out front.

These soldiers are sneaky, like ants. Sometimes you don't realize those bastards are on you until you feel the stinging bite. I have no doubt they're watching from God only knows where.

Journey hops off the porch, loops her arm with mine, and whispers in my ear.

"Everything is going to be okay. We're going to my place to get you something to wear, then we're going into the city to shop. Birdie can handle the kids for a few more hours."

I stifle my groan. I know she's trying to help, but I don't want to go shopping right now. I want to clean up the mess inside, then curl into a ball and wallow in self-pity. Is that so much to ask?

On the porch, I hear the vacuum inside. When we enter, I see Ivey bent over the couch, lifting cushions.

Glancing around, I land on Bay's tall, lean body. The sunlight beams off his muscular arms, making them look even more prominent.

I love that I am the only person he's ever given himself to. He's the only man I've honestly ever given all myself to.

When his lake eyes meet mine, he gives me a heart-stopping grin. He is gorgeous. My own smile widens when he winks at me. The flock of butterflies in my stomach wakes from their slumber and takes flight. Just looking at him eases my tension.

I knew I was falling in love with him, but yesterday I realized I had already fallen. I told him as much, but it's deeper now, since our connection last night. It's raw and powerful.

It's in my soul and bones. My lungs forget how to breathe when he's not near. I feel like I can't survive without him now. I would do anything for him. I would die or kill for him. Is that normal?

Would he be upset if I pushed past everyone and claimed the mouth I can't get enough of? How bad is it that the house looks like a chaotic mess, and all I want is to feel his arms around me?

Bryce and Summer are right. I still have so much to be grateful for. I still have Bay, the boys, and this family. I can hear Journey's voice, but I don't listen as my feet propel me forward, and I make my way to the sliding glass door.

Opening it, I step past the other men around him. Lifting my arms, I wrap them around Bay's neck and bury my face in the crook. He doesn't waste any time slipping a warm hand up the back of my shirt and rubbing my lower back while his other arm splays between my shoulder blades.

His scent mingles with mine, and warmth begins to calm the chaos in my mind. Even with the threat hanging over our heads, I don't regret this. I can't regret a love like this. I know he will do everything he can to protect us.

"Are you ok, Angel?" he whispers.

Shaking my head, I inhale him again. "Holding you helps."

His hold tightens, and he kisses my head. His large arms around me make me feel small in his embrace. "I like you."

I fake a gasp, draw back, and look at him. "You do? I didn't know that."

"Then I am definitely doing something wrong." Bay leans in and whispers in my ear. "Guess I'll have to try harder next time. Perhaps I'll give you the necklace that lit up your eyes the last time it was mentioned."

I bite my lip as the thrill runs through me, knowing he will. Last night was slow and gentle; both of us needed it that way. But now it's game on. I have no doubt he'll use that filthy mouth next time and fuck me into another dimension.

"Mm"

"Oh my god, you two had sex," Journey shouts.

"Journey, seriously, what the actual fuck is wrong with you?" I snap. "We're leaving."

Bay laughs as I kiss his cheek in a hurry. I don't miss the smug look on his face before I drag Ny through the house. I need to get her out of here before she embarrasses me even more than she already has. No one needed to hear her outburst. I should have denied it, but my brain wasn't quick enough to think of it.

I open her car door and get in. I swear, if the kids didn't need anything, I wouldn't be going. I would have hidden in the room until all the strangers left.

During the drive to Nys, she finally breaks the silence.

"Was it good? How did it happen? Are you living with him now? You two have animals together, so it makes sense. When are you telling the boys? Did I hear him say I like you?"

"Damn woman, what's with the rapid-fire?"

"I'm too excited. My two besties finally banged. Answer."

"It was amazing and life-altering. I created a romantic night to make it perfect for both of us. Yes, we have pets together now, and we will be living together. Even if I wanted to stay somewhere else, he would follow me. Yes, we said, "I like you"-it's our version of "I love you" for now. I'm going to tell the boys when I tell them we're living with Bay." Fidgeting with the hem of my shorts, I start to feel nervous about telling the kids. "Do you think they'll mind?"

"Not at all. They love Baylor and already stay with him all the time. I'm sorry about the house. How long have you been dealing with this?"

"Since the speed-dating night. Tony threatened Bay and the kids if I talked."

Journey sighs and parks in her driveway. "That explains why Briggs wasn't as upset as I was when we heard about the house. They all knew something was going on."

"Yeah. Bay got suspicious and looped everyone in."

I glance around for any bodyguards. Huh, Col was serious when he said I wouldn't see them, or maybe they're not there.

"They're here. I watched the SUV follow us," Journey says, then gets out.

Ugh, I need to learn to pay better attention.

Inside Journey's house, we go to her room, where she hands me some jean shorts and a t-shirt. Then we go to her design room for a bra and underwear. Guess that's a perk of knowing an underwear and lingerie designer.

"Was it easier having Briggs by your side when you were going through everything?" I ask while I change behind the dressing screen.

"It was. I don't think I would have survived it without him."

"I'm scared, Ny. I'm scared he'll get hurt next. The house was a warning, just as the warehouse fire was. What if his next call…" I trail off, holding back the sob that wants to break free.

Ny steps behind the screen and rubs my arms.

"You can't think that way. I felt that way, and it didn't help. I wanted to run to protect Briggs, but I didn't. Hold onto the feeling you have when you're with him. Don't let this break you or your new relationship. One thing about the Banks men is that they love fiercely, and nothing will deter them once they find their person. You are Baylor's person. That man will not let you go now."

Shaking my head, I slip my sandals back on, and we head to the store so I can spend what little money I've managed to save.

Five hours of shopping is exhausting. Trying to pick out new clothes, shoes, and everything else I could think of left me mentally drained. My brain feels like spam, and my arms feel like jelly from carrying clothes. I want a hot bath and to forget this entire day.

Journey wouldn't let me pay for anything and smacked me every time I tried. I know she wanted to help, but it made me feel like shit that she always seems to be paying for my kids and me. I hate it. I don't want people to take care of me. Sometimes I wish I had done things differently. I don't regret my kids; I regret sticking by their father for as long as I did.

While we were shopping, I kept trying to think of ways to sneak away from my family and the damn army Summer called in. I came up with nothing. My new plan is to watch a few thriller movies and read a few books to see how other people dodge their bodyguards. Then I have to pray Troy will see me when I go to visit him.

As we open Baylor's front door, we're greeted by laughter and the scent of grilled food. My stomach gets the memo and growls. We didn't stop our mission to eat. I wanted to get in and get out.

Looking through the sliding glass doors, I notice Birdie is here with all the kids. Shit, I'm an ass. I should have checked in on her and the kids.

When I step outside, I see Summer in the yard with all the kids sitting in the grass. Col is with her, and they are all laughing. He looks to be the only one still here. Then I notice

Nila, her head on Dylan's lap, as he pets her. It's a beautiful sight.

Bay and his brothers are close by, still watching Summer. How can they still not trust her? Ivey is holding Everett and talking to Journey now. Birdie is walking over to the kids, Blue babbling in her arms. Bryce is at the grill, doing what he loves. I swear the man would cook all their meals on the grill if Ivey would let him.

It's like any other typical day, except it is anything but that.

Everyone in the vicinity whips their heads toward the kids as they scream, then laugh. I let my own laughter out when I see Summer flop her stump around dramatically.

Damn it. I missed the treasure story.

My eyes flick to the four brothers, who look like they're about to unleash hell on my sister. When she's done, she lets the kids touch her leg.

When Dyl and Dan notice me, they jump up and rush over, with Nila following closely behind.

"Mom, are you okay? Did you get hurt in the fire?" Dyl asks, his hazel eyes full of concern.

"Are we going back to Aunt Ny's? I don't want to. Bay got Nila for us. We should stay with him and her," Dan says in a sad voice, making my heart ache.

Shaking my head, I hug them both and kiss their heads. I glance over and see Bay walking toward us.

"We're not going back to Aunt Ny's," I tell them, then wait for Bay to stand beside me. Releasing the boys, I look down at them, and they look up at me with watery eyes.

Squatting down, I cup both of their smooth cheeks. "How would you boys feel if I told you Baylor is my boyfriend and that I like him very much?"

"Does that mean he'll be like a stepdad? Because that would be awesome," Dylan says with excitement.

"Wait, if he's your boyfriend, can we live here with Bay, Nila, and Stormy? Stormy likes my bed and my window. Do we call Bay dad now?" Dan asks.

"Yes, he's so much better than our dad. He's always here."

"And he doesn't make mom cry," Dan says next.

My heart clenches, and tears prick the back of my eyes, a mix of happy and sad. Bay's warm hand on my back helps soothe the depression that's threatening to take over.

I knew they weren't fans of Troy, but it still hurts to hear how they really feel about their father. It hurts to know they know Troy has made me cry.

"You don't have to call me dad. You'll be living in our home. I want you boys to know I will always be here. I will always take care of you and your mom. And the only thing I might steal is your Halloween candy," Baylor jokes, and they both start laughing.

"But if we want to call you dad one day, can we?" Dyl asks with round eyes.

Baylor looks at me, and I nod. He's a better father to them than Troy ever could be, and if this is what they want, I'll let them have it. I've accepted that Bay will always be a constant in their lives. Even if things go sour with us, he'll never leave them. Baylor loves them too damn much to walk away. My heart knows that now.

"If that's what you want, then of course you can. But you don't have to," Bay tells them with peaceful satisfaction, as if being their father has completed him.

"Cool. We get to live here, have pets, and call you our dad. Now, Russell can suck it," Dyl says, then does the floss dance.

“He’s a jackass. Bay is cooler than his dad,” Dan joins in the insult.

“Language,” I tell him, then blink rapidly at Bay, who is using all his control to hold back his laughter.

Who the fuck is Russell? And whose parents’ ass do I have to kick because of him? Bay must sense my anger. Leaning over, he whispers he’ll tell me later. Damn it, how does he know about Russell?

Have I been so disconnected from my own children that they couldn’t tell me a bully was picking on them? Are they at an age when they no longer want their mom's protection and are resorting to secrets? The questions swirling in my head are making me motion sick.

“Hey, why don’t you guys go unload the car for us? Shopping is exhausting.” Ny shouts, breaking the tornado of thoughts.

Bay kisses my cheek, and we both stand. As he walks by Ny, I see her hand him a card before he steps past her.

The breath leaves my lungs, and my body stills. Ny didn’t pay for everything Baylor did.

Inside my brain and heart, the deck of emotions shuffles. Once they’ve passed the cards out, I flip the first one. Love. I love Bay, the kids, and my newfound family.

CHAPTER 19
BAYLOR

Dylan's door creaks as I open it. Nila shuffles and stretches at the foot of his bed. I walk over and wake him from his slumber. Over the past week, Winter has been exhausted from the stress of dealing with insurance and is still questioning Troy's choices regarding the kids.

I've been playing dad, getting the boys up, making them breakfast, and getting them to school. I never loved mornings as much as I do now that they've all moved in with me. Being their father has been phenomenal. In my heart, I know Winter loves me, and I understand why she wants answers from Troy. My brain can't comprehend how little he cares for these amazing kids.

"I don't want to," Dyl murmurs sleepily.

When his tousled hair and sleepy face peek out from the covers, a smile crosses my face. My heart expands as I look at him. I love them both so damn much. I'm happy to take Troy's place in their lives.

"I know you only have a couple more weeks until school is out, and then we can plan gaming marathons. But today you have to get up. Do you want fruit and yogurt or eggs for breakfast?" I've learned those are his two favorite breakfasts.

"Can I have both?" Dylan finally opens his eyes and stretches big.

"Absolutely. Get dressed so you can eat, then brush your teeth."

Dylan sighs, sits up, and starts petting the dog. "Ok."

I'm not stupid. He's going to lie back down as soon as he's dressed, and I'll have to wake him again.

Daniel's door is silent when I open it. I see Stormy perched in his window, soaking up the morning sunlight. Dan is already dressed, his hair neatly brushed back, and he's putting on his socks. Winter and I got each of them a phone for emergencies; he's been using the alarm on his. He said he wants to be ready for middle school, starting with waking up on his own.

"Hey, bud, good job getting up on your own. What do you want for breakfast?"

"Can I have strawberries and a toaster waffle?"

I swear he's as bad with toaster waffles as Winter is with pizza rolls. I caught her eating them twice this week after midnight. She laughed and told me she didn't want to hear me tell her how bad they were.

"You got it."

Nila's nails click behind me as I head into the kitchen, where I open the sliding door and let her out. I installed the wireless fence so we wouldn't worry about her running off. Not that she would. The dog has attached herself to us like a tick.

With a slight pull, I open the refrigerator and freezer, pulling out everything I need to make today's meals and coffee.

Once I have the skillet ready, I crack two eggs, scramble them, and pop two waffles into the toaster. While they cook, I slice the berries and prepare the yogurt. With both breakfasts ready, I plate them and set them on the island in front of the kids' usual seats. Then I get the bagels, break one apart, and pop it in the toaster for my angel. The smell of toasted grains and Winter's apple air freshener fills the air. I've grown accustomed to the mixed scents.

"I can make their lunches today. I've been a shit parent this week," Winter says behind me. Her angelic voice is a sweet symphony.

My breath catches when I see her up and looking more refreshed than she has in days. She needed the extra rest. Color is back in her cheeks. Winnie looks bright and vibrant in her green flowered Maxie dress and jean jacket. She took the time to put on some makeup and curl her hair.

Stunning

"I enjoy doing it," I say, making her coffee the way she likes it. All caramel creamer, a splash of coffee, and 4 teaspoons of sugar. Once it's stirred, I tap the spoon on the rim of the glass and hand it to her.

Winter makes sure to graze my fingers with hers when she accepts it. I watch as she brings it to her lips and lets out a low hum of delight. A smile cracks at the corner of my mouth. With a lick of her lips, she looks at me through her thick lashes.

My cock doesn't understand timing. Everything about Winter Anderson makes the cum cannon ready to blow.

"I have everything that matters most. But every time I talk to Henry about the explosion or the insurance, my gut feels like it's crawling up my esophagus. I hate lying. I want to tell them I know who did it, but there's no proof. And I'm." Winnie trails off. “Why is my heart broken? You’re a better man and father to the boys than he ever was. Why is it bothering me so much?”

My sweet angel, I reach out and take her hand, pulling her into me. Winnie wraps her arms around my waist, then rests her cheek on my chest. I let my hands fall to her hips and give them a gentle squeeze. I know she finds comfort in my embrace.

“Because, babe. He’s still technically their father. He should love them like he loves the others.” I answer honestly.

I hate this for her. I hate that I can’t make it better. There’s no way to. All I can do is be here, for her, for the boys.

“I get not caring about me, but the boys. It’s not right. How could anyone ever choose which of their children to protect?” The sadness in her voice is crushing.

“I don’t know,” I answer with a sigh, kissing the top of her head. “I wish I could take away your pain. All I can do is tell you I will always care for all of you. I would always choose them. If you want answers, then we’ll go and see if he’ll talk.”

Winnie’s head snaps up so fast. The woman doesn’t know what it means to be disingenuous. I’ll admit it pained me to know she felt she couldn’t come to me. “Again,” I think. I’m starting to think she’ll never fully trust me, that she’ll always feel she needs to hide things from me.

“If I wanted to, would you go with me?”

Finally, she’s going to admit what she’s been up to.

“Of course. I wouldn’t let you do that alone. You want answers from him. And a small part of me wants him to know you have a good man in your life and that the boys have someone they can count on.” I lift a shoulder, locking my gaze on her crystal-blue eyes.

“Can I confess something?”

Nope

"You were already planning to go?" I say. I want her to know she can't get shit past me.

Winnie's jaw drops, and she gives me a 'what the fuck' stare. "How did you know that?"

"You left your Kindle open with a bunch of thrillers. I opened one and read it. You only read romance or fantasy. Then our TV app was flooded with movies, TV shows, and documentaries about women running from someone. I know you weren't trying to run from me because, well, you can't quit me. Besides, I am fucking amazing, so I connected the dots." I shrug and sip my coffee.

"Who are you and what have you done with my boyfriend? Your sleuthing skills have been on point, and you are absolutely amazing."

I bark out a laugh and kiss her forehead. "Winnie, babe, you may not know this, but you were as inconspicuous as a penguin wearing a top hat, sunbathing on a beach. Now, do you believe I've read all those mystery books I buy?"

"Not at all. I believe you watch too much TV and hang out with your suspicious cop brother too often." Winnie lets out a cackle, tosses her head back, and smacks my chest. "You read? That's funny, hotshot."

"Damn it, woman, I read." Burying my face in her neck, I blow raspberries, making her laugh harder.

Once she's regained her senses, I snake my arm around her waist. I consider my words. Very calmly, I say what I need to. I need her to know she doesn't have to do anything alone anymore; she doesn't have to worry about upsetting me. I'm a reasonable guy.

"At some point, you have to stop hiding things from me, Winter. We said no more secrets, but you were planning a great escape because you didn't think you could trust me to be understanding, or I don't know the reason, but that's what it feels like. If you feel like you can't trust me, I need you to tell me how I can help you get there. Tell me what else I can do."

The guilt and pain flickered in her eyes before she hung her head. She knows I'm right. Before she can say anything, Daniel's voice carries through the air.

"Morning, Mom," Daniel says, hugging Winter around her waist and looking up at her with big eyes. "Do you feel better?"

I let Winnie go, walk over, and let Nila in while I watch Winnie run her fingers through Dan's thick brown hair. The smile on Dan's face brings one to mine.

If it came down to them or me, I would happily accept my fate as long as I knew they were safe. My love for them is no different than it would be if I had a child with Winnie. They would all share the same space in my heart equally.

"Yeah, honey, I'm feeling better. Bay's been pretty great taking care of you kids while I rested."

"Yup. I hope we never have to leave. He makes the best breakfast. Yours is good, too," he stammers.

"I do have impressive toaster skills." I wink at Daniel, pop a strawberry in my mouth, and head back to Dylan's room while Winter packs their lunches.

Peeking into Dyl's room, I knew he would be asleep again. I smiled at my correct assumption. Walking further into the room, I brush his shaggy hair from his face. "Dylan, you need to get up. I have breakfast ready, and your mom wants to see you before you go to school."

"Is she feeling better?" he mumbles, stretching his long arms and legs again.

"She is. Come on, kid."

"Okay. Can we get ice cream after school?"

He finally relents, gets to his feet, puts on his shoes, and grabs his backpack.

Chuckling, I pat his back as we walk out of the room. "We'll see, but you have to go to school first."

"Why do we have to go to school? Mom owns a bookstore. She could teach us," he argues.

"I don't think it's the same thing, big guy," I tell him, and he lets out an exasperated groan.

In the kitchen, he goes straight to his mom and gives her a big hug.

"Morning, sleepy head," Winter says with a big smile.

I love seeing her with the boys, and I can't help but imagine her with at least two more clinging to her.

"Do you want to ride with us?" I ask her.

"Sure. I was thinking about going to work after."

My eyes snap to her when she mentions going to work. I'm not ready to leave her alone yet. I don't trust anyone right now. I know Summer has Winter well watched, but I don't like it.

"Relax. I have some planning to do."

She sips her coffee and lifts a brow at me, and it clicks. She needs to plan for us to see Troy. I meant it when I told her I want that son of a bitch to know she has a real man now. I have to keep my cool while we confront him. I can't exactly kill the son of a bitch where he is.

"Don't forget the charity event tomorrow. I'll hang out with you. I don't go back on shift for a couple more days."

"I remember. I wanted to go shopping with Summer for a dress. Do you think she's going? Come to think of it, you should check in on Baxter. I'm sure Summer has him on his last nerve." She chuckles.

A burst of laughter breaks free from me.

"He doesn't know what to do with such a strong personality. I'm not sure if she's going. You could always text and ask her if she is."

"Ugh, my head is somewhere else."

When the boys go to wash their teeth, I tug Winnie into my arms and cover her mouth with mine while my hands grab as much of her ass as they can hold.

When I knead her ass cheek, she moans, making my dick want to come to life and burrow inside her for the rest of the day. I would, I want to, but there isn't time for that.

My hands release her as if she has the plague, and we laugh into each other's mouths when we hear both boys at the same time.

"Yuck."

"Are you going to do that all the time?" Dylan asks.

His scrunched, disgusted face makes me laugh even harder when I look at him.

With everyone ready, I grab my keys from the hook and lock up while they all pile into my car. After I lock the door, I look around. I want to see one of the snipers Summer has watching the house, but damn, they're good at staying covered and out of sight.

Sliding into the driver's seat, I start the ignition and head to the school. My mind races with what to expect when she confronts her ex and what excuse he'll give her.

The boys are on their phones, completely engrossed in whatever game they're playing. That happens when they get older. I remember when I got my first phone. I forgot I had a family most of the time. All I paid attention to were the games, then social media, and eventually texting girls. We are not ready for them to have girlfriends yet.

Winnie's warm, slender hand slips into mine, and I look over and see her staring out the window. Her fingers lace with mine, and she holds on as if I would float away. Giving her hand a light squeeze, I reassure her I'm not going anywhere.

No matter how annoyed? Irritated? Hurt? I'm not exactly sure I can explain the feeling I have about her not trusting me. It's a mix of several, and I can't pick which is strongest. Perhaps it's not just that, but everything. Honestly, I hate that her sister came to the damn rescue. I'm the man; it's my job to protect my woman.

Fuck, that made me sound like a chauvinist.

Winnie's phone starts to chime just as the boys say bye and get out of the car in the drop-off lane. Glancing around, I notice one of the guys here to watch over the school today.

"Who was it?" I ask when she ends the call.

"I'm not sure. Maybe another bank I tried to apply to."

Nodding, I pull out of the school and head to the bookstore. Winnie finally breaks the silence, and I catch her shifting in the corner of my eye.

"I'm sorry for hatching an escape plan to see Tory on my own. A part of me thought you would be upset that I wanted to confront him. You're right. I should have trusted you and told you my plans. You have done everything to show me I can trust you. I promise to try harder, Bay. I promise to stop thinking I need to do everything on my own." Her voice comes out soft and genuine.

Inhaling, I bring her hand to my lips and kiss each knuckle.

"It's okay. I want the same trust I give you. What if Tony followed you, Angel? The thought of you sneaking off to confront Troy on your own, and what could have happened." I shake my head and pull into the parking lot behind the store.

With the car in park and the ignition off, I turn in my seat and take in her striking beauty.

"I can't take it. I can't bear the thought of anything happening to you. I'm always here for whatever you need, Winter. If you say a fly kicked a bear's ass, I'm right there with you, backing your story. If you want to join the circus, we'll start a family of clowns. If you want to fight or confront someone, I'm your backup. If you need to cry, I'm the arms you run into. I'm always here. Please believe I'm with you 100%. You never have to do anything on your own again, and you don't have to hide anything from me."

"Damn it, hotshot, that was beautiful," Winter says before leaping from her seat and straddling me.

Her warm mouth captures mine, and our lips part. Her tongue swipes and twirls mine. I will never tire of tasting her. It's been almost a week since I've been inside her, tasted her, or touched her, and my cock is ready. Gripping her plump ass, I pull her flush against me as she rolls her sexy hips. I'm about to take her right here, in the open, in my car.

Before I can go further, there's a tap on the car window. I wrench my lips from hers, and my eyes narrow when they make contact with the group of women hunched over, peering in through the car window.

Great, I'm being cock-blocked by my two sisters-in-law. Why did my brothers have to get married? Winnie giggles and buries her face in my neck when she sees them. I lean forward and gently kiss her delicate shoulder.

"They didn't tell me they'd be here," she says into my neck, then bites it lightly, making me groan.

"You shouldn't do that, babe. It's taking all my control not to fuck you right now."

I chuckle as she huffs into my neck. I know my sweet angel wants it as much as I do.

"Fine, but I really need you, baby. Like, I feel like I'm starving, and you're the only thing that can fill me up." Her sultry voice fills the car. Tonight is not soon enough.

Fucking hell

I lift and scoot her back when another knock comes on the window. I hate the women outside right now. I hate them all.

"I will give you everything you want tonight. All night long."

"Yes, please. I want dirty talk and hard fucking, Baylor."

"Goddamn it, Winnie. You're making it worse. The clam hammer is ready to smash into you."

Winter bursts out laughing at my stupid joke, kisses my cheek, slides off my lap, and gathers her things. "Oh my god, Bay, that was lame but adorable. Guess I have to go out there before Journey gets in the back seat."

"Yeah, I'm not a fan of them around while I'm sporting a baby batter blaster."

Winnie holds up her hand, laughing, and opens the door. "Just stop."

"I will never stop making you laugh and smile. Call me when you're ready for me to pick you up. I like you, Angel."

"I will. I like you, too, hotshot." She gives me a whisper of a kiss and jumps out of the car.

I watch her take off with her friends and think about how lucky I am.

CHAPTER 20
WINTER

"I see you and Bayritto are getting along well," Ny says, looping her arm through mine. "Let Ellie open today. Birdie and I met Summer at the firehouse this week, and she's going to meet us at Birdie's parents' house. We three need dresses for the charity ball."

I pinch my brows and look at my best friend. "Three of us?"

"Yeah. Dad asked me to go with him, and you know I love a reason to wear a fancy dress."

The three of us laugh because she's lying. She's only going because Henry asked her to. He loves telling people he has a daughter, even though she's twenty-seven now.

"I want to go. Beau hasn't had an event like this before. But I do think Mom and Ivey are planning a Victorian ball for Halloween this year, so there's that, I guess," Birdie chirps as we get into Ny's Bronco.

"That sounds fun. I can't wait for that," I tell her, snapping my seat belt in place.

I'm supposed to be planning a trip to Atlanta, but I do need a dress for tomorrow, and Summer will be meeting us there. Guess it's the same as going shopping, and this way we can avoid the crowds.

While Ny drives, I glance in the rearview mirror and see the black car following us. I'm working on being more observant of my surroundings.

Today is the first day I've left Bay's house all week. He's been letting me relax and has been playing dad. Baylor is the most patient person I've ever had the pleasure of being around. All week, he didn't try to touch me; instead, he held me. He projected his love so I would feel it, and damn, did I feel it.

Bay is tender and gentle. Yet he's protective and strong. It made me realize that saying I like you isn't enough anymore. I want him to know how much I love and adore him.

"Do you think it's acceptable for a woman to ask a man to marry her? Specifically, do you think Bay would rebuke the gesture? Not now, but maybe in the future."

The words fly from my lips before my brain can stop them. When the car falls silent, I glance at Ny and Birdie, both in shocked silence.

Even though our relationship is new, the intensity of my feelings for him is overwhelming—a full hurricane. His absence is a violent whipping wind inside me. When he is near, it is the calm center, the eye of the storm, where peace settles, and the winds fall still. But when he leaves again, the full rage of the storm returns.

The feeling of having your person is tranquility and serenity. It is powerful and addictive. I can't picture my life without him anymore. If I don't have him, then who am I?

"Oh my god," Ny finally squeals.

"Yes, I love this. Wow. It's so romantic," Birdie says, starting to tear up in the back seat. "Shit," she says, starting to cry.

"What's wrong?" I ask, turning in my seat. A frown dips my lips as tears streak her cheeks. Does she think Bay would be against the gesture?

"I think I might be pregnant. I told Beau the pill wouldn't hold up to his turbo tadpoles. The big fucker has a breed kink, and I swear he projects it past the barriers I put up," she sobs.

Ny and I both burst out laughing at her sperm joke. I need to know what a breed kink is.

"No offense, but that's why I'm glad I don't have a uterus. It'll be okay, mama. You two want a big family," Ny says with a small smile. I look back at Birdie, reach out, and give her a reassuring pat on the knee.

"Right, yeah, it's fine. Today is about Winter and you. To answer your question, I think you should do it if that's what your heart tells you. I think Bay would accept. He's letting you lead."

Huh, she's right. He's waiting for me to make the next move. Bay tried to be the one to dive in first, but I shut him down, and now he's letting me take over.

"Maybe I'll start with I love you."

"That seems appropriate," Ny says as she parks next to Summer's Range Rover in Birdie's parents' driveway.

Excitement zings through me. I haven't seen Summer since the cameras were installed, and I miss her. She and I need a night to catch up and get to know each other. I want to know whether she ever found love and learn more about her career. I want time with her, uninterrupted.

Jumping out of the car, I notice hers is empty. Huh, she must be inside already.

"Your sister isn't shy, is she?" Birdie laughs as we walk to the front door, and she opens it. Laughter echoes through the house.

"She is definitely not shy, and we should be worried about what comes out of her mouth."

As we move closer, we hear her telling her story.

"Needless to say, we failed the drill, but the worst part was that I wore Powerpuff Girls underwear that day and ripped the ass out of my pants on barbed wire, so everyone saw them. I was swiftly nicknamed Power Puff."

Freddie and Tilly's laughter grows as she finishes the story.

"That's why Colburn called you that? I thought it was because you did something badass. And here I thought you were a tough girl," I joke with her as we enter the room.

Summer's sapphire eyes meet mine, and she gives me a broad grin. "Well, an ass was involved. There just wasn't anything bad about it. And tough chicks like fun underwear as much as the next girl," Summer laughs.

"It's good to see Bax hasn't killed you yet," Ny says lightly. I know she's trying to give her a chance.

Summer cracks up at that. "The big Yeti likes it. He needs to be reminded how to find his shine again. I gathered the information and can see why he's so dime."

"How the hell do you do that so quickly?" Birdie asks.

Summer lifts a shoulder as if her ability to get information on demand isn't a big deal. "I'm a whore for knowledge, and quick with my fingers on a keyboard."

"Are you girls ready to look through dresses?" Tilly asks, getting to her feet.

"Hellz yeah. I don't have my dress uniform yet, so I get to feel like a lady tomorrow night. Fancy me up, Mama T," Summer says enthusiastically.

"Summer, I mean no offense, but have you ever worn a dress?"

"Many, many moons ago, back when I was a wee fairy. They have since been replaced with armor and weapons." Summer throws her head back and lets out a dark chuckle.

I'm starting to think something happened to her brain. We all shake our heads and follow behind her and Tilly.

Awe strikes me when I enter Tilly's dressing room. It's huge. Every wall is lined with extravagant gowns in every color. Summer b-lines to the green section and starts shuffling through them. Ny goes for blue, and I gravitate to the deep reds. I want to feel beautiful and sexy. In my mind, red is a sexy color. Red says fuck me until I can't walk for three days.

"Excellent color. A bold cherry will be gorgeous with your blonde hair and porcelain skin tone," Tilly says beside me, then slides through dresses until she lands on one she wants, and her eyes light up.

Lifting it from the rack, she hands it to me and points to the other room. "Try this."

My fingers graze the heavy satin. This is no cheap dress. It's rich, sophisticated, and screams fuck me.

A grin spreads across my face as I stare at it, completely mesmerized by its beauty.

In the changing room, I slip into the cherry-red mermaid-style dress with a draped back. It's a snug fit that hugs all my curves, accentuating my best qualities. An asymmetrical sheer one-shoulder drape adds flair. The bodice is embellished at the bust with black jewels, features a dramatic dip between the breasts that shows the perfect amount of cleavage, and includes a bold high side slit up the thigh. As I walk, the skirt flows and sways behind me.

Holy hotness, this might be too much. But damn, I look good. This dress is luxurious, powerful, and unapologetically glamorous.

When I step out of the changing room, the girls whistle and hoot at me.

"Yes. That's the one—hot, mama. If I were into girls, Briggs would have to worry right now. Hell, he might have to anyway. Damn, Winter, you look stunning." Ny compliments me while continuing to eye-bang me.

"It's not too much?" I blink into the floor-length mirror, loving how I look and feel in this dress. I've never worn anything this nice.

"Hell no. Bays is going to cum in his pants just looking at you," Summer pipes in.

"You're a queen. I love your hair and complexion," Birdie says, not taking her eyes off me.

"Are you bringing Baxter?" I ask, then turn to look at my ass in the mirror.

"I'm not sure. He didn't answer when I asked, but Col said he would if Baxter didn't."

"I have to ask because he is a gorgeous man. Have you, you know..." I ask, genuinely curious.

Summer lets out a laugh and shakes her head. "He's pretty, but let's say I'm not his type, and neither are any of you," she says without saying.

"Got it. I think Baxter will cave. He has a hard time saying no to beautiful women," Birdie pipes in cheerfully.

Summer snorts. "I won't be pussy-punched either way. I don't think he classifies me as a woman."

She's completely unbothered as she grabs the dress she's been eyeing and steps into the next room.

While we wait, Tilly pins a few spots on my dress. After a few minutes, my jaw hits the floor as Summer steps out in a floor-length, body-hugging dress made of sheer nude mesh, revealing bare flesh. Over the mesh is an intricate emerald-green vine-leaf lace fabric. The deep V-neckline reaches the middle of her stomach, with long, sheer sleeves. The dress is fitted to her body, showing off her petite hourglass figure and the same bubbled ass that I have. Her freckles look like fire embers covering her flesh.

"Holy shit. Bax will see you as a woman in that fucking dress. The green makes your hair look like flames," Ny says as she steps out next.

Her dress is a long-sleeved, velvet, floor-length gown that covers her well while still showing off her gorgeous body. The mid-thigh slit gives it a little extra. I get it. She's going with her father, and Briggs might stroke out if she wore something too sexy. She still looks like the model she is.

"I want to go," Birdie whines.

"Damn it, Birdie. When will you and Beau learn?" Tilly huffs, but a grin spreads across her face.

"Shush. I'm just having a weird day," she fires back at her mother.

"Oh, sweet beauty. Do you want to be my date?" Summer asks Birdie, rubbing her arm.

"I want to, but I think you should have someone stronger than me there, just in case anything happens. Winter's safety is more important than my selfish desire to wear a dress. I need to text Beau." Birdie sniffles, pulls out her phone, and leaves the room.

Summer whistles once Birdie's out of the room, and Birdie's comment reminds me of the threat I'm still facing. I should be focusing on booking flights to Atlanta, not playing dress-up.

"Can you wear heels?" Ny asks Summer.

“They make prosthetic feet that make it possible, but I prefer flats. It’s easier to run in them if I need to. I have a pair of gold strappy sandals I can wear. I was never a fan of heels, so I have a few other options.”

“I can hem the bottom for you,” Tilly tells her, then starts pinning the length of Summer's dress when she’s done with mine.

“Ok, Winter, I need to know. Is Bay,” Ny stops and puts her hand at the base of her neck, wiggling her brows.

“I bet he’s a dirty talker, isn’t he? He has that personality. I bet he calls you a good girl and smacks your ass.” Summer laughs.

Embarrassment makes my face heat up. I know I’m as red as the dress I’m wearing.

“Dear lord, do you girls have no shame?” Tilly laughs and shakes her head.

“I agree with Tilly,” I tell them, then start moving toward the bathroom. Ny stops me and unzips the back for me so I don’t have to struggle with it. Holding the chest of it up, I refuse to respond to their perverted conversation.

“She didn’t answer, which means we’re right. Bay’s a dirty boy. Good for her. Personally, I like to watch a man crawl to me, then call him a good boy for doing what he’s told. You should try it. It’s hot watching a man do what he’s told,” Summer says.

“Are you going to make Bax get on all fours?” Ny chuckles.

“Hm, don’t underestimate my femininity. He may be a Yeti, but I could get him on all fours, barking like a dog. Though I have a feeling he’s rough in the sack, and I could use a good, angry pounding. If he fucked me hard enough, I might call him Daddy.”

"Oh my god, I think I might actually love you. I was skeptical at first, but I like you." Ny throws her head back with a laugh.

"I'm kidding about Baxter. He has ex baggage. Sex with someone carrying all that around is the worst. You're guaranteed not to bust a load," Summer says, scrunching her nose.

"Wow. It just keeps coming out of you," Tilly chuckles.

"I have a leak in my brain that causes word sewage to seep out of me," Summer jokes as I close the dressing room door and shake my head. She isn't lying about that.

I slip off the dress and hang it neatly back on the hanger. I put on my own dress and jacket, then gathered my belongings.

I'm not the kind of person who enjoys talking about what it's like to be with the person I love. I don't want them picturing what Bay is like in bed. I know it's innocent, but I don't like it. Bay prefers to keep what happens between us private. He shows me I'm the only person he sees and wants to be with.

When my phone rings, I dig it out of my purse and check the caller ID. It's the same number from this morning. I inhale, then swipe to answer.

"Hello."

"Hello, is this Ms. Anderson?" a gruff male voice says on the other end.

"May I ask who's calling?" I'm not saying shit until I know who this is.

"This is Agent Sampson. Is this Ms. Winter Anderson?"

My brows shoot up. Panic takes hold, and I end the call. Shit, I just hung up on an agent. Wait, what if it wasn't an agent? What if it was someone pretending? Oh god. I do not need this added to the pile of dog shit that is this disaster right now.

My face must show my anxiety as I walk out of the bathroom. Summer's eyes meet mine, and her smile fades into a serious look.

"What's wrong?"

Stepping away from Tilly, she walks over and holds my shaking hands.

"I, ah, I just got a call. The guy said his name was Agent Sampson."

"Okay, remember, I told you this would happen once Beau's search hit. If he's calling, he's likely already here and gathering information."

"What are we going to do now? If Tony finds out, Bay," my voice cracks at the thought of what could happen.

"Hey, I'll take care of it. If it's Agent Sampson, I'm thinking he'll listen to me."

"Who are you? Are you a spy or something?" I ask, my voice shaky.

"Or something. Nothing will happen to Bay while I'm helping with this. I need to change. I have an idea where Sampson is. I'll meet you at your place tomorrow, and we can get ready together." Summer leaves no room for further discussion as she steps away.

Glancing at Ny, she gives me a slight tilt of her lips. Taking a seat, I wait for her to change and take me back to the bookstore, where I can start planning my and Bay's trip next week.

CHAPTER 21
WINTER

As I stare into the mirror, I consider my next move. The kids asked to stay with Ox and Lux tonight. Bay and I finally have a night alone, and I'm deciding what to do. Food or sex?

Bay is in the kitchen, cooking a recipe he wanted to try, while I'm looking at my wet, naked body in the mirror. I should leave him alone and let him cook, but I haven't stopped thinking about him all damn day.

Tonight, I'm going to tell him how much I love him. I know he loves me and is waiting for me to say it first. Is it too bold to walk out naked? It tells him what I'm thinking, and I'm not in the mood to fuck around with clothes tonight. I want him on top of me, under me, behind me, and beside me all damn night. Just the thought of all the positions I want him in sends heat radiating from my core. The thrill makes my nipples peak.

My mind is made up; I slip on the glasses that make his dick hard and start moving. He can burn the food for all I care. I want him now. I don't want to think about the agent or the plans to see an ex. I only want him inside me, distracting me from reality.

Swinging the bathroom door open, I stroll through our bedroom and open the next door. My feet patter silently on the cold hardwood. The savory scent of beef, pork, and onions fills the air, making it feel homey and comforting.

I almost stop to take in Bay's sculpted back muscles showing through his tight shirt, the backwards hat on his head, and his perfectly rounded, taut ass. Fuck, he is too damn pretty, and he is mine.

Bay's back is to me. I see his arm muscles flex as he reaches out and turns the stove off. Good, dinner won't be ruined. We're about to have a hella workout, and we'll need the carbs afterward.

When I stop behind him, I say nothing. I grab the hem of his shirt and start lifting. Bay chuckles, reaches up, takes off his hat, and lets me remove his shirt. As I press my body to his, I feel him melt as my bare flesh meets his.

"Mm, babe, are you naked or shirtless? Please tell me you're naked," he says, both hands out, fingers crossed.

My lip tilts up. I step onto my tiptoes and bring my lips to his ear.

"You should turn around and find out, but first, I want your pants off. Can you do that for me like a good boy?" I ask, turning the dirty talk around.

Holy shit, who am I right now? It's all the sex talk earlier. I run my fingers lightly down his side, almost like a secret on his skin. My palms flatten as I reach his V-line, and I let the feel of the dipped muscle send a fresh shock through me. The wetness is starting to coat my inner thighs.

I bite his shoulder blade as I flick open his jeans and unzip him. Slipping my hands inside the waistband of his boxers, I slide his clothes off. Bay steps out of the restraints and kicks them aside. He doesn't try to take control. He's allowing me to take what I want from him.

"Fucking hell, Angel." He groans, and his hips jerk when I wrap my hand around his hardness and stroke.

His control finally slips, and he stops my hand. Spinning in my arms, I catch my breath as his mucky lake-green eyes meet mine. The need to possess me has taken over, and I can tell he's about to take what he wants and needs.

Bay lets out an animalistic growl. "You're wearing the glasses."

I knew he would like them. He's got that nerdy-girl, bad-boy fantasy.

Large, thick fingers dig into my ass, and my arms fly around his neck just before he lifts me. My legs lock around his waist, his hardness positioned perfectly between my slit.

I could cum just like this. Molten heat rocks my core with the feel of him nestled on my bud. My hips move, stroking his length against my clit.

Bay grabs my neck with his free hand and pulls my lips to his. Reflex has me opening for him, my tongue racing out to meet his on the battlefield of our lust. Bay's kisses are promises of love, filthy words, and fierce conviction.

I hold him tighter, deepening our kiss, and move my body so my clit rubs up and down his massive length while he moves us to the couch. He's skilled and fluent in kissing; hell, he's adept at everything he does.

Bay sits, digs his fingers into my hair, and yanks my mouth away from his. My eyes meet his, and he gives me a dark smirk.

"I want you to ride my cock and take whatever you want. You're going to fuck me until you milk us both dry. Can you do that, baby?" Bay asks, biting his bottom lip as his hand twists and teases my breast.

"Y-yes." I moan.

Bay leans in and licks my lips, then trails kisses along my jaw. He stops at my ear and bites my lobe.

"Good girl. Now, ride me." He commands, and fuck me, I obey.

His strong fingers grip my upper thighs, bruisingly tight, as he lifts me, positions me so he can slip his tip in, and slams me down as he thrusts up hard. My scream rips through the house. Pain and pleasure sear through me from the impalement.

Full. I'm so damn full. I'm tightly stretched, and I think he just hit the bottom of my stomach.

"It's all yours, beautiful." Bay lifts me again and pounds me down.

We both want a rough, dirty fuck, and he's about to deliver. I finally regain control and take over.

My fingers pierce his hair, and I pull hard as I glide up his shaft to the tip and back down. Hard and relentlessly. I fuck him like he's my breath and I need air.

"Yeah, baby. Like that. Christ, Winnie." Bay groans and holds my hips as I roll and snap quickly. The feel of him hitting what seems to be every organ in my lower half is too good. Shifting my angle, I let each movement tease my swollen clit.

When his hand wraps around my throat again, and he starts thrusting up, sparks begin to flicker in the darkness. My pussy tightens, and I know I'm about to explode.

I want him to feel the raw, rough desire fueling me. Releasing his hair, I move both hands to his pecs and dig my nails in as I ride him faster.

With my climax on the horizon, I drag my nails down his tight, taut stomach.

"Mm, make me bleed. Leave every mark you can. I want everyone to know this cock belongs to you." His voice comes out hoarse, and his head tips back.

"Are you going to cum for me, baby?" I ask, picking up the pace.

"So fucking hard," he grunts, pumping faster.

"Ah," I cry out when he hits my G-spot. "I want to spend forever with you, Baylor. I want to be your wife. I want your babies. I want your love. I want it all. You're mine. Only mine. Tell me, baby. I need to hear you say it." I beg, bouncing in rhythm with his thrusts.

My breath quickens, and my heart swells to a new size to accommodate the love flowing through me like a river.

"Holy shit. Yes. Yes, to all of it, Angel. I'm yours. Only yours, and you're mine." He rasps, grabs my hips, and holds me in place as he slams into me with each word. "All. Fucking. Mine."

"Oh, God, I'm cumming, baby. I love you, Bay." I scream and squeeze my eyes shut as my pussy sucks and pulses around him. The orgasm takes hold with a force that feels like the biggest explosion I've ever experienced. Love, devotion, strength, trust, lust, and passion rain down inside me. My vision blurs from the intensity of my climax.

"I love you, Winnie. So goddamn much." He roars, slamming me down one last time, bringing me closer, biting my shoulder, and holding me there as warm ribbons of liquid fill me until I'm overflowing.

Bay cradles the back of my head and brings my lips to his in a slow, lazy kiss while we ride out the orgasm and the feelings of our confessions to each other. Our tongues dance and twirl together.

It feels good to tell this man how much I love him and what I want. It feels good to hear he feels everything I do. Drawing back, I cup his flushed cheeks and look at the claw marks where blood beads in some spots. Shit, I got carried away.

"I didn't mean to tell you all of that like this. It was supposed to be special when I told you, and I made you bleed."

Bay chuckles and moves the damp hair from my face.

"Babe, I was balls deep inside you when you told me. I think that was special enough. I wanted the marks." He thumbs my cheek and gives me a breath-stealing smile. "You meant it, though?"

"I did. All of it. I love you, Baylor Levi."

"I love you, Winter Sky. That's such a hippie name." He jokes, and I playfully slap his chest.

"Stop. That's why I don't tell people." I giggle.

"I'm kidding. It's a beautiful name because it's yours." Bay kisses each cheek, then my forehead, before he holds me to him, stands, and walks us to the bathroom, where he tentatively sets me on the counter, slips from me, and cleans me with a warm cloth, as he always does.

"After we eat, I want you again," I tell him.

I'm ready now, but we should eat and let Nila out first.

"I'm all yours whenever you want," he tells me, helping me off the counter.

Once we were dressed, Bay reheated the meal he had cooked while I let Nila out. Stepping onto the porch, I inhale the fresh, warm late-evening air. I watch the sun set in the distance and take in the beautiful, vibrant reds, oranges, and yellows.

A loud pop, pop, pop, and a *'WHAT THE FUCK'* scream have me whipping around to see Bay rushing to the front door and flinging it open. I enter the house and wait. My heart hammers and skips as I wait to see what's going on.

“Karson, what the hell are you doing here? You never come to my house,” Baylor yells at the man outside.

I take a few steps and tilt my head to look out the door. There's a tall, skinny young guy on the stairs, hands up.

“Seriously, someone just shot at me, and that's your question?” Karson yells back without moving a muscle.

The snipers Summer has here aren't playing around. I forgot they were even here.

“Who are you?” Col appears out of nowhere behind the man.

“Is it safe to move? I work with Baylor. I came to ask if he had an extra white dress shirt.”

“No. It’s not safe to move.” Col’s voice is commanding, authoritative. I hear the shuffle of feet before Col speaks again. “Why do you have this?”

“I have a permit. Plenty of people conceal carry.”

“You could have texted Karson. Why show up?”

My body stiffens for a moment, but Col must be overreacting. The man works with Bay and Henry. Surely he’s harmless, and he’s right about carrying.

Turning on my heels, I stride to the bedroom, grab one of Bay's extra shirts, and stomp outside. I’m not stupid about how Bay feels about men seeing me, and I’m in short-ass shorts and a crop top, so I stay behind him and hold the shirt in front of him.

“Here,” I tell him. Bay takes it and places my arm around his middle.

“Next time, call or text.”

“What the hell is going on, Baylor?”

“It’s not your business. There's the shirt. You can give it back to me at work on Monday. I’m serious, Karson. Do not come back here unannounced.”

“Sure, okay. See you Monday. Thanks.”

I look around Bay's puffed-up frame and see Col step aside, keeping his weapon trained on the target, while Karson gets into his car and drives off.

"Thanks. Sorry about that. He's never shown up like that," Bay tells Col.

"That's why we're here. I'm going to look into him. You two are safe. We've got eyes, and I'll stop Power Puff from storming in here. I'm sure the snips called her already," Col says.

"Yeah, ah, thanks again."

Bay turns, blocking me from Col's view. I assume not many people know the man is gay, and that looking at me is the last thing he would do.

Inside, I take a seat at the island, and Bay sets a plate in front of me.

"It's weird he decided to show up. I've known Karson for a few years, and he's never been here," Bay says, then sits with his plate. He's clearly still annoyed with his co-worker.

"Do you think he's dangerous?" I ask, take a bite of the Swedish meatball with potatoes, and moan. Holy shit, it's good. "This is amazing," I say with a mouthful.

"I'm glad you like them. I don't think he's dangerous. I think I'm paranoid and suspicious of everyone right now. He probably wasn't thinking and just needed the shirt."

"I'm sorry. Maybe Troy will slip next week and give us information about the flash drive. Maybe that will be enough to get Tony to leave. If that doesn't, I'm sure federal agents will."

"What?" Bay looks at me questioningly.

"Shit, I wasn't hiding it. I swear. I was focused on one thing when you picked me up. I told you I was seeing Troy next week. I wasn't thinking about the agent who called me. Summer said she would take care of it. I assume that means she'll make sure they're discreet."

"What did the agent say when he called?"

My face burns, and I look down at my food. This is embarrassing.

"I panicked and hung up on him as soon as he told me his name. All the thoughts that he could be lying ran through my head, and then I panicked, thinking about what might happen to you if Tony finds out they're here." I rush out.

For a second, I worry he thinks I'm lying again until he brings his other hand out with a laugh and thumbs my cheek.

"You're adorable. Nothing is going to happen to me. Tony had to know it was a matter of time."

"What if he thought I was some stupid girl who didn't know her feet from her ass? He probably thought I would roll over and do what he said without question."

"Then he's an idiot for underestimating you." I scoff at that. If it weren't for Summer, I'd be a sitting duck. I'm still a sitting duck. I haven't heard from Tony this week, but today was the first day I left the house, and I was with friends or Bay. I know he won't track me down if I'm with people. Baylor might be right, though. Tony or one of his goons may follow us to visit Troy.

"I don't know. It's nerve-racking not knowing what the next move will be. At least for tonight, we know we're fine, and the kids are safe with Ny and Briggs," I say.

"Both things are true. So how about you finish eating so I can fuck you again?"

A smirk crosses my face when I see the devilish mischief in Bay's eyes.

Not wasting any more time, I shovel the rest of my food into my mouth, making him laugh. As soon as I swallow, Bay picks me up, tosses me over his shoulder, and strides to the bedroom without another word.

CHAPTER 22
BAYLOR

"Can you come by?" Baxter asks on the other end of the phone.

"Sure. The girls are getting dressed here. I can change at your place."

"Sounds good. See you in a few."

That's all he says before the call ends. Alrighty then. He's in a mood today.

In the closet, I adjust myself. Winnie and I fucked so much last night that my dick hurts today. I shuffle through my clothes and pick out my dress uniform and shoes. Summer and Ny showed up about twenty minutes ago and have been waiting for me to leave so they can all get ready for tonight. They all know I do not want them in my and Winnie's room, so they have decided to get ready in the living room once I leave.

With my shit in my arms, I exit the room and see Journey already starting Winters' makeup. I stop in my tracks, and they chuckle when Winnie looks at me. Only one eye has black makeup. It looks like she got punched.

"Trust the process, Homefry. She will be stunning by the time we meet you there," Ny says, then keeps working.

"I have no doubt she will be gorgeous no matter what." I walk over and kiss her temple. "See you in a bit. Love you, babe."

"Love you too," she says with a big grin.

"I love you both, too. Now go," Ny says, pushing me aside.

Chuckling, I kiss Winnie once more and walk out the front door.

"Bay," Summers' voice calls out behind me as I'm loading my clothes into the car.

"Yeah."

"Listen. Tonight, you need to watch your surroundings. There's been movement among Tony's guys, and I'm not sure what it means yet. He could be shuffling them, or they could be planning something. Col is with a few agents, keeping an eye on them. I don't want to worry, Winter, but I need you to stay sharp. Beau and his partner, Noah, will be patrolling the area. Stay close to her." Summer says in her professional, authoritative tone.

"I will. I'll protect her with my life. I won't get distracted."

"Okay." Summer nods and steps back inside. It's weird seeing her so concerned and less confident. I need to stay focused. If she's worried, I should be too.

I sit in the driver's seat, start the ignition, and grip the steering wheel so tightly that my hand starts to sweat and my knuckles turn white as I drive.

As I arrive at Baxter's place, I park and grab my shit. Anxiety I haven't felt before is rioting through me, shaking me. I need to calm down. I cannot let this feeling control me; otherwise, I will make a mistake. "Treat it like you do when you're in a fire," I tell myself.

When I step inside, I'm greeted by the scent of vanilla cupcakes. Must be Summer's doing, since it usually smells like cologne and motor oil in here.

"What the fuck am I supposed to wear? I'm huge, and I don't have suits that flex well. By that, I mean Summer told me we need to be on alert. I'll have my weapon, but if we need to run or fight, I can't have a suit restricting me," Baxter grumps. I look at the couch and see multiple suits. My eyes flick to him, and I burst out laughing. Baxter has a fucking mustache.

"What's on your face?"

"I'm trying something new," he says, using his pointer and middle fingers to smooth it down, making me laugh harder.

"Ok, Sam Elliot. What are these?" I ask, gesturing to all the suits.

"I got them from Freddie since we're the same size. I own one suit, and I've worn it three times. Grams' funeral, Gramps' funeral, and that stupid masquerade ball two years ago. And well, it's tight now," he says, staring at the suits.

"Put on some weight there, buddy?" I joke.

"I told you I sat around on my fat ass. Just help me pick one so we can get this night over with."

"So sorry, my girlfriend's life being in danger is such an inconvenience. Col was going to do it before the FBI got involved and is busy with them," I snap.

"Shit, I didn't mean it like that. Summer gets under my skin and riles me up. She's infuriating, but keeping you and Winter safe is her priority tonight. She was, I don't know, different before she left, which is troublesome. Her silly craziness wasn't there. She was all military."

I toss my clothes onto the end of the couch, then walk around, feeling the fabric for one that stretches.

"I know. She stopped me before I left," I tell him, then toss him a suit that might work. "That one has stretch in the fabric. It shouldn't restrict your movements."

"Thank you. Look, I didn't mean to be an ass. You and Winter have a ton of people looking out for you tonight. Summer wanted it to be legal, so the FBI brought in their own team for tonight." Bax says, then starts taking off his pants.

"Dude, what the fuck."

Bax rolls his eyes. "I'm wearing underwear, and you're my brother. Stop making it weird."

"You made it weird. I don't want to see you tuck your dick into your pants."

"What's wrong, little bro? Are you worried mine's bigger than yours? Don't worry, yours is still growing. You'll get there." Bax laughs and turns away from me to finish getting his pants on. I can't help but laugh, too. It's nice to hear him joke again.

"Is that always going to be a thing because I'm the youngest?"

"Probably. Better," he says, turning back around with his pants in place. "Are you going to freak out if I change my shirt now?"

"No, you asshole. I'm going to the bathroom to get dressed."

I turn and walk upstairs to the bathroom to change into my own clothes. We can do this. Winnie will be safe tonight.

Back in the living room, Bax is put together and has all the other suits put away. He even brushed his overgrown hair back.

Checking the time, we have about an hour before the event starts. I'm sure people will be showing up sooner, like we will, so we can survey the area.

"Ready? I want to get there to look around before this thing starts." I check with Bax.

“Yup, one second,” Baxter says, then jogs up the stairs. A few minutes later, he stomps back down and tucks his weapon into the back of his waistband.

Time to get this night started.

As we wait out front with Baxter and Henry, we keep our eyes open. He told me Summer filled him in on what’s happening, and according to Briggs, Henry is some badass.

I straighten my posture, and my stomach dips as the red Range Rover approaches. I inhale and wait impatiently as Summer pulls in, and she and Ny get out on the same side.

Baxter sucks in a breath and whispers, “Fucking hell.”

I knew it.

Summer is still in protective mode when Winter's door opens, and she steps out in the most stunning red dress I have ever seen on a woman.

My heart stops, and my lungs still as I take in the magnificent beauty of my soon-to-be fiancée. I definitely plan to propose. The dress hugs every curve, pushing her breasts up. So much porcelain cleavage. Ny did her makeup in a black smoky eye, I think they call it. Her thick blonde lashes are now black, and bright red lipstick is painted on her plump lips.

Winter's blonde hair is up in an intricate, curly style. I can’t believe she's mine.

My feet move when Baxter nudges me. I quickly go to her, scoop her up in my arms, and lock my mouth to hers. The explosion of candy and innocence hits my taste buds as our tongues twirl together.

Winter giggles into my mouth, and I break the heated moment before I go Tarzan on her.

"Gorgeous. Absolutely, incredibly gorgeous," I whisper to her.

"Thank you. You look quite handsome yourself."

"I almost don't want to show you off in this dress. I don't want anyone else to see what's mine."

"Mm, I will always be yours, and everyone here will know it."

"I know. I'm being selfish. Come on, it should be starting soon."

Winter happily loops her arm through mine and lets me guide her inside.

Inside, the place is decorated in a sophisticated, elegant style with bold red, black, and gold. There's a hum of conversation and music in the background. Men and women walk in dress uniforms or formal attire. Scents of perfume and cologne linger in the air. The tables are decorated with miniature fire hydrants as centerpieces, and elegant plating surrounds them.

In the corner, the silent auction was set up. With my hand on the small of Winters' back, we moved through the tables.

The crowd moved easily as people stopped to read and bid on auction items. Looking through, we saw all kinds of things: a boat, basketball tickets, spa certificates, autographed items, and a mini vacation.

"They have some neat stuff," Winter said, looking at the couple retreating into the mountains in the fall.

"Do you want to put in a bid?"

Winnie snorted with a small laugh. "No. I'm happy being at home and watching scary movies with you for the weekend."

I roll my eyes, put down a number, and move her along. Six grand might get it. We'll need it after all this shit with Tony is wrapped up.

At the table, I pull out Winnie's chair, placing her between Baxter and me. Neither of us will let her out of our sights. After a few minutes of silence, Winter looks at her sister and tilts her head.

"Are you ok, Summer? You haven't said much tonight."

I flick my gaze to Summer and see her mindlessly playing with the skin on one of Baxter's knuckles, like she doesn't realize she's doing it, while scanning the room. Baxter isn't moving either, watching the area with her.

"Hm," she says, then brings her other hand up, touches her ear, and nods. Huh, I didn't realize she had an earpiece in.

Winnie giggles and leans forward. "You haven't said much, and you've been fidgeting with Baxter's hand since we sat down."

Summer yanks her hand away, murmurs sorry under her breath, then pastes on her signature smirk.

"Perfect. Baxy's so hot in that suit it's taking all my brain power not to pork him in front of everyone. Have you seen his beautiful mustache? I mean, wowza. It makes me want to ride his face." Summer reaches up and fingers the corner of his mustache.

"And she's back," Baxter grunts. Summer winks, then goes back to watching the room.

"You like it, Yeti."

"Debatable."

My eyes land on Karson pulling out a chair. I pinch my brows when I see he's in a standard black suit. I assume he came by to borrow a white shirt to go with his dress uniform.

“Thought we were supposed to be in our dress suits?” I ask him.

“Yeah, I burned the pant leg while ironing. Cap said this was okay.”

Karson rakes his fingers through his hair and leans forward on the table.

“No date?”

“Nah. I wasn’t dating anyone when I sent my RSVP. Megs wasn’t too happy, but there wasn't much I could do about it.”

Of course, she was. The woman is a bitch who thinks the world should revolve around her.

“There’s always next year.”

“Yeah, are we going to skip over what happened last night?” Karson asks with a squint.

“That’s the plan.”

Karson grunts and leans back in his chair, but I don’t miss the way he watches Winnie's cleavage. My skin heats with annoyance. I know Winnie is stunning and people will look, but I don’t like it, especially when he’s staring at her tits.

The conversation stalls when the food arrives. I scan the room while everyone eats, watching for anyone who looks off, but I’m not trained for this. The place is crawling with people I’m not used to seeing. There are only two people I recognize by face. I doubt Tony will show up, but the sister might.

Dinner goes smoothly, with the girls making light conversation. I’m not really paying attention until I feel Winter's hand on my thigh. I turn my attention to her and relax somewhat when I see the smile on her face.

“Do you want to dance?” Her soft, feminine voice is like a siren's call. I’d dance even if I didn’t want to, just because she wants to.

“Sure,”

As I rise to my feet, I hold out my hand. Winnie's cold palm slips into mine, our fingers twine, and we walk to the dance floor.

I smooth one hand behind her back and leave the other in hers. Winnie places a hand on my shoulder, and I lead the dance. Soft, melodic music flows around us. Our steps and sways fall into rhythm.

A smile stretches my face when I look down and see her bright eyes and grinning face staring up at me. Tugging her closer, I make her giggle. I love that she's happy right now. I wonder what she's feeling. Is she excited to be here, letting all these people know she's mine? I am. I want every fucker who's staring at her right now to know she's off limits. That's a partial lie. I want to stab their eyes out, too.

When the music ends, I dip her and brush my lips against hers.

"Are you having fun?" I ask once she's upright and back in both my arms.

"I am. Thank you for bringing me. I feel like I'm at a gala. I do have to use the restroom, though. You kept a tight hold on me, but nature is calling." She says, with a little wiggle.

"Okay, I'll walk you," I tell her, leading her to the restrooms.

"I'll walk with her. I have to go," Summer says, taking Winnie's hand. There's no doubt Summer isn't letting Winter out of any of our sights.

I keep my eyes on her until she enters the restroom. After a few minutes of watching, I decide she's safe with Summer. I turn to head back to the table, but Karson intercepts me.

"Hey, man. I want to say I'm sorry," he starts.

The moment he speaks, the fire alarm blares, and the smell of smoke hits me. Chaos erupts when someone shouts, "There's a fire!" and everyone rushes for the door. I spin back to face Karson.

"What did you do?" I demand, turning away.

"He said if I didn't, it would be Megan," Karson blurts out. "All I had to do was cause a distraction and keep you from leaving." He then throws a punch that lands squarely on the bridge of my nose, making me stagger back.

What the actual fuck?

Not happening. I lunged, grabbed his shirt, pulled back, and punched him twice, each landing hard on his jaw. I released him, and he stumbled back, trying to regain his footing before lunging at me again. I landed two more swings before Bax materialized, locking Karson in a headlock from behind.

"Get the girls," Bax snarled at me, his grip tight on Karson.

I spun on my heels, shoving through the crowd. My eyes fell on Summer as she stumbled into view, her face bloody and a slash across the side of her dress.

"West exit. Now," she shouted.

I turned and raced left, tearing through the smoke-filled building. I wouldn't stop until I found Winter.

My heart hammered against my ribs, driven by a surge of pure adrenaline and instinct. I flung the doors open to the night. Sirens cut through the silence. I scanned the scene and spotted a black SUV speeding past. Through the window, I saw Winter's wide, terrified eyes.

I pumped my legs and sprinted after the vehicle. Around the corner, I spotted Beau's cruiser and two other black SUVs. A volley of sharp, loud cracks pierced the air as glass shattered. The vehicle Winter was in swerved violently to the right, slamming into the back of another SUV.

My forward motion stopped abruptly as Beau, Noah, and several other men in suits drew their weapons and pointed them at the vehicle. Red and blue flashing lights illuminated the black sky.

"Stop. Winter is in there," I shout, but Baxter grabs me from behind, preventing me from reaching Winnie. I start yelling and struggling against him. "What are you doing?"

"You need to let them do their job. They won't let anything happen to her. This is why they were here." He's being logical, I know, but I'm not. Not at all. I can't breathe; the world is slowly crumbling around me. Standing here, waiting, watching, while doing nothing is one of the hardest things I've ever done.

"Get out with your hands up," Beau's voice travels.

Just let Winnie be okay.

I don't give a damn about anyone else in that car. My lungs freeze, and my heart pounds as we wait for the standoff to end.

Finally, two men exit the SUV. As their arms rise, weapons in hand, shots ring out. Both men are on the ground. The gunfire ceases, and silence stills the air. After a few moments, Beau shouts again.

"Get out with your hands up."

Everything has stopped, as if time has paused.

The SUV's back door opens agonizingly slowly, and Winnie steps out. I thought she was okay, but that hope shatters when the second woman, Tony's sister, emerges, a gun pressed to Winter's head. My stomach plummets, and the air rushes from my lungs.

No, no, no.

Baxter held me firmly, forcing me to watch. My sweet angel's crystal eyes filled with tears; her whole body trembled. The fear radiating from her sent a sharp ache through my heart, and I fought back my own tears.

“I have to say I’m impressed. It appears my brother misjudged this town's capabilities. I’ll let you have her,” she shouted with a smirk.

My eyes darted behind them. A shadow shifted, and then Summer stepped into view a short distance away. Blood still stained her face. Her weapon was aimed, and her finger rested on the trigger.

“Lower your weapon and let her walk to us,” Beau yelled, lowering his own weapon and stepping forward.

The woman, Liz, nudged Winter with the gun, compelling her unsteady feet to move, and slightly lowered her own weapon.

Liz raises her arm just as Winnie is four feet away. Two sharp, whip-like shots split the air, followed by Winter's piercing scream.

“Winter,” I yell, my voice catching in my throat as tears burn my eyes. My legs propel me forward. I can't process what's happening or who was hit. All I know is that I have to reach Winter and hold her.

I shut out the surrounding chaos, my entire focus fixed on her—the love of my life. She's standing; she's okay. Her bloodshot eyes find mine, and she rushes toward me.

When we collide, I crush her against me, holding her as tightly as I can while she sobs into my neck. Her fearful tears soak my skin and shirt.

“I'm here, baby. Always here.”

Winnie's sobs intensify, and only then do I truly notice my surroundings. Beau is pressing something against Liz's arm. My gaze shifts to Baxter, who walks past us, carrying Summer.

“Henry,” Baxter shouts.

I set Winnie on her feet, hiding her face as Henry rushes over and checks Summer.

"Where's Summer? Liz caught her off guard. She was hurt, Baylor," Winter says, trying to shove me away.

"Henry's checking on her, and Baxter won't let her out of his sight. She's in good hands. She's going to be okay."

Winter holds on to me tighter and starts crying again. I need to tell Henry about Karson, but I have a feeling Baxter will make sure he knows.

"Take her home and stay inside. Col is putting more people on the house until this is over," Beau says behind me.

Nodding, I scoop Winter into my arms and carry her away from the scene. As I approach the front of the building, I see Karson being held outside by officers. Good. That son of a bitch is the reason they almost got away with Winter.

I assume the fire is out since the firefighters are walking out of the building. A calm, beautiful evening gone before it ever really got started, but we knew this might happen.

At my car, I open the passenger door and set my sniffling angel inside. All I can think about is how grateful I am that we had backup here tonight. If we hadn't, I don't want to think about what could have happened.

The drive home was quiet, and Winnie clung to my arm the whole way. Once I've parked, I get Winter from the passenger seat. Col steps off the porch and nods as I walk past him.

Inside, Nila yips at the back door and wiggles her tail. Not letting go of my precious cargo, I let the dog out, then walk to the bedroom, where I help Winnie out of her dress, strip off my suit, and carry her into the bathroom. I open the shower door and turn the water on.

Setting her on the counter, I keep my eyes locked on her red-rimmed blue eyes as I remove the pins from her hair. I smooth the hair from her face and kiss her pink cheeks while she clutches my sides.

"I'll be right back. I need to let Nila in."

"Take me with you. I don't want to be alone," Winnie whispers, wrapping her arms and legs around me like a koala. I will never deny her.

I lift her from the counter and carry her through the house. We let the dog in, shut and lock the door, then head back to the bathroom. Stepping into the water, I set her on her feet, keeping her as close as I can while I wash her hair and body.

Carrying her to the bed, I pull back the covers, slip her under them, and cuddle up behind her. I hold her tightly until she cries herself to sleep.

This has got to end, and soon. She can't take much more. Closing my eyes, I kiss her shoulder, then drift off to sleep.

CHAPTER 23
WINTER

I need to get out of bed. I know that, but after last night, I don't want to. Instead, my eyes roam the bland, masculine room. You can tell he was a single guy. The empty spot next to me tells me Bay is already up and likely making coffee or breakfast.

Taking a deep breath, I try to calm my anxious heart and racing brain. Had it not been arranged that everyone under the sun was expecting something to happen, I would still be with Liz. I would be God knows where with Tony, and who knows what he would be doing to get the information he wants.

Now I'm lying here, trying to decide whether seeing Troy is worth the risk. Tony will likely follow us there. With only Baylor and me going, I know Tony will kill him. I don't even know if Troy will see me.

Summer was hurt last night, and I don't know how bad it is. All I know is that Liz came out of nowhere and got Summer from behind, but damn if my sister didn't give up. I watched their legs kick, punches swing, hits blocked, and blood spill in what was probably the fastest, most badass girl fight I've witnessed live or on TV.

Then I saw silver. I cowered in the corner, and before I knew it, Liz had me by the wrist while Summer pulled herself off the floor, bleeding from her side and face. Liz's face was just as fucked as Summer's. I saw the knife. I know Liz stabbed her.

God, what if my sister dies because of me? She survived an ambush in another country just to come home and die because of me.

Unable to hold back a sob, I turn to my side and pull my knees to my chest as the salty water flows freely. It feels like it's too much. The anxiety, fear, and panic of the unknown are too much for my brain and nerves to handle.

I squeeze my eyes shut when I hear the door open. I'm not ready for human contact. The world can wait a few more minutes. I feel a light weight crawl onto the bed, and a slender arm come around my middle. The scent of lilies and honey surrounds me, making me sob harder.

Peeling my lids open, I see the summer-themed tattooed arm holding me as new sobs rock through me.

She's here

She's ok

I turn into her hold and come nose-to-nose with a bruised face. Her nose has butterfly stitches, two black eyes, a purple cheek, and a busted lip.

"I'm so sorry you were hurt," I whisper.

"Hey, you remember me saying I'm like a cat. Nine lives, though I might be down to five now." Summer chuckles and tucks my hair behind my ear. "I'd lose all them if it meant keeping you safe."

"You shouldn't have to. Did she stab you?"

Summer snorts. “Tried. I only needed a few stitches. She only got me down because she kicked my bad leg.”

“Was it you? Were you the one who took her down?”

My eyes meet her sapphire gaze. Summer inhales deeply, and her breath fans my face when she releases it.

“She wasn’t going to let you walk away.”

More tears leak. Will they ever stop?

“This is my fault. It’s too much. I don’t think I have anything left. I don’t know if I can survive this,” I say, sobbing again.

“Hey, no, this isn’t your fault. It’s Troy’s. I know you want to give up, but you can’t. We’re going to get him. We need to talk to Troy and see if he’ll give anything up. For now, we’ll hole up here as a group. Tony is not going to be happy that his sister was shot and is going to be in a federal cell soon.”

“Y-you didn’t. You didn’t kill her,” I stammer.

“No. I wanted to, but I knew where to hit to bring her down without doing that. We needed her alive. And the bitch tried to stab me; she deserved it.”

“What do we do now?”

“Now, we get out of bed, I call the prison, and we see if Troy will give anything away. Then we brainstorm where he might have hidden the flash drive if he doesn’t. You’re not in this alone. Out that door is a man who loves you and will do anything to protect you. His right eye may have a shiner.” Summer chuckles.

“How? I didn’t notice it last night.”

The tears have finally dried. Somehow, she managed to pull me out of the darkness I was heading into.

“Karson was a distraction. He started the fire, then tried to fight Bay. Bay kicked his ass, and Baxter headlocked him until he passed out. Guess Tony threatened his girlfriend if he didn’t.”

"That's why he showed up here the night before?"

"He was going to tell Bay about it. But when my snipers shot at him, he knew something was up, and Tony was likely serious." Summer says, taking my hand.

"This is insane."

"Yup, now it's time to get up and handle this shit. Oh, and I brought a tiny little guest to brighten your mood. Baxy calls him Everett, but I call him little Kingly. Kingly is a way cooler name." Summer beams, and I think about how she can be so damn happy all the time. She had the shit kicked out of her, and here she is, making me feel better with a smile on her face.

A small laugh bubbles out of me. Everett is adorable. Okay, I can keep going. I can finish this. With the support of the people I love, I can do this; we can do this.

Summer kisses my forehead before rolling out of bed, and I toss my covers back. I get out of bed, stretch, and start moving.

With renewed determination, I swing the bedroom door open and stride into the kitchen, ready to fight to end this. My eyes widen at the sight of multiple people gathered in the kitchen. I know some, but not others.

Bay finally notices me and walks over quickly. He doesn't miss the chance to give me a brief open kiss before hugging me to him. I wrap my arms around his narrow waist and inhale his warm, soothing scent.

"Who are all these people?"

"A couple of Summers people and a few agents," he tells me.

That makes sense. Last night's events would call for them to be here.

"Oh,"

"They're working together to hatch a plan. But they know we were going to see Troy, so Agent Sampson is arranging a call instead. It's too risky to travel right now."

“Yeah, that sounds right. When is the call?”

“Once you're ready. There’s no rush. Have some creamer and breathe for a minute.” Bay chuckles when I give him a playful smack.

“I’m going to hold Kingly and think for a minute. I still don’t know what I want to say to Troy. The need for certain answers isn’t that important anymore,” I tell him as he guides me into the kitchen.

Stopping beside Baxter, I hold out my arms without a word. He gives me a warm smile and places the sleeping baby in them. Staring down, I stroke his smooth cheek with my index finger, and the corner of his lip lifts in that cute baby smile.

I ignore the chatter around me and give all my focus to this sweet boy. I lean against my man and smile down at Everett. I lift him, breathe in that new-baby smell he still has, and kiss his little head, full of brown hair.

He is too precious.

God, I can’t wait to have another one. It wasn’t something I thought I would ever have again, but I know with Bay I will. I know I’ll have all the support I’ll ever need.

“We can start as soon as you’re ready. We can start it all now. You’re already the mother of my children. I want you to be my wife, Winnie. We can piss mom off and go to the courthouse tomorrow morning if that's what you want. You know you can’t quit me, so we might as well lock it in,” Bay says. He squeezes my hip with one hand, then brings the other up to smooth Everett's head, making the little cutie smile again.

“That’s either the sweetest or the worst proposal I’ve ever heard,” I chuckle. “Your mom would kill us. Beau and Briggs have already done that to her.”

“Eh, it’s the Banks brothers' policy, apparently. Elope or randomly propose.”

I laugh lightly and shake my head. “We’ll get married this fall, on September 29th. I think it would be perfect to do it in your parents' backyard, with the trees changing for the season.”

“Did you just propose to me, Winnie Anderson?” he asks, resting his chin in the dip of my neck.

“No, baby, I’m telling you what we’re doing. We don’t need fancy words or grand gestures. You can’t quit me, either, hotshot.”

“You’re damn right I can’t. We’ll have a hell of a story to tell our kids and grandkids. Nan and Pop got engaged while plotting the take-down of a crime boss in their kitchen, surrounded by FBI agents and soldiers,” Bay jokes.

A burst of chuckles sounds out, and suddenly, I realize the entire room heard our conversation. I look away from the baby and see everyone smiling at us. Summers' eyes soften, then she reaches into her backpack and pulls something out.

I flinch a little as she winces while standing. Summer walks over, takes Bay's hand, and places something in it. When Bay opens his palm, I see the white gold sapphire ring with two small diamonds on either side, along with its matching band. It lies in his palm like a beautiful offering. The air leaves my lungs, and I hold my breath. I never thought I would see that ring again.

She steps up to me and gently takes Everett from my arms.

“It was our grandmothers. It was supposed to be Sky’s, but our parents kept it. I was going to give it to you once I had the chance.” She tells Baylor, who is speechless, staring at the ring he's holding.

“How?” I ask, swiping a stray tear from my cheek.

“I can’t answer that in a room full of lawmen. I'd incriminate myself. I plead the Fifth,” she says sarcastically, giving me her signature smirk.

I can’t tell if she’s joking. Knowing her, she’s not.

Bay takes one ring, slips it onto my trembling ring finger, and gives me the sweetest kiss. It will be an interesting story to tell.

Bay breaks our kiss and presses his brow to mine.

“I love you, Angel,” he whispers.

“I love you, hotshot. Now, let's plan how to take down the crime boss.”

Pulling myself together, I look around the room. “What’s next?” I ask, clapping my hands in front of me. I’m ready. I have a life to start living.

An average-height man with greying hair takes the floor. “I’m Agent Sampson, but you can call me David. We have a couple of options.”

“So help me, David. One of those options better not be hiding my sister and nephews in some backwoods town we can’t even pronounce, where fucking pigs are common. I told you no WITSEC. Choose carefully,” Summer growls.

“This is the only time you will ever hear this, but I agree with her. Hiding won’t stop him from looking,” Baxter agrees.

Summer turns and gives Baxter a sly grin, bouncing Everett in her arms. “I knew you loved me. Repeat it. I like hearing I was right. It gives me a chubby.”

“And that is why I said this would be the only time. Her mouth doesn’t know when to let her brain take the reins.”

“You keep playing hard to get, Yeti. You don’t realize the chase only makes me harder.”

“I blame you, Winter.” Baxter circles Summer with his hand. “She’s your fault. You just had to be her sister.”

“Hey, I had no choice in the matter, but I wouldn’t change it,” I say, shrugging unapologetically.

“Okay, people, I think we’re getting off topic here,” David says, exasperated.

Col barks out a laugh. “Summer is laser-focused when it counts. Right now, her untreated, undiagnosed ADHD is in control. Just start talking, David. She'll circle.”

“The other option is to contact Troy. You’ll talk to him and see if he’ll give you any hints about where he hid the drive. If he does and you think you know where it may be, we’ll set up the sting to catch Tony because you can bet he will be following you, and we’ll let him.”

“You want Tony to catch her? How the fuck will that help?” Bay says with annoyance.

“This is theoretical right now. If he says nothing, we brainstorm every place Winter can think of where he might have hidden it. I know it was a dicey relationship, but he had habits. He wouldn’t want it close to his norm when he was with Tony's crew, so leaving it somewhere you might think of makes sense,” David says.

“Ok, yeah. There were a few places I knew he would go. So, we call him now?”

David nods and takes a phone from one of the other agents. “The call will be recorded, and two agents will listen in.”

“Does it? Does it have to be the agents? Can my sister and Col do it?” I ask, gnawing on the inside of my lip.

I don’t want these people to hear if he talks down to me or says the kids are unimportant to him. They don’t need to listen to it.

David tilts his head and gives me a questioning look before his hard stare softens. “Of course. Then they can copy over what they think is necessary.”

I nod and lean further into Bay for support. He doesn’t disappoint. Both arms come around me from behind, holding me close for a moment.

“We’re up, Power Puff,” Col tells Summer.

Summer kisses Everett, then hands him off to his dad, walks over to me, and takes my cheeks in her hands. “It’s just me, and Col. Do not let anything that man says hurt you. You are the strongest woman I know, and you have the man you were meant to be with here, supporting you.”

“Thank you. For everything.”

“We're family. Once David hands you the phone, go into your room,” Summer says, nodding toward the room.

Summer pats my cheek, goes to her spot at the island next to Col, and slips on her headphones. I steady my racing heart as I watch the nods. David steps away, phone to his ear.

Twisting in Bay's arms, I hug him tightly, kiss his cheek, and step back.

“I’ll be right here waiting,” Bay reassures me.

I nod and look back at David, who gestures for me to go over to him.

Stealing my heart isn’t working. I’m a nervous fucking wreck. I step over. David finishes his call and holds out the phone. With shaky hands, I take it and walk to the bedroom, where I close the door and take a few deep breaths before bringing it to my ear.

I don’t say anything. I can hear him breathing on the other end. I feel like I’m negotiating a ransom.

“I tried calling, Win. I was trying to warn you.”

“The kids and I shouldn’t be in this situation, Troy. He blew up our home and tried to abduct me. What if the kids had been in the house?”

“It was a threat. He wouldn’t have done it if anyone had been in the house. I’m sorry, Win. I might have a few other things to explain.”

“You think?” I snap, unintentionally.

Troy sighs into the phone. "When we met, I fell hard. You were bright and so damn beautiful. One of my favorite times together was when I first got to the compound. You and Summer came and got me. We snuck off and walked for what felt like miles until we reached a riverbank. We spent hours swinging into the water and swimming. It was the day I knew you'd be mine and the day I knew Summer, and I would be best friends."

Why is he telling me this story? He and Summer hated each other. She warned me about him the day we met him.

"We were just kids then," I say.

"Yeah, my second favorite memory was the night we spent eating s'mores by the campfire. I told you I loved you before we got there. I thought we'd be together forever. Then my last favorite memory was the night you got pregnant."

"Why are you telling me this, Troy?" I huff into the phone.

"Because I needed to tell you before this next part." Troy clears his throat, and I hear clothes wrestling in the background. "I hated you, Winter. After we found out you were pregnant, I hated you for it. I was already using by then and felt like I was living the high life. When you told me you were pregnant, I blamed you for destroying my high. I was going to leave. I didn't want to be a father. I didn't want to be tied down to you—none of it. But Summer showed up. She offered to pay for everything. I still hated you, but you had to think I was a somewhat decent person for getting us a place to live after your parents kicked you out." He says in a flat, uninterested tone.

The pangs keep hitting. I knew this would be rough, but I didn't expect him to be so honest.

"When the twins were born, I resented them too. I let the hate I thought I had for you spill onto them." He sighs and continues. "When I met Jasmine, God, being with her was a fucking rush.

The thrill of being with the boss's wife was better than doing drugs. I kept coming back to you so Tony wouldn't get suspicious of her and me. I ended up falling in love with her. When Trevor was born, fuck, I loved him as soon as he opened his eyes. Then I had the same feeling when Izzy was born. I didn't feel that with Dylan and Daniel."

Tears pour from me as I hear his confessions. The hurt I've never felt before stabs me like 1000 daggers. Pain for my kids. Pain in knowing he has always resented them.

"Tony eventually found out the two kids were mine, and that's when I stole the money and the drive. I hid Jasmine and the kids, then I tried to blackmail Tony with the drive. It didn't work, so I broke into your house and came to your job to put him on your tail." Troy admits everything.

"You put us in danger on purpose? You're so fucking weak and pathetic. You're not a man, Troy. You're a piece of shit that deserves whatever happens to you. I don't want to hear anymore. I need to know where the drive is." I shout into the phone.

"I can't tell you, Winter. I know my apologies mean nothing. What I'm most sorry for is not knowing my kids. I'm sorry I resented them and couldn't love them. I hope you'll hold onto those good memories instead of dwelling on the bad. I hope you find a man who deserves you, Win."

Oh, this is a new form of anger. I feel like a pissed-off tiger on cocaine, ready to shred Troy. The pain is replaced by a burning need to let him know he's nothing to us. He's an afterthought now.

"I have. He's amazing. You don't need to apologize for not knowing the kids. They're not yours anymore. They're his, and he has earned the right to call them that. He has earned their love, respect, and happiness. He earned the right to be called

Dad. I hope you get ass-fucked by the biggest dick every day you're in there, Troy."

Without another word, I hang up on him. Before I can crash onto the bed, the door flies open, and large arms catch me.

"I'm here," Bay whispers.

Holding onto him, I cry tears of rage as I replay the entire conversation. He gave me the location without telling me.

CHAPTER 24
BAYLOR

As I hold Winnie to me, I comfort her as she rides the rapid wave of emotions. I didn't hear the conversation, but I can tell it pissed her off and broke her a little. I wish I could take this from her. All I can do is show her she'll never feel this kind of pain again, and I will spend the rest of my life showing the boys and her how loved they are.

While she was on the phone, I tried to keep my distance and let her handle the call, but fuck, as soon as I heard her yelling, I lost the little control I had. I want to kill the man. I want to strangle him with my bare hands.

Feeling her push off my chest, I take in her bloodshot eyes and the pink spreading across her cheeks and nose. Winnie wipes her cheeks, then reaches up and strokes mine.

"We can go out now. I think I figured it out."

Winnie now looks determined and ready to confront this threat. She's being brave and pulling herself together to finish it. I know she wants to move on with our lives. She wants to get married and have more kids. She didn't say that part, but I could tell she does by the way she looked at Everett.

"Are you sure? There's still time. We can make them wait."

Winnie shakes her head. "I'm ready."

I nod and place my hand on the small of her back, leading her through the door. In the kitchen, I notice everyone sitting quietly.

David notices us first and waits. Winnie stops, rubs her hands together, then clears her throat and finds her voice.

"It's in one of three places. He told me the good memories as clues. He couldn't give me one location, so he gave three. One of the places will be almost impossible to reach unless it's just Summer and me. The village won't allow government personnel near the property. The second place should be okay because it's outside their property line. The third place is the same."

"Okay, that's good. What do you think is most likely?" David asks, arms crossed over his chest.

"I'm not sure, but I think it's the first one. He tipped it off by saying it was the day he knew Summer would be his best friend. She always fucking hated him, and he hated her. They would never be friends of any kind."

"You're damn right we wouldn't. I hope he gets ass-fucked with a big dick while he's there, too. In fact, I can arrange that," Summer says, digging in her back pocket.

"Summer, don't," Col says, shaking his head and stopping her hand. "Law people, remember."

"I'm not the one fucking him," she argues.

When a laugh croaks out of me, I cover my mouth and cough, hoping to disguise it. My body is rumbling, trying to keep it in, though.

"Let's all pretend we don't hear the woman with a swinging cock running her mouth," David says, looking at the group before glancing back at Winter. "Okay, the first location. Give us the second location outside the compound, and we'll have a team there as well. Tony won't let you know he's there until he sees the drive. Would the compound let Baylor and Baxter on the property?"

"Maybe if they think they're our husbands and all tattoos are covered, Summer will also have to tone down her alpha female energy," Winter responds with a giggle.

"I will do no such thing," she huffs, rolling her shoulders. "I mean the energy thing. I will definitely pretend to be the Yeti's wife."

Laughter erupts from the room because she can be so serious and yet so damn childish. Poor Baxter.

"Dear, sweet mother of God, give me the strength not to strangle her," Baxter says, tilting his head back.

"Dude, you might as well bang one out with her, or she'll never stop," Col jokes with Baxter.

"This is why we're besties," Summer tells Col with a grin.

"Yeah, I'm not fucking her. She wouldn't be able to walk for a few days, and we can't have that right now," Baxter fires back, and my brows nearly shoot off my face.

"Oh, Baxy, you have no idea what door you just opened. When this is over, rawr," Summer claws the air and bares her teeth at him.

"You mean, meow, kitten," Bax smirks now.

"Ohhhh, shots fired. He retaliates. Finally," Col laughs so damn hard he holds his guts.

"Dear Jesus, how the hell did you survive in the military?" David snaps at Summer.

"Uh, have you seen my leg, fucker? It was a spotty survival," she quips.

"This has got to be the most unprofessional team I have ever been part of. Winter, can you show us the locations?" David asks, pointing at the computer.

"Sure."

Winnie steps away and starts typing. I walk over and watch her zoom in on the first location, then the second, and finally the village she grew up in.

The houses you can see look nicer. They have barns, gardens, and something that looks like a church.

"The village has armed guards." Winnie stops and thinks for a minute.

"What are you thinking?" I ask her, rubbing her back.

"The village would make the most sense to hide something you never want anyone to find. They won't let anyone in. But I still think his pointing out a fake friendship was important. I don't know. Maybe I think it's important because I don't want to see my parents."

"What does your instinct tell you? There's no wrong choice. We'll check all of them if we have to, and we both know I can be super charming. Don't worry about your parents," I tell her.

"The first location, and of course, you can be charming with that cute baby face."

"Damn it, Winnie, we talked about this. I'm not cute. I'm manly. You're supposed to tell me I look very manly." I tease to get her to laugh.

A burst of laughter escapes her before she grips my chin in her small hands. "You are very manly, but you will always be cute to me. Now, go put on your big boy undies. We're taking a road trip." Winnie pulls my face to hers and gives me a smacking kiss.

"Fine, but this isn't over," I growl when she pulls away.

"I'm looking forward to the closing arguments," she says.

The playful glint in her eyes has my dick twitching. She wants a rough pound and ass-slamming.

Exhaling deeply, I watch my breath fan across her face like a raging dragon's huff. When I stand to my full height, I narrow my eyes at her, then step back.

"I need to call Journey to make sure it's okay for the boys to stay there for a couple of days."

"I need to make sure Mom and Dad can keep Everett while we do this," Baxter says next.

"I'll pack a bag for us," I tell Winter.

"Oh, no. I need to, in case we have to go to the village. There's a specific dress code for Summer and me."

"Boo. We have to wear a long-sleeved turtleneck under a matching dress. We can't talk unless you tell us we can, and we have to follow you. The men must grant permission. It's so gross," Summer gags.

"I think my prayers just got answered. Please let us go there so I can control your sister," Baxter says with a grin.

"I will break your dick, Yeti," Summer says, pointing and glaring at Baxter, who is still smiling as he feeds Everett.

"I'm going to assemble the teams and send them out. You four will leave in a couple of hours. Whose car are you taking?"

"Mine," Baxter answers.

"I'll put a tracker on it. Col and I will follow from a distance," David says as people start dispersing from the house.

"I'm going to ride with Baxy. My shit is at his house, and I'll call Henry to cover our shifts," Summer says, hugging Winnie.

"You owe me, Bay. I'm thinking unlimited babysitting hours," Baxter says, arching a brow as he carefully straps his son into his car seat.

"Deal. Thanks for doing this."

"Well, that's what family is for. Winter and the boys were family before the engagement."

Shit, I'm engaged.

Damn, that hits me in the feels in the best way. I didn't think I would ever be here with Winnie. How bad is it that a small piece of me wants to thank Tony for pushing her into this? If he hadn't, I'm not sure she would have ever caved.

"I knew he had a heart under all that broodiness. Come here, big guy. I'll dry your tears for you," Summer teases, stretching her arms out. Bax shakes his head and walks past her, carrying Everett in his car seat.

Once they leave the house, Winter stares down at the ring on her finger with a big-ass smile. I love that she loves that ring. It was essential to her, and her family tried to keep it from her.

Noticing Nila wagging her tail at the door, I walk over and let her out.

"Babe, do you own any turtlenecks?"

Winnie sighs and walks into the room. As I pass her, I stop at the dresser and pull out a pair of jeans and boxers. Winter steps into the closet and pulls out a blue dress and a pink dress. Both feature floral prints and are floor-length.

"No, I'm hoping your mom might have some. I'm really banking on not having to go to the compound at all."

Glancing over at her, I notice the worry lines on her face and her chewing her bottom lip as she looks at the dresses.

I toss my shit on the bed, stride over, and wrap my arms around her. Her warm body leans back against mine, soaking up the comfort I give her. I bring my hand up and lightly tickle her neck, making her giggle and wiggle.

"There ya go. Don't stress about what we don't know yet, babe. I'll be right beside you no matter what. We're going to finish getting ready and go to Journey and Briggs so we can see the boys before we leave."

"Okay. Have I told you how lucky we are to have you?"

"Hm, not today." I dip my head and kiss her flawless shoulder.

"We are. I wouldn't have survived this without you, baby. You're the only person I want to catch bad guys with," she says.

I chuckle and kiss her again before letting go. "Let's hope this is the last time we have to do this. Once is enough, but if it's not, I'm glad I'm doing it with you, too. We make a good team, Winnie."

Moving into the closets, I pull out the duffel bag and start shoving our clothes into it. I'm not sure how long this will take, so we packed three days' worth of clothes. Hopefully, we have this wrapped up by then.

"I'll let Summer know to meet us at Journeys."

"Okay, shit, we need to drop Nila and Stormy off with Beau or my parents." I almost forgot. We're still getting used to being pet parents.

"We'll take them to Beau. Your parents will be busy with Everett," Winnie says, walking out of the bathroom and zipping a small bag.

Striding out of the bedroom, I move through the house, pack the pet supplies, and put the cat in the carrier. She would be fine here with enough food and water, but Harley will appreciate the companionship.

As soon as I hook the leash onto Nila, Winter comes out of the room, now wearing all black, combat boots, and her hair in a high ponytail. Holy shit, she's sexy as hell, looking like an assassin.

"You're wearing that again when we get back to finish the closing arguments. Fuck, babe, if we had more time." I clamp down on my bottom lip and groan. I want to be balls deep, pounding into her.

"After all this, your wish is my command, hotshot. Literally." Winnie winks, then tosses the bag over her shoulder.

"Yeah, you're going to toss those little pills so it counts."

"Not until we're married. I want to look good for the wedding pictures. I got huge with the twins." She laughs and opens the front door.

"Babe, you would be stunning carrying our babies, but I can wait until after the wedding."

Once I've locked the door, we load the car and start our trip. I want to make sure I see the boys before we leave, in case this little plan goes sideways. I need them to know I love them more than anything in the world.

After we drop the animals off and Winter gets the turtlenecks from Birdie, we park outside Briggs's house.

Dylan and Daniel race out the front door.

"Aunt Ny said we're staying here for a few days," Dylan says, hugging his mother, then moving over to me. I hug him close and ruffle his hair. They don't need to know my nerves are barely holding.

"Where are you going?" Daniel asks, hugging my other side.

"Just a little trip. We won't be gone too long. You two better be good for Aunt Ny and Uncle Briggs. When we get back, you boys can have a sleepover at our house," I tell them.

"Yes. You're the best dad ever. Oh, ah, is that okay?" Dylan asks, looking up at me.

"Of course. I love being your dad. I'm the coolest man at the firehouse because I have you two as my sons," I tell them. Their eyes light up with pure delight, and they hug me again.

I can't help but squat and hug them as Baxter and Summer pull up. I kiss the tops of their heads, stand, and let them go.

"Give your mom hugs, and we'll see you in a couple of days," I tell them.

They both go to Winnie, who looks like she's hanging on by a thread. She kneels and hugs them. We're both anxious about this entire thing.

When she stands, the boys wave, smiling.

"Bye, mom, bye, dad, love you," they say in unison.

"We love you too," I say, my voice thick with emotion. Nothing could be truer. I nudge Winter toward the truck while I grab the bag from the car.

I open Baxter's back door and get in next to Winnie, who has foggy eyes. Taking her hand, I give it a reassuring squeeze.

"It's going to be fine, babe. We have a good team watching over us."

"I know, but it doesn't make it easier. So much could go wrong."

"It won't. I'll make sure of it. We've got this. It's like my treasure-hunting story. Except in this one, a crocodile won't bite off my foot. A yeti might, but not a crocodile," Summer says.

Winter shifts and leans in to see Summer better. "Can you tell me the treasure story when we get back?"

"Argh, I shall tell the story of how I lost me foot now." Summer doesn't waste any time jumping into the story. She holds to her character and talks like a fairy pirate the entire time. I know she wants to distract my worried fiancée.

"I was drifting along the Nile in search of a cave. A cave no woman fairy had ever sought. The river was too calm. Trouble lurked beneath the dark waters. I watched the ripples, waiting for the monster to emerge. The wind puffed, and water fell from the sky. I prepared me sword for battle. Then, whoosh, one crocodile, two, three. I fought like a mighty warrior. I slashed and stabbed. One jumped, aiming for me hand. I drew up me sword and came down with all me might." Summer goes through the motions.

At this point, Winter is smiling broadly, wholly engrossed in the story. She watches while Summer acts out the ridiculous battle.

"Standing there, I scream in victory as I conquer them all. Then the cave reveals itself. With a laugh, I enter, and there she be, me treasure glowing, waiting for me. I toss the anchor, jump over the side, and move through the water. Holding the chest, I carry it back to me boat. Victory was mine. Then, just as I load the prize, the air stills, the air puffs, and water rains down. Then I feel it, the pain, oh, the pain. Water covers me like a blanket. In the river, I open my eyes and see him. I missed one. I withdraw me sword, fighting the crocodile and the water. He wants me treasure, but he shall not have it. With one final swing and one final clamp of the jaw, he lets go. I swim to the surface, adrenaline running high,"

Summer shifts in the front seat, so her back is against the center console, and she's looking at us.

"Pulling myself on board, I lie there breathing. Now victory is mine. Lifting myself, I wiggle me feet, no, not feet, foot. Glancing down, I see I have only one. I lift my leg and see it. Ahhh"

Summer shouts and throws out her amputated legs and wreaths in the front seat. Winter lets out a little shriek and jumps, making Baxter and me laugh.

"Me foot, the bloody bastard got me foot. Looking around, I see me treasure resting comfortably next to me. He got me foot, but not me treasure. Acting quickly, I tear off my jacket, rip it, tie off the wound, and cover it. From this moment on, I will be known as Sgt Foot, but I did it. I did what no woman fairy has done before."

At this point, we are all losing it. She has managed to turn this gut-churning drive into an adventure for my angel. I haven't heard her laugh this hard in over a week. I reach over and rub Winnie's back. I need to feel her. The smile on her face steals my breath when she looks at me with her crystal-blue eyes.

"That was fantastic. I can see why the kids like it. You should turn it into a book," Winter tells her, wiping away tears of laughter.

"Nah, I just like saying the words. I could never type them. Do you feel better?"

"I do, thank you. Do you have any more? Is that why you got the fantasy tattoos?"

"Sure, and it is. Want to hear about the fairy farmer and her deal with the warlock?"

"Yeah," Winter nods, unbuckles, and scoots to the middle seat. She reaches over and holds my hand while she listens to the fairy adventures.

CHAPTER 25
WINTER

The seven-hour drive went by quicker than I imagined. I was graciously entertained for the entire ride, but my body was happy to be out of the vehicle and checking into a hotel. We kept the stops brief, so there wasn't much time to stretch out.

Agent Sampson booked a room for himself and Col so they would be close to us in case anything happened. I was so exhausted when we got here last night that I crashed while Bay was in the shower.

I spent seven hours listening to tales of adventure and victory. Today will be a real adventure, and victory has to be ours. Looking down at the outfits on the bed, I feel my stomach churn. I had hoped I would never have to return to my childhood home. Fingers crossed, the flash drive is at the first location.

When Bay walks out of the bathroom, his eyes darken, and he bites his bottom lip when he notices I’m in all black again. I wonder what it is about this outfit that makes him hot?

"When do we have to leave?" he rasps, striding up behind me.

Bay's long fingers come around to the base of my throat, forcing my head back. Bay's lips take mine in a warm, open kiss before he plunges his tongue into my mouth, dominating mine into submission. Liquid heat pools between my thighs as Bay grinds his hardening cock into my ass.

Unadulterated need floods me the longer the moment lasts. My fingers fumble to unbutton my jeans. Behind me, Bay follows my lead without breaking our kiss.

With our jeans down, Bay pulls his lips from mine.

"Bend over, babe. This is going to be rough and fast."

"God, yes," I moan, doing as I'm told.

Bay guides me down, placing one palm between my shoulder blades and gripping one hip bruisingly tight. Bracing myself on the bed, I scream with pure euphoria when Bay slams into me without warning. His cock is an anaconda, and my pussy is its prey.

The sensations of pain and pleasure move through me like waves. Bay fucks me so hard I see stars. I'm about to lose it and cum already.

"Mm, you like taking my cock like this, Angel? Are you ready to cum for me?" His voice is hoarse and breathy.

"Yes," I cry out as he slams into me, rolls his hips, and hits my G-spot. Waves roll through me like a tsunami, liquid gushing and drenching his cock, running down my thigh. Shit, Jesus, that's never happened before. Did I squirt? Glancing down, I see glistening wetness leaking down my legs.

"Holy fuck, Winnie," Bay groans, slamming into me one last time and gripping my hips. He holds me there as he stills, and his warm cum fills me, mixing with my own.

"I'm sorry, baby. That hasn't happened before."

"Don't you dare apologize for that. I just made my fiancée squirt all over my cock. That was, fuck, phenomenal."

Bay lifts me so my back is against his chest. He brings his lips to the shell of my ear and traces it with his tongue. "When we get home, we're going to see how many times you can do that in one night."

A breathy giggle slips from my lips. I clamp my thighs together as our combined mess leaks past the barrier of his cock.

Bay kisses and teases down my neck, stopping at my shoulder and biting it.

"Don't move," he commands, then slowly slips from me.

I hear the rustle of his jeans. Looking over my shoulder, I catch a glimpse of him before he's covered and firming back in place. I watch his every move as he strides to the sink and warms a washcloth.

When he returns, he carefully cleans up the mess we made. Once he's done, he bites each ass cheek, then lifts my pants, making me laugh. He's so cute and gentle. His heart and love are so wholesome.

"That may have been a record-breaking quickie. I'm pretty sure we still have a few minutes," Bay says, leaning in for a kiss, but it stops abruptly when the pounding on the door starts.

"Are you cum guzzlers done?" Summer shouts outside the door.

My face scrunches, knowing they all probably heard us. When Bay notices, he bursts out laughing.

"It's not funny. They heard us," I say, pushing him away and gathering the clothes I might need later.

"I don't give a shit. Now they all know my woman is thoroughly satisfied. I'm not ashamed of it."

I roll my eyes, walk to the door, and double-check myself before swinging it open.

Summer leans on the railing with a tilted half-grin. The guys all look away, avoiding eye contact with me.

Damn it, they all heard.

"Well, those rosy cheeks make you look like a dirty little sinner. I always say a good pounding helps prepare for battle. It relaxes the mind and body."

"Please stop," I groan, moving past her. My face feels like I just walked through flames. Col doesn't bother hiding his laugh as he trails behind us.

"You still get embarrassed easily. Okay, I'm zipping it. The team is set up at the first location. Do you think he would have put it in the water? It's pretty mucky, so visibility will be nonexistent if it's at the bottom," Summer says, changing the subject.

I shake my head as we all load into the elevator. "No. I would say he buried it. The problem is, it's been thirteen years since we've been there."

"Which means we have no idea how much it's changed yet. Are you sure about this location?" Summer asks, rolling her neck.

"Not a hundred percent. I thought yes, but now I'm not sure. Saying you two were best friends could have meant this location, or it could have been a hint about the clues. Honestly, I never really knew him, so I'm winging it." I shrug and step into the elevator.

"I say trust your first instinct. If it's wrong, that's fine. We'll move on. It will only be you four. The team will be close," David says as he steps in.

Easier said than done. I need the first spot to be the right one. I don't know why I'm so worried about seeing our parents. Do I fear the resentment I know I'll see on their faces, or do I fear Summer's mouth running and getting us shot? It may be the ladder.

Baylor grabs my hand and squeezes as we step off the elevator into the lobby. Summer and Baxter follow behind us, while Col and David stay in the lobby as our group exits the building.

Outside, the warm spring air blows across my face, lifting the hair from my neck. The sun is high, beaming down on us. We're in a little Podunk town about forty minutes from Atlanta and five miles from where we grew up.

In the backseat of the truck, I glance through the window. I take another look at the rundown gas station with an attached garage and the outdated hotel. The old general store appears to have been abandoned for the last ten years, and the hardware store's windows are now boarded up.

Summer and I would often sneak off to the general store. The older man who owned it would sneak us a soda and a piece of candy when we came in. He knew we weren't allowed that treat any other time. Those were the good days here. Summer and I were constantly rebelling against the cult's rules.

The town is being forgotten. Outdated, rundown houses with grass as tall as my waist line the street as we drive past. With jobs only in the larger cities, I can see why towns like this can't survive. Even the trees look like they've given up.

Baylor's warm hand gliding over my thigh pulls my attention from the not-so-scenic view.

"Was it like this when you were here?"

Shaking my head, I lace our fingers together. "I don't recall it being this bad. It's almost desolate now."

"Hm," Bay hums and looks ahead.

When Baxter comes to a stop, I take in the overgrown dirt path.

"How do we get there now?" Bax asks.

"We hike, yeti," Summer tells him, swinging her door open.

Hopping out of the truck, I stretch my legs. I haven't hiked in years, and I have a feeling this is going to kill me. Bay grabs our pack and tosses it over his shoulder.

"Do you like hiking?" I ask as we start our trek through the overgrown trees and brush.

"I'm neutral about it. We have to do it from time to time for work. What about you?"

"I haven't hiked since I was a teen. I didn't mind it then. I'm older and bigger now."

Bay stops and spins me so I'm looking at him. The scowl on his face says it all. He didn't like that response.

"You're joking. You're tiny, babe. There isn't a big thing about you."

"Well, not to you. You're a giant. Everything is tiny beside you and your brothers."

Bay shakes his head and tugs me to him. My body melds to his, where it belongs.

"You are my perfect angel. Don't call yourself big again. Okay?"

His words are a plea, as if it pains him to hear me say them. I reach up and stroke his cheek. Bay's murky lake-green eyes bore into mine.

"I won't repeat it." Damn, my voice came out shaky and weak.

With a nod and a kiss on my hand, we continued walking. As we followed Summer and Bax, I took in the dense undergrowth of trees and saplings that blocked the sun's rays. It was a chaos of broken branches and vines, covering the ground like blankets. The scene was creepy yet somehow peacefully undisturbed. The smell of earth and nature made my senses tingle.

I feel the resistance around my ankle just before my body stumbles forward. Gasping, I stretch my arms out to stop my fall. Bay's long, defined arms catch me before I face-plant into a tree trunk. Lifting me, he gets me back to my feet.

Man, I'm grateful to have him here. I'm sure I would have gotten a tree rash on my face. Looping my arm through his, I hold him tightly. This time, I pay attention to my feet instead of the scenery.

"It's just up here," Summer says as we reach the riverbank.

The breath leaves my lungs as I take in the rushing water. The water is murky but beautiful. Smooth stone lines the bank. Different vegetation leans toward the water, silently asking for replenishment.

Glancing higher, I see a waterfall. My face scrunches at the sight. I don't remember it being here before, or the water ever moving this fast.

"Found a rope," Baxter shouts.

My eyes flick to him at the top of a hill. Guess we start scouring and digging now. Bay and I walk over to where Baxter is and start climbing.

By the time we get to the top, I am completely out of breath. Hunching over with my hands on my knees, I control my breathing.

"How far are we from the compound?" I ask Summer, then start looking for anything that looks recently disturbed.

"About a mile. Do you think it could be within that range?"

Shaking my head, I squat down and lift a few rocks.

"No. I think it would be here, and that's why he mentioned the river and swinging into it."

Silence descends on us as we search for any clues. Rock after rock. Dig after dig—hours of scouting and nothing. Not one search proves fruitful. That means we have to go to the second location.

The thought of going brings tears to the back of my eyes. I refuse to let them fall.

"Damn it," Summer murmurs under her breath.

I feel the same way.

The three of us sit on boulders while Summer makes the call to check the next location. Thankfully, I have my emotional support person with me. Bay massages the nape of my neck, easing the growing tension.

"Let's go," Summer barks, then stomps off.

My brows shoot up at her annoyance. This is the first time she's lost her gleeful attitude. Her mood screams pissed-off fury. I hate the guilt that starts to rise in me. She wouldn't have to go back. She wouldn't have to risk seeing him if it weren't for me.

The hike back took half the time. Summer flings the door open and yanks out clothes. Then she pulls out two gun holsters and straps them to her thighs. She doesn't bother taking off her current clothes. Following her lead, I slip on the turtleneck and dress.

Ugh, I can't see myself, but I'm positive I look ridiculous.

Once we're all in the truck, Summer digs into her bag and pulls out multiple rings.

"Here, I picked up cheap silicone bands for the guys. I wasn't kidding about pleading the fifth. Put this on, Sky."

I slip off the engagement ring and replace it with the thin gold band.

My face blanches as I look at the bland jewelry. I do not like it.

Yuck

Bay's chuckle draws my attention away from my finger.

"You don't have to wear it long."

"Still don't like it." Huffing, I slouch into the seat. I know I'm throwing a mini tantrum, but I don't care.

Within a minute, the village gates come into view. It hasn't changed since we were here last. It almost looks like a peaceful community behind the 8-foot chain-link fence.

Whitewashed homes dot the property. Bright green gardens take up more space. The worship center has doubled in size. The closer we get, the clearer it is that the peaceful view is staged, like a laugh that's gone on too long.

When we come to a stop, two old pickup trucks kick up dust and rocks as they speed toward the entrance. The sound of exhaust and revved engines echoes through the air as they stop, revealing four armed men from each vehicle.

Bay and Baxter each exit our vehicle and wait for us to step up beside them. Outside, we're still a decent way from the entrance.

Glancing at Summer, I see her nails digging into her palms. I know not to comfort her. We have to stay in a submissive role.

"What can we do for you, strangers?" one of them shouts.

Bay's body stiffens, but he nods for me to answer.

"My name is Winter Anderson. Daughter of Patrick and Milly Anderson. The woman with me is my sister, Summer Anderson, and these are our husbands, Baylor Banks and Baxter Banks. We're here to speak to our parents," I shout back to them.

Bay's arm snakes around my shoulders, and he drags me into his side.

"You two were shunned. Why would they want to talk to you?" a familiar voice says.

Fucking Kirk.

As Kirk's form comes into view, my heart starts hammering against my ribs. My gaze darts to Summer. Her body is taut, her knuckles white from clenched fists, and her jaw locked. Baxter notices and wraps his arm around her.

"My sweet Summer. How I've missed you. Come closer so I can see you all," Kirk shouts.

The four of us move closer, and I finally see the snide man. He looks the same. Short and thin, with a receding hairline. The same dangerous brown eyes and black hair. He's what Journey would call a demon wearing a meat suit. I don't miss that Bay and Bax both look like they've doubled in size, like balloons being filled.

When Summer takes a step, my heart spasms. Shit, she's about to blow this whole thing up. Before I can stop her, Baxter steps in.

"In the future, I'd appreciate it if you didn't address my wife. Summer, stand behind me, then give me your hands," Baxter says firmly, never taking his dark glare off Kirk.

Summer reluctantly does as she's told; she moves behind Baxter, stretching her hands out from behind him. He takes them and places them on his chest.

"I see someone was finally able to train the beast. Winter, how is your bastard child?"

I dig my elbow into Baylor's ribs when I feel him start to move. Good grief, they're both going to blow this. I look up at him, waiting for permission.

"Speak, woman," Bay snaps, and his shoulders roll as if the demand were the hardest thing he's ever had to do. It is. The Banks men treat their women like treasure; they're the dragons that guard and care for the shiny metal.

"My children are doing fine. They flourish where we are."

My voice comes out calm and collected. Inside my head, I already have a thousand ways to kill this man. That helps steady me.

"And your husband doesn't mind raising them?" Kirk asks, leaning against the back of his truck with an amused look.

"Our leader believes in molding young minds. No matter the heritage. We seek a government-free future. We train all who are willing," Bay responds now. Huh, he paid better attention to what I told him than I thought.

"I can agree with that. What about you?" Kirk shifts his gaze back to Baxter now. "How did you manage to get Summer to see the way?"

"You must have missed the bruises on her face and the missing foot. If you do enough damage, they eventually listen," Baxter replies with a twisted smirk. I know Summer is seething right now. Bax is lucky she has to stay in character.

Kirk bursts out laughing, staring at Baxter. Envy swirls in his eyes, as if he's jealous of the thought of Bax beating Summer into submission. Fucker doesn't know she'd kill half the men standing here within seconds if she had the chance.

"Open the gates. We'll let them see their parents," Kirk says, nodding at his brother Boyle. I remember his smug face, too. He's just as hideous as his brother.

When the gates start to open, Baylor shifts me behind him to mimic Summers' position. Once I'm able to look at her, she rolls her eyes dramatically. Then she mocks Kirk as he explains everything to the guys. Every ounce of my self-control goes into overdrive to keep from laughing. If I don't look away from her, I'm going to crack.

When I pull my eyes from hers and scan the area, I notice no kids are running around. When I was younger, I remember the kids running freely after our schooling and chores were done. Hell, there's no one outside.

What the fuck is going on?

The area is still, as if everything here has been paused. The wind chimes on the house porches hang motionless and silent. I notice a curtain twitch in the windows. It's quiet to the point that chills spread down my spine.

Our footsteps crunching on the gravel ground are the only sounds. The smell of soil and something I can't quite put my finger on. It's a chemical smell, but what chemical? I don't know.

As we walk, my breathing quickens. I feel like we're walking to our death, like a man about to be hanged or a watch about to be burned at the stake. It's terrifying.

We stop when Kirk halts outside my childhood home. The door creaks open slowly. I swear my heart is no longer pumping in rhythm. So many thoughts race through my mind. We're about to come face-to-face with the family that so easily cut all ties to their kids.

"Who are they?" My mother's voice cracks like thunder in the once-silent space.

Baylor takes my arm and pulls me to stand in front of him. Baxter does the same with Summer. I watch the color drain from my mother's beautiful face. Wrinkles crease her eyes, and gray streaks her hair. Her blue eyes look gray and drained. The past twelve years seem to have aged her.

Behind her, my father steps into view. He's quick to hide his surprise, but his shaking body gives him away. White sprinkles his hair and beard. New wrinkles have formed along his forehead and eyes. The blue of his irises looks as drained as my mother's.

“I’ll take care of this, Kirk,” my father says, stepping in front of our mother. “Girls, inside.”

Baylor puffs out his chest and squares his shoulders. “They don’t go anywhere without us. You may have been their father once, but we are their husbands now.” Bay gestures between himself and his brother. His tone and stance leave no room for argument.

My father's face hardens as his glare bounces between the four of us.

“Very well,” he says, stepping aside, still blocking my mother's view.

The control these men exert over women here is truly warped. I'm not naturally violent, but I'd fight any man who tried this kind of thing in the outside world. The people here are trapped in a delusion. Despite how awful my life was with Troy, being here now makes me see that it was worth leaving with him and escaping this.

Baylor takes the lead, walking ahead, while Baxter stays in the rear. Inside, the house looks exactly as I remember it. The living room is completely open-plan. It contains only the bare necessities: a four-person oak table and chairs, a sofa, a coffee table, and plain white curtains over the windows. There is no TV, no lamps, no books, no pictures—nothing. The air is heavy with the smell of dampness and woodsmoke from the fireplace.

At the table, Summer and I take a seat, and both men with us hover behind us, hands on our shoulders. It’s an act of possession. An act that must be shown.

Our mother sits at the table, and our father takes the same possessive position behind her. We all sit in silence. No one wants to make the first move.

CHAPTER 26
BAYLOR

Silence stretches as we all sit here, staring at each other. I'm not sure how long it lasts before Winter clears her throat. The sound ricochets through the house.

"You two shouldn't be here," Winter's mother finally says.

"Trust us. It's not by choice," Summer snarls. Now that we're inside, she lets her mouth run.

"Then why?"

"We won't take much of your time. I believe Troy came here sometime last year." Winter stops, twisting her fingers together.

When I notice Winter's discomfort, I decide I don't give a shit about these people's weird control issues. On an exhale, I shift, pull out her chair, and squat in front of her. Winnie's wide, crystal eyes meet mine as I reach out and frame her face. I can see the vein in her neck thrumming erratically.

"Relax, angel. As soon as we find the drive, we're out of here. I promise."

"You're not like the men here? It was an act?" Milly asks. My eyes don't leave Winter's.

“Troy hid something of great importance here. We need it back, then we’ll be on our way,” Winter says, her eyes never leaving mine.

Neither of us answers her mother's question.

Milly doesn’t say another word before getting to her feet and walking to another room.

“What your mother said about being here has nothing to do with you,” Patrick says, leaning in and whispering. “You four need to be out of here soon. If not, you’ll all be trapped until it's over.”

“The fuck does that mean?” Baxter doesn’t hide his aggression.

Patrick rakes his hands through his hair, then scratches his beard. “Shortly after Winter left, Milly and I realized how fucked up this place is. Your absence woke us up. We were in town trying to leave when an FBI agent approached us.” Patrick moves closer, keeping his voice low. “We’ve spent the last seven years feeding them evidence to build a case. The raid is happening today. At any minute.”

“Do they know about it? Is that why everyone is inside?” Winter asks. Patrick shakes his head.

“No. They saw you four by the river and had everyone go inside in case you came here.”

“Listen, there are bombs. You four need to get what you're looking for and leave.”

“That’s the smell in the air?” Summer asks.

“Yes,” Patrick says, not elaborating. Milly comes back into the room with something in her hand.

She stops beside Winter and waits for me to move. I kiss Winnie’s nose and stand to my full height. I keep my eyes on the two and watch Milly place the flash drive in Winter's hand.

"I saw him. The night he buried it. I watched him sneak into the compound while I was gathering evidence. Once he was gone, I dug it up. I figured I'd give it to the FBI."

"Thank you."

A second passes before an alarm sounds throughout the village. My protective instinct kicks into full gear. Baxter and I rush to the window and see two large SUVs waiting outside the gates.

I've seen enough movies to know it's not the FBI. A raid of this scale would bring tons of enforcement. My heart quickens as we watch. The back door opens, and a minute later, Tony steps into view.

"Damn it," I grumble under my breath.

"What?" Summer asks, squishing herself between Bax and me. "Ah, fuck. Dad, you said the raid was happening any minute?"

"Yeah, why?" Patrick asks, joining us now.

"We need to stall until then. Mom, you and Winter go to your room and stay on the ground. Hide the drive."

Without another word, she steps back. I don't look to see what she's doing. Instead, I watch Kirk talk to Tony. Seconds tick by, and the gates start to open. Tony and three men follow the militia toward the house.

A nudge on my back pulls my gaze from the group headed our way. I can almost feel my pupils dilate as Summer hands me the weapon. She has shed the dress and turtleneck and is back in her jeans and T-shirt, ready to do what's necessary.

Winter rushes over, wraps her arms around my waist, and buries her face in my chest. "Stay in here," she whispers.

I can't do that. She knows I can't. Protecting her is my responsibility. Not Summer's, not Baxter's, and sure as shit not her father's, who shunned her. Milly comes over, hands Patrick a rifle, and steps away.

"You know I can't, babe. You and our boys are mine to protect. That's what I plan to do. I'm going to be okay. Go hide with your mother." I keep my voice calm and even. Inside, I'm a wreck.

I'm not nervous for my life. I'm worried about what Tony will do if he gets past us. What will he do if he makes it to Winnie? I cannot let that happen. So I will walk out those doors, becoming the first line of defense to protect my future wife.

Tears pool in her eyes, threatening to spill. "I won't survive, Baylor. The kids and I need you."

"I will always be here. We don't have to keep him distracted long. Please, angel, go with your mom. Now." I nod toward a worried Milly.

"Please be careful." Winter hugs me tightly, then pulls away and follows her mother.

"Baxy, you good?" Summer asks my brother, who nods. His arm moves behind him, removing his own weapon, then slips it into his front waistband.

"If anything happens, do not let him get to Winter," I tell Patrick in an assertive tone, making it clear I am not fucking around.

"Understood," he replies.

With a deep breath, I steady myself. All we need to do is stall him. Summer steps up next to me and pats my shoulder.

"It's all good, bigfoot. Our team is moving in. Stay focused, but try to relax your body. Don't tense up. It worsens any injuries. Think about your wedding day. I'll do the talking," Summer says, pulling a flash drive from her pocket.

It feels like we're at the final scene of our movie. The monsters are at our gates, only three warriors remain, and it's up to us to protect the city. Is this where we shout 'For Cedar Creek,' 'For the innocent,' or 'No guts, no glory'? I wish I had a cool catchphrase for this moment.

Summer reaches out and flings the door open. Calm confidence surrounds her. Kirk's eyes narrow as he takes her in.

Outside, the sun is setting, and darkness is slowly taking over. Our vision will decrease as it ascends. The scent of soil and chemicals is thicker now. Or maybe my senses are heightened, along with my vision, which is in complete focus. To the right are Kirk and five other men. On the left are Tony and three of his goons. Then there are the three of us and Patrick inside the house. We are significantly outnumbered.

"I thought you had a handle on that bitch," Kirk snarls at Baxter, who fucking laughs.

"One thing about my kitten here is that no one, and I mean no one, can control her," Baxter chuckles. I hide my shock at hearing his nickname. It's all for show, I'm sure, but it still sounds weird.

I should speak up, but I know Summer will run her mouth long enough to keep the men distracted.

"Hm, and who are you exactly? I have resources you can't even imagine, but there's no information on Rayn Cooper. Winter is important to you. You're also the one who took down my sister. Government or vigilante? Who are you, red?" Tony says now.

"Well, duh. That's not my name, you silly pigeon. You know. You're not as bright as I thought you'd be. The pretty ones usually disappoint in that department," Summer says casually.

Tony tilts his head and takes in the woman. You can tell he doesn't know what to make of her.

“I quite enjoy the title of vigilante. I know some talented people myself, Mr. Lopez. It’s amazing how easy it is to erase someone's identity,” she says, popping her hip out and inspecting her fingernails.

“You intrigue me. Tell me your name,” Tony asks. A hint of a smile crosses his face.

“Naimh Raindrop. I assume you're here for this?” Summer pulls out the flash drive and holds it out to him.

Tony’s stance stiffens. The men with him stand tall and ready. Kirk adjusts his weapon across his chest. We are now in a three-person deadlock.

“Amongst other things.”

“Ah, yes, the 60K. There’s a travel bag in the truck parked outside the gates. Go on. Have a look.” Summer waves her hand toward Tony’s men.

My head whips toward her. Winter doesn’t have the insurance money yet, so how the fuck does she? Summer stays focused on Tony. I flick my gaze back to him. Tony nods to one of the men with him. The guy steps back and heads to the vehicle.

Out of the corner of my eye, I see one of Kirk's men inching toward the house.

I let out a whistle to get his attention. “Don’t even think about it,” I warn in a low growl.

The man stops, locking eyes with mine. I shift my stance to face him. His finger moves to the trigger of his weapon, and my hand instinctively rests on mine. Terrific. I feel like I'm in an old western movie.

A movement behind the man draws my attention. I know better than to give it away. Instead, I keep my sights set on the guy. I’m hoping it’s the backup.

"I'll take that little trinket in your hand as well," Tony tells her.

"Hold on. You're on our property. If it's worth anything, I'd say we have rights to it," Kirk says, stepping closer to Summer. Baxter moves next to her, broadening his chest.

"I want what she has. Hand it over, Summer," Kirk tells her, as if she'll listen.

Commanding her is like telling a wild squirrel to spit out the nut it's holding. When the guy I'm watching moves, I draw my weapon and point it at him. Bax and Summer draw their guns next. Dad made sure we each knew how to shoot from a young age. Over the years, we've all stayed sharp.

"I said, don't do it," I shout, and the man aims back at me.

There's no doubt he wants to drag Winter out here. For what, though? Kirk wants what Summer has because he thinks it's valuable. Winter has the one they really want.

"Now, boys. There's no need for all of this hostility," Summer says as Tony's guy returns with the travel bag of cash.

At this point, everyone has drawn their weapons. It's insanity. Thirteen people are surrounding each other, each waiting for the other to pull the trigger first. The sky has turned a deeper purple. The pink and orange are melting away quickly.

"If you want it, Kirk, you have to take it from its owner," Summer says, tossing the drive to Tony, who catches it mid-air.

Kirk and his men shift their sights to Tony.

I sense a change in the atmosphere just before the silence is shattered by loud cracks, like branches snapping in rapid succession. Sparks leap, skittering like angry fireflies in the night. Shouts pierce the air. Kirk and his men return fire into the darkness as uniformed men and women emerge from the shadows.

Tony and his men fire back while trying to make a hasty retreat. Summer and Baxter's weapons respond. A single shot rings out. I raise my gun and peg the guy running toward Winter's house, hitting him in the back of the knee. The pungent, acrid, metallic scent of sulfur floods my senses.

The chaos of shouts and gunfire deafens me. Summer shoves me toward the house, yelling for me to go. Lights suddenly illuminate the fenced property. Then two massive explosions boom, shaking the ground and lighting up the night sky. Ashes now join the bullets in the burning sky.

A searing pain shoots across the side of my head, as if a fire poker had been dragged across it. Blood streams down my face. My leg threatens to buckle, but I hold steady. My breathing is uneven and erratic. I need to stay calm. With a deep breath, I focus on the events unfolding around me.

I exchange fire until my clip is empty. My vision blurs as liquid leaks into my eyes. Before I can react, I'm yanked and shoved into the house.

Inside, I stumble and land on my ass. Summer runs over, tilting my head from side to side. Was I shot? Is that why my head is bleeding? Was it debris from the explosions?

"It was a graze. Dad, I need a first-aid kit. If you don't have one, bring me any towels you have." Summer shouts at her father.

"Baylor," I hear Winter's panicked voice before she comes into view. Dropping to her knees, she cries uncontrollably, tears streaming down her face. She keeps apologizing, blaming herself.

"Baby, I'm okay. It was a graze. Nothing a few stitches won't fix." I try to calm her.

When shots start hitting the house, I swiftly gather her in my arms, pull her to the ground, and shield her. Winter's screams pierce the air, as loud as the gunfire outside.

"Shh, I got you. Not much longer," I whisper, though I'm not sure I believe it.

In this moment, all I can do is hold her and shield her until this is over. Bullets chew chunks from the wall, and plaster dust and wood float down on us. The scent of metal and smoke fills my nostrils.

It feels like it's taking an eternity for the shots to slow.

When the shots stop, I peek out and see Patrick and Baxter shielding the other woman. We all wait as the minutes tick by. Once we've decided it's over, we start to move. My body shifts as I still hold onto Winter, and I sit up with her.

Patrick and Milly are both sitting up now. Baxter gets to a sitting position and pulls Summer into his arms, hiding her face from the rest of us. Winter crawls across the floor and grabs a cloth. When she returns, she presses it to my head and holds it against the wound.

"Is it over? Do we wait in here until they come to get us?" Winter's voice cracks, and a new sob escapes her. My hold on her tightens. That's all I can do right now.

"They know we're in here. They'll get us when it's safe," Patrick answers, holding his weeping wife.

No one says another word. We sit in silence while we wait. I can't help but wonder if they got Tony. If they didn't, he'll be back once he discovers he got a blank drive. Things erupted so quickly that it's hard to say. The fence seemed surrounded. I doubt anyone got out.

Winter moves and sits in my lap, still holding the cloth. She still doesn't feel close enough. My arms tighten around her waist. Tonight felt like the beginning of the apocalypse. The world around us was being destroyed, and the sky was falling.

Time ticks by slowly. Minutes feel like hours. Seconds feel like minutes. Never in my life did I think I'd end up in the middle of something this big. The only thing keeping me together is having Winnie safe in my arms.

When the door flies open, Patrick moves quickly. He points his rifle at the men standing there. As my vision sharpens, I see Col and David. Col comes over to me, moving Winter's hand and the cloth.

"Graze. It's clear outside," Col says, digging in his bag and pulling out gauze. Col presses the gauze to my head and helps Winter and me to our feet.

"Did you get Troy?" Winter asks, holding out the drive to Col.

He takes it from her and nods. "We got him. You won't have to worry anymore," he reassures her.

Winter visibly relaxes and holds back a sob. Col escorts us outside to an ambulance. The paramedic loads me into the back. Winter jumps in and sits across from me. She holds one hand and caresses my cheek with the other.

"It's over," she whispers to me.

"Yeah, babe, it's over. I love you, Winnie."

"That's not my name. And I love you, too, hotshot."

We both let out a small laugh as we ride to the hospital together.

EPILOGUE
WINTER

I jump to my feet from the bleachers when Daniel gets the soccer ball. He moves swiftly across the field. With the goal in sight, he draws his leg back and kicks with all his might. The anticipation tightens my chest. I watch the ball fly through the air. The goalie dives to block, but he's too late—goal for the Tigers.

My arms fly up as I jump and shout. Bay launches to his feet and starts rooting and shouting. Our baby scored his first goal. He's been practicing with Baylor all summer for this moment. The game isn't over yet. There are ten minutes left, and I can see the determination on Dan's face. He's aiming for a second goal.

Bay guides me back down to the bleachers, and we watch. It's been five months since everything exploded. Life since then has been extraordinary. I twirl the ring on my finger and think.

My parents moved nearby and have been trying to make amends. I've accepted their efforts, but Summer hasn't. I haven't introduced them to the kids yet. I'm not ready for that.

Ivey has been helping me plan the wedding scheduled for two weeks from now. It's going to be magical. I want it small, and I've invited my parents. I have been thinking about asking my father to walk me down the aisle. Baylor won the mountain vacation at the silent auction. He won't tell me how much, but we've decided it will be our honeymoon.

The boys now call Baylor 'Dad' instead of Bay. I ended up getting the money from the house, and instead of rebuilding, we decided to keep the land to give us a bigger yard and expand our current home for a growing family. I paid Summer back the 60k she lost during the raid. It was marked as evidence.

Everyone was apprehended that night. Turns out we didn't see any children because they had been separated from their families and were housed across the compound. The kids were given an hour a day to spend with their parents.

We learned the compound's leader had been murdered by Kirk years earlier and that the leader wasn't the only one Kirk took out. Tony later died from the injuries he sustained that night, but the FBI used the evidence on the flash drive to take down several others. Troy is still rotting in prison, and I can't say I'm sorry about it.

The bookstore's business has grown since Birdie partnered with Nyx to add a mini coffee bar, and she has also partnered with the town's new baker to offer limited baked goods. Oh, and she was definitely pregnant with a boy this time. I swear, Beau almost cried at the gender reveal. The man was set on having only girls.

Summer is still staying with Baxter and Everett. She wants to buy a home and says she doesn't want to rent. She has Everett when she's off shift, which helps Baxter. He only has to take Everett to Ivey two days a week. It works for them, I guess.

A light rub on my back pulls me from my thoughts. Butterflies take flight when I meet Bay's mesmerizing gaze.

"Are you okay?"

My heart skips a beat when I meet his lake-green irises. I melt into his side, and a smile stretches across my face. I love that he is always concerned about us.

"Perfect. I was thinking, that's all."

"Mm-hmm, and what were you thinking about?"

"About how happy I am. About how much I love you and how much the kids love you. You're too pretty not to love," I say playfully.

"I heard you think I'm pretty," he jokes back.

I roll my eyes to the back of my head.

"Is that all you heard?"

"Yup. I didn't hear the part about you being happy, or how much you love me and want to kiss me. But if you did say those things, you should know." Bay leans closer and whispers in my ear. "The feeling is mutual."

A thrill runs through me, making me giggle. He never misses a chance to flirt with me. I shake my head, look back at the field, then check the time—only 30 seconds left.

Daniel brings the ball back down the field, running as fast as his legs will carry him. 10 seconds remain. The goal is in sight. I rise to my feet as he kicks. The goalie tries to block, but fails. The buzzer sounds just as the ball hits the inside of the net.

Another goal.

I repeat my usual energetic praise. Two goals. He did it. I have no doubt he'll go far in this game.

Baylor takes my hand, and we walk to the fence where Dylan is talking to a girl in his class. I am not ready for this. Seeing him with her reminds me that this is the next stage. The little shit doesn't even notice us behind him. He started football this year. Tomorrow, we have a game to attend for him. I have a feeling the next seven years will be about sports and girls.

Once Daniel's done, he doesn't run to me. No, he runs straight to Bay and hugs him. His hair is soaked with sweat, and his cheeks are flushed. He's still adorable to me.

"Did you see me, Dad? I made two goals. Two." His voice shrills with excitement.

"I saw, bud. You killed it out there. I'm so proud of you." Bay tells him, hugging him back. Dan finally comes to me once he gets the praise he wants from his dad. Bay takes Dan's soccer bag and slings it over his shoulder.

"Did you like watching Mom? I was good tonight," he tells me confidently.

"You were amazing. I love watching you play," I tell him.

As we walk past Dylan, he still doesn't notice us.

"Dylan. We're leaving," I call over my shoulder.

"Coming," he says, and I hear his feet thundering behind us as he catches up.

"Hey, Mom, do you think I could get a touchdown tomorrow night?" Dyl asks as we walk to the car.

"Absolutely. You've been practicing nonstop with Uncle Baxter. I think you'll kick ass tomorrow."

Baxter has spent the summer teaching Dyl how to play. I know he'll crush it.

"Sweet. I hope I do."

We all pile into the new SUV we got a few weeks ago. Baylor decided his car was no longer suited for two growing boys. Doing my usual thing, I reach out and turn the music up a little. I bob my head to the tunes while the boys talk Bay's ear off about sports. I'm interested in the games when the kids play, but that's it.

I'm a little anxious about how tonight will go. The boys and I have a surprise planned for Baylor when we get home. I know in my heart it will go well, but the pesky anxiety still shows up sometimes.

As soon as we park, the boys jump out of the vehicle and race each other to the front door. We both chuckle at their antics. I like the little reminders that they're still kids.

Inside, they let Nila out, then dash off to take their showers and get their surprise ready. Over the months, I have slowly decorated the house. I asked if Bay minded, and he said that if I'm happy, he is, too. He only cares about us, not the color of the rug or whether there are flowers on our comforter.

In the kitchen, I pull out the pizza rolls, earning me a 'really' look, but Bay doesn't say anything. He's learned I'll eat the damned things regardless. While they heat, I let the dog back in.

"Dad, close your eyes," Dylan shouts. Bay gives me a look. I lift a shoulder and play dumb. He twirls on his stool and does what he's told.

"Don't open them," Dan says as they enter the room.

"I won't."

"Ok, Dad. You are the best father we've ever known," Dylan starts. Then Daniel.

"You've taught us how to play sports."

"And how to fish."

"You show up when you say you will."

"And you never make promises you can't keep."

"You've taught us how to be happy."

"And how to be kind to others."

"You've given us a lot of aunts and uncles."

"And a ton of cousins."

"We love you with all our hearts."

"You will always be our only dad."

I walk around the island and put my arm around his shoulders. Bay reaches up and holds my waist. Dyl steps forward and hands the papers to Baylor.

"You can open your eyes," Dyl tells him.

Bay looks down at the adoption papers in his trembling hand and wipes his eyes.

"Dad, will you adopt us?" they ask at the same time.

"Yes. A thousand times, yes." Bay stands and rushes over to the kids, dropping to his knees. He hugs them both, and they laugh. "I love you both so much."

Once Baylor stands up, he steps back beside me. The boys look at me, and I nod.

"We want to be a family," Daniel says.

"We want to have the same last name," Dylan says.

"As their other two brothers or sisters," I finish, stepping in front of Bay and holding up the sonogram of baby 1 and baby 2.

I take Bay's hand and place it on my stomach. His eyes bounce between the boys, the pictures, and my stomach. I wait patiently for it to sink in.

"You're pregnant? The boys are going to have a brother or sister?" he whispers, and I hold up two fingers.

"I told you, twins run on my side." I hand him the photos. He studies them for a moment, then looks back at me.

"This is the best night of my life, Angel—the best night. My boys want my name, and they're getting siblings. We're having a baby. Babies. We're going to have four kids." Bay pulls me into him and buries his face in my hair. "I love you. I love you with everything I am. Thank you, Winnie. Thank you for letting me adopt them."

"You are the best father I have ever met. They made this decision, baby. I love you more than words can say."

I could feel him gesture for the boys to come over. They both squeezed us tightly. It was the best family hug, but it didn’t last. When the boys had had enough, they told Bay they loved him and ran off to their rooms to play video games.

My poor future husband was still reeling from all the information tonight. I cupped his cheeks, bringing his gaze to mine.

“Is this the life you’d hoped for?”

Bay shook his head. “It’s better. What about you? Are you ready for this life together?”

“I am so ready. You're mine, Baylor Levi.”

“And you're mine, Winter Sky.”

www.ingramcontent.com/pod-product-compliance
Lightning Source LLC
LaVergne TN
LVHW010641110826
845149LV00014B/2920

* 9 7 9 8 9 9 3 4 3 6 3 5 7 *